NEW YORK REVIEW BOOKS
CLASSICS

OTHER MEN'S DAUGHTERS

RICHARD STERN (1928–2013) was the author of more than twenty books of fiction and nonfiction, and was best known for *Other Men's Daughters*. His other works include the novels *Stitch* and *Natural Shocks*; the short-story collections *Packages*, *Noble Rot*, and *Almonds to Zhoof*; a collection of essays, *The Books in Fred Hampton's Apartment*; and a memoir, *A Sistermony*. He taught literature and creative writing at the University of Chicago from 1955 until he retired in 2001.

PHILIP ROTH is the author of thirty-one books, including the Pulitzer Prize–winning *American Pastoral*.

WENDY DONIGER is Professor of the History of Religions at the University of Chicago and the author of *The Hindus: An Alternative History*, *On Hinduism*, and, most recently, the volume on Hinduism in *The Norton Anthology of World Religions*.

OTHER MEN'S DAUGHTERS

RICHARD STERN

Introduction by

PHILIP ROTH

Afterword by

WENDY DONIGER

NEW YORK REVIEW BOOKS

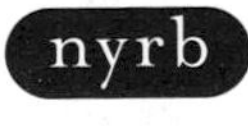

New York

THIS IS A NEW YORK REVIEW BOOK
PUBLISHED BY THE NEW YORK REVIEW OF BOOKS
435 Hudson Street, New York, NY 10014
www.nyrb.com

Library of Congress Cataloging-in-Publication Data
Names: Stern, Richard, 1928–2013, author.
Title: Other men's daughters / by Richard Stern ; introduction by Philip Roth.
Description: New York : New York Review Books, [2017] | Series: New York Review Books classics
Identifiers: LCCN 2016040725 | ISBN 9781681371511 (alk. paper)
Subjects: LCSH: Middle-aged men—Fiction. | College teachers—Fiction. | Biology teachers—Fiction. | Young women—Fiction. | Cambridge (Mass.)—Fiction.
Classification: LCC PS3569.T39 O8 2017 | DDC 813/.54—dc23
LC record available at https://lccn.loc.gov/2016040725

ISBN 978-1-68137-151-1

Printed in the United States of America on acid-free paper.
10 9 8 7 6 5 4 3 2 1

INTRODUCTION

In Memory of Richard Stern

I MET DICK in the fall of 1956, and thus was initiated a fifty-seven-year-long literary conversation and friendship. In 1956, Dick had only recently joined the English department of the University of Chicago where I was teaching freshman composition. He was twenty-seven, I was twenty-three. I had just returned from the army to Chicago, where I'd earlier received an MA in English. Dick and I started to talk immediately about writers and books and didn't stop until a week or two before his death.

His assiduous engagement with everything literary never diminished. He was reading fiction, writing fiction, teaching fiction (over the phone to me; in bed with his wife, Alane) right down to the end. For me, as his friend and fellow writer, his appetite for book talk was an inexhaustible treasure.

Dick played an important role, maybe the most important role, in straightening me out when I was first getting going in the mid-fifties. One noon shortly after we'd met as colleagues, we were having hamburgers together at the old University Tavern and, for no purpose other than to amuse him over lunch, I recounted my adventure a few summers back in Jewish suburbia with the dazzling daughter of a prosperous dealer in plate glass. Because Dick was such an eager listener and so enjoyed laughing, I was encouraged to tell the story in all its fullness, embellishing along the way for comic effect.

When lunch was over and we were walking back to campus, Dick said, "Write that, for God's sake. Write that story." It hadn't occurred to me. Write the story of an ephemeral summer romance in inconsequential Maplewood, New Jersey? I wanted to be morally serious like Joseph Conrad. I wanted to exhibit dark knowledge like Faulkner. I wanted to be deep like Dostoyevsky. I wanted to write *literature*. Instead I took Dick's advice and wrote *Goodbye, Columbus*. I would remain responsive to his literary wisdom forever after and would put before him, for him to challenge with his critical vigor, the final draft of virtually everything I wrote.

What did I prize in him? What do I most miss about him? His scrutinizing engrossment with every last vicissitude of existence, his raptness and his rapture, his lucidity, his being perpetually wide awake as if he were being *stung* by life, his childlike geniality, his gentle and not-so-gentle force, the swiftness of his perspicacity, his impulse to celebrate, his miniscule antipathies and his benevolent urges and his wide-ranging fellow feeling, his imaginative merging with other lives, the bonding of his vulnerability to his fortitude, a steely literary integrity—beyond everything, the way he was weighted down by love. Because the wellspring for his daemonic attentiveness was, in the widest sense, love.

Frequently, while listening to Dick speak of a new colleague, project, sorrow, hardship, idea, improbability, of another blast of news from the great fallen world—while listening to his vivid, focused, unfailingly unhackneyed responses—the same three words would be catalyzed in me: "You're so human."

A large, excitable man, highly delighted and of marvelous intelligence, with his face pressed tight to the window.

A man for whom nearly every encounter was unforgettable and for whom fulfillment was no fantasy.

A man who could conceal little and from whom little could be concealed.

His mindful presence here, his joy in being among us, his absorption in everything both within and beyond his ken, seemed never to slacken. Living, for Dick, was an unceasing stimulant and the engagement with life never ceased to evolve. Everywhere this urbane and not entirely unwily man went, mankind flabbergasted and enkindled him. His direct apprehension of the real was amazing.

He wrote many wonderful books, beginning in 1960 with the comic gem *Golk*, a prophetic fable, as it turns out now, more than fifty years later, of the tyranny of mass entertainment and the insidiousness of surveillance. To me his masterpiece is his sixth published novel, *Other Men's Daughters*. I've reread it twice since Dick's death. If I may, I'd like to repeat what I wrote about *Other Men's Daughters* at the time, in 1973, in the first flush of delightful discovery.

> There's much to admire in this book—the precision, the tact, the humane feeling, the tremendous charm—but what stands out particularly is the intelligent Harvard physiology professor who is (truly) its hero. A blend of restraint, decorum, rampant courtliness and atrophied eroticism, he is a perfect target for the wise and witty Cambridge student-beauty of the Sixties, coutured in jeans and armed with the Pill. And she is his text in the physiology of Love.... The theme is Leaving Home, departing the familiar and the cherished for erotic renewal. Richard Stern's accomplishment (here, as in all his work) is to locate precisely the comedy and the pain of a particular contemporary phenomenon without exaggeration, animus, or operatic ideology.... In all, it is as if Chekhov had written *Lolita*.

Aside from being a novel shapely, penetrating, accessible without being simple in any way, perfect in all its parts and proportions—in its distribution of sympathy, in its graceful narrative jumps as in its artful shifting points of view—*Other Men's Daughters* belongs side by side with the strongest of the books that have been written about the historical upheavals and extreme transformations that made so astonishing to the Americans who lived through it the turbulent decade—to be exact, the eleven years—beginning with the shock of President Kennedy's assassination, extending through the horrors of the Vietnam war, and concluding with the resignation of that most devious of all devious commanders-in-chief, Richard Nixon.

In its modest way—precise and elegant at every turn, no page of prose that isn't unostentatiously bejeweled and intimately evocative while simultaneously dense with spot-on intelligence—*Other Men's Daughters* illuminates a decisive turning point in American mores. The novel reminds us of where we were, morally speaking, when the vast assault upon convention, propriety, and entrenched belief began to challenge authority, high and low, and of the wreckage that caused, the theatrics it fostered, the hope and euphoria and intemperance it quickened. The novel reminds us too of the casualties that were taken by the generation of previously hidebound adults who comprised the first wave to hit the beaches of protean American prudery.

I would contend that in its own felicitous small-scale way, *Other Men's Daughters* is to the distinctive character of the sixties what *The Great Gatsby* was to the twenties, *The Grapes of Wrath* to the thirties, and *Rabbit Is Rich* to the seventies: a microscope exactly focused on a definitive specimen of what was once the present American moment.

Golk, *Europe*, *In Any Case*, *Stitch*, *Other Men's Daughters*, *Natural Shocks*, *A Father's Words*, *Pacific Tremors*, exquisitely imagined and surpassingly executed by one of our era's most distinguished, if unheralded, novelists and men of letters, Richard Stern, who was born in Manhattan on February 25, 1928, and for decades, in the environs of the University of Chicago, lived to the hilt the life of the mind and the imagination (to be sure, tempered, as his biographical record will show, by the daily trials, the inescapable crises, the stunning losses and unavoidable conflicts engendered simply by going about one's business for eighty-four years) and who, after enduring everyman's thousand ups and downs, died beside his adoring, brilliant, devoted wife, far from brainy Hyde Park and its renowned university, in his unlikely last home, on little Tybee Island, the easternmost point in Georgia, a very simple place with one main street and a nature sanctuary, on January 24, 2013—a magnanimous friend, a formidable writer, an exceptional man.

—PHILIP ROTH
November 2013

OTHER MEN'S DAUGHTERS

For A

Cavalcando l'altr'ier per un cammino
pensoso dell'andar, che mi sgradia,
trovai Amor nel mezzo della via,
in abito leggier di peregrino.

Dante, *Vita Nova*

PART ONE

I

The Merriwether House—as it was known in the neighborhood for most of its ninety years—is a three-minute walk from Harvard Square. The second house from the southwest corner of Acorn Street—a hundred yards between Ash and Hawthorne—it is wooden, gabled, bellied with bay windows. "Autumn-colored," said a Merriwether child. It rises three stories behind a large acacia tree set in a tiny oval lawn whose few feet of renewable earth stuff supplied a large proportion of ordinary Merriwether exchanges: "The tree's leafing out." "Time to mow again." (Mowing took sixty seconds.) "Your bicycle's on the lawn."

A resident of Manhattan might think of Cambridge as "country," but it is urban in marrow, which is to say that whatever grows there bears the mark of human toleration or display.

Until the day of Merriwether's departure from the house —a month after his divorce—the Merriwether family looked like an ideally tranquil one. Parents and children frequently gathered in the parlor reading in their favorite roosts, Priscilla, by firelight, the others by the light of old lamps whose bulbs were shielded by pies of rose and amber glass. Years of fire-heat have bulged the room's striped wallpaper and, with other pressures, lumped the armchairs and velveteen sofas.

Merriwether had complained for years that his wife Sarah hadn't rejuvenated Aunt Aggie's house. The reason, he believed, was a form of Cambridge indolence disguised as ascetic contempt for body comfort. For years such Cambridge platonism brought the rear ends of Merriwethers against the coils of what should ease them.

"Darn it all, Sarah. I wish there were chairs we could sit in."

"Of course, Bobbie."

"I guess I'll have to go out and buy some myself."

"That would be practical."

"Practical all right, but where do you find them?"

"I'll inquire."

A bit of charade: Sarah, "the earnest, bright-eyed, agreeably useless antiquarian," Merriwether, "the helpless man of thought." Two decades before, they had fornicated on one side of a double bed while Sarah's roommate pretended sleep on the other. Even then much more of the world was in their heads than in talk with each other.

In the warm, crannied, silvery parlor, parents and children formed an irregular crescent around the fire. Albie, the eldest, home from Williams, stretched on a sofa reading Machiavelli's *Discourses*. He is stocky, shaggy, sharp-faced, with soft, near-sighted, deep brown eyes. A political conservative—he runs quietly against all discernible tides —his preferred manner is oblique irony. Priscilla tells him he looks hip but smells medieval. Priscilla lies a yard from the soft mesh firescreen. She wears a green buckskin vest and scarlet bell-bottoms, wide bells at bare feet. The flames raise gold welts in her long brown hair, gold chips in her green eyes. She reads pamphlets on Metal Fatigue sent her by NASA. For years, she has corresponded with them about becoming an astronaut, has done the exercises, mathematics and engineering prescribed by their education specialists, and though, recently, it is poetry which takes up more of her time, she keeps her hat in the spatial ring.

Beneath Grandpa Tipton's portrait sits Esmé. On the edge of greater beauty than Priscilla, she is a flat length terminated by ringmaster boots. A little bra shows through the unbuttoned upper half of a blue work shirt. Blonder, clearer-featured than Priscilla, a dreamier girl, she reads the magazine *Glamour*.

The youngest child, George, has bangs to his eyebrows, his father's blue eyes and his mother's stocky build. Pencil in hand, he corrects the typescript of a children's book written by a Merriwether neighbor who has already dedicated one book "To my punctilious critic, G. M."

Dr. Merriwether feels an antique safety here. He drinks a New York State Chablis and reads *Cymbeline,* a play he hasn't read since an undergraduate course in Shakespeare twenty-five years ago. The difficult, magic language and the mild wine enrich the calm. The parlor, the fire clicks, the tiny clinks and rattles of supper-making from the kitchen, the beauty and momentary seriousness of his children dissolve the anxiety which has gripped him for months. The play is such a mixture of strangeness, precision, extremity and restraint. It sits on the old rock of ethic: "Self-fulfillment is self-denial." He reads, "The breach of custom is breach of all." "But is it true?" wonders Merriwether. This parlor, thicker with custom than life, holds like a microscope specimen his own breaching.

"The parlor is for dusk," said Aunt Aggie Tipton. Aunt Aggie, too, was a breacher. For thirty years she lived unmarried with Mr. Louden Stonesifer. The house is still laced with the debris of wires, speakers, buzzers and colored lights installed so that he and Aggie could communicate wordlessly with each other. (One never knew when a stroke would disable speech.)

"The Merriwethers never felt the need to add to the Gross National Product. Or to coddle provincial morality," said Aunt Aggie. Such boastful maxims supported her breach of Cambridge burgher life; though it seemed to her nephew that she gauged to a turn the bounds of Permitted Eccentricity.

"Pray you trust me here—I'll rob none but myself," he reads in *Cymbeline*. If he could make his children understand that. If it were true. Even as he thinks, "I'm peaceful, happy, this is a beautiful moment," he is aware that in four or five hours he will walk out of their earshot, down the backstairs and telephone the source of his breach, Cynthia Ryder, a young girl for whom he is almost ready to give up the thousand formulas which compose this beautiful human hour.

"Love," Dr. Merriwether thinks. Famous, frozen word concealing how many thousand feelings, the origin of so much story and disorder.

When he teaches the Introductory Physiology course, he begins one lecture, "Today, ladies and gentlemen, we will talk about love. That is to say, the distension of the venous sinuses under signals passed through the third and fourth sacral segments of the spinal cord along the internal pudendal nerve to the ischio cavernosus, and, as well, the propulsive waves of contraction in the smooth muscle layers of the vas deferens, in seminal vesicles, the prostate and the striated muscles of the perineum which lead to the ejection of the semen."

His seriousness does not invite the concessionary laugh to pedagogical wit. If he wants laughter, he will say, "That, gentlemen, and perhaps ladies, is what is making you toss in your beds. One way or another." Usually, though, he explores mind-body problems, peripheral sense filters, spinal lesions, the swelling and beading of myelin sheaths, the fragmentation and disappearance of axis cylinders. A careful lecturer, he does not forget love. (For non majors, it is important to relieve the technical complex with more manageable views.) He cites a definition of John Locke, " 'Any one reflecting upon the thought he has of the delight which any present or absent thing is apt to produce in him has the idea we call love.' Philosophers among you may note the distinctions between 'delighting,' 'thinking of delight,' and 'reflecting upon the thought of delight.' I believe later analysts simplified this scheme. Freud, for instance, speaks of love as a mild psychosis." Or Dr. Merriwether will vary his decorative allusions and speak of "such amateur physiologists of love as Balzac, Maine de Biran, Rémy de Gourmont and Stendhal. I suspect French analytic power is revealed in their literature more than in their science." In the same lecture, he draws on Sarah's master's thesis on Courtly Love. Those rough maps of feeling had precious little congruence with physiological ones; yet without the internal pudendal nerve, the invention of love would not have tamed the ferocity of medieval western life. Sarah had argued that the

Rebirth of Women began in that old deflection from war to love. (Now, *her* direction was reversed.)

In those days, he'd been enchanted by her work. As she finished the chapters of her M.A. thesis, she read them to him. How had that stocky little dynamo with the cameo head learned so much? Provençal, Old French, Spanish. Those beautiful bird sounds spun out of her husky little voice. A Dietrich voice without the parodic sexuality; enchanting out of that sweet stump of girl.

He explained his work to her. The black pearl eyes lit with excitement: how she wished she'd studied science so she could really follow. How long was it before they both realized she not only didn't follow but was bored stiff pretending? Dr. Merriwether retreated. Then, five or six years ago, Sarah stopped pretending. She opened a door inside her to a very tough little lady. The lady said, "This is it. I am no doormat. You are no Einstein." Venus in armor. A new Sarah who corrected everyone, who lectured everyone. When Priscilla got interested in French poetry, Sarah fetched down her old text and began passing out the Radcliffe word. "*The Spirit of Romance* is NOT an authoritative book, sweetheart. Pound was enthusiastic, he was gifted, but he knew NOTHING. He bought a copy of the *Chrestomathy* and he thought that made him a scholar." In Provençal, Sarah scored high; at least there was no one around to grade her. She moved on to politics: no "mushy liberal squash" for her; Cambridge was a swamp of soft-headed muckers, what did they know about running the world? She stood with Bill Buckley (who'd dated her cousin when he was at Yale): she'd rather have the country run by the first thirty people in the Boston phone book than by the Harvard faculty. Albie got out the directory: "Triple A Cleaners, Aamco Transmitters, Felicia R. Aabse. Looks pretty good, Mom. Who do you want for Defense, Felicia or the Cleaners?"

For months now, Sarah specialized in her husband's moves. She classified his gestures, checked his bills, noted his new suit, his brighter ties, the extra shag in his hair. He has spent more time *in the lab* than he has for fifteen years. There is new ease in his speech and dress, yet he has long since stopped asking her what she had even longer refused him.

She used Albie as weapon and fortress. Albie, indolent and charming, accepted his mother's flirtation along with her checks. In his cruder moments, his father is a conversational ploy, a backdrop for truancy. "Dad gets everything through the test-tube. There's more to life." What there is mostly is sleep, touch football, reading Burke and *The National Review*. Sarah took the temperature of Merriwether's silent distaste. "It does no good at all to get after Albie."

"Get after?"

"He sees your face harden when he sleeps late."

"He can't see it if he's sleeping."

"Do you want a debate or the truth?"

"It's you who have the truth, Sarah. But it is true that Albie is happier horizontal than vertical."

"You may stay vertical, but he sees through that."

"I stay vertical, because you don't want me any other way."

The black eyes burned in her pale face. Angry, she is less puffy, almost the white cameo he'd thought so beautiful. "I am no legal whore."

When he came back from the summer in France, he told her. "Of course there's someone, Sarah. I'm not a cactus. I couldn't endure without intimacy. I've been driven to the wall." He'd kept from saying, "You've driven me to the wall." Part of his fear and guilt had been converted into pity. Even to him, Sarah often seemed his victim. Despite the harshness of their life together, pity enabled him to care for her. She'd been so decent. She was basically—whatever that meant—and he was to learn there were endless "bases" of Sarah and himself—decent. But this woman who had almost never lied or cheated or done much more than hold back the truth went into his files, read his mail, listened in on his phone talk.

"You think I don't know," she said. Cambridge neighbors were as hungry for gossip as their notion of Iowans. (Hungrier: fluent passivity was an appetizer.) Sarah herself gossiped little. But for years now she had kept an inner catalogue of his weaknesses; each year added to them, every book she read gave her new material. *Double Helix,* Jim Watson's charming boy's book of genetics and tourism, was a treasure trove for her. "You never had Jim's free spirit. You're a grub, you go to the lab like a bookkeeper to his accounts. Without verve, without creative spark." And he lacked Jim's tenacity. "I can't see you rushing off a train to a bookstore and swotting up a subject the way he swotted up Pauling's *Chemical Bonds* in Heffer's."

"Blackwell's."

"Yes, a pedantic grub. You'd remember you had to play tennis, or have lunch or take one of your girls to the movies." He didn't have any girls then. And was this what a grub did? She described him the way Jim described himself. Yet it worked, as did anything in his dark moods, to sap his self-confidence. Her latest find was Lévi-Strauss. "You're a *bricoleur,*" she said over the Corn Flakes she "insisted" on buying against his lectures about protein breakfasts. "A mental garbage collector. Your life is made of left-overs. You don't plan, you don't have long views of your own.

You've got the mind of a primitive." He vaguely thought Lévi-Strauss had wiped out the notion of the human primitive, but he knew the joys of lecturing, he waited her out. "It's clear why you're not an important scientist."

Women, thought Dr. Merriwether, did have difficult times, particularly women who grew up between the Twenties and Sixties; they smelled new freedom in the air, they saw young women who enjoyed it, yet felt they themselves hadn't been prepared for it. Even scholarly, New England girls such as Sarah had been raised as charmers, dreamers. If they were almost content, they sensed they shouldn't be. Like the new blacks of the Sixties—Merriwether's experience was mostly second-hand—they assigned every pain to one conspicuous wound, they were this way or that because they were women, being a woman was a misery, an inflicted misery, and who were the inflictors but men, and what man in particular but the husband, or, at least, the husband one no longer loved, that is, the man who no longer loved them. So the progression went, and women of intelligence and education were the prime sufferers or complainers, activists, gossips, haters and corrupter/liberators of others. Merriwether feared for his children. Sarah did not hear hatred in her voice, but the vitriol leaked into the children's heads. Poor Sarah, yes, but also, yes, curse her, curse her blind egoism, her self-righteousness and curse her hatred.

A strange, released summer for Dr. Merriwether. Most of the day he was alone. Sarah had taken the children to her parents' summer place on Duck Isle, Maine. He stayed behind in Cambridge and moped about the laboratory. Most of his friends were away. Three afternoons a week, he dusted off his M.D. and did the doctoring chore for the Summer School at Holyoke Center.

For a month, he ate most meals by himself, breakfast on a stool at Zum-Zum's—toasted bacon rolls with strawberry jam, fresh orange juice, a terrific tonic after the winter of frozen cylinders out of the Minute Maid cans, two cups of coffee and the New York *Times*—lunch at the Faculty Club, sometimes with a colleague, and dinner at the Wirthaus where he had the same table every evening, just behind a little Korean gourmand who ate nine-course dinners. ("Where do they go?" he wondered.) The first week, he hit on an excellent golden *Graves;* he drank most of the bottle every night. The waitress pointed him to the evening's delicacies. It wasn't unpleasant. Bolstered by thousands of meals with family and friends, he did not have the bachelor shame of solitary eating, and he could do without talk.

After dinner, he walked the jammed, astonishing summer streets, then home, and in the silent house, watched television movies or read books of a sort he hadn't read since his literary youth, Dante, Montaigne, Shakespeare.

Longtime skeptic living in a sea of skepticism, Merriwether needed something more that summer. The Cambridge heat, swampy, intimate, almost visible, drained that energy which, most summers here, drove him down to the boathouse for a shell, or to running in sweatpants along the river. Now and then he did play tennis with his colleague Davison, but that energy which for years he'd at least partly dispensed in a thousand competitive games (even solitary rowing was competitive for him: he rowed against clogged arteries, against the clock), turned inward. "About time," he thought. "But where to take it?"

Day after day that summer, the *Times* obituary pages contained news of deaths which gripped his heart. The deaths were seldom of people he knew personally, yet they touched him deeply. People who were fixed stars in his cosmos of expectation were suddenly no more. Day after day another: Walter Gropius (whom he had passed for years in the Yard); Red Rolfe, his boyhood baseball hero; Senator Dirksen; Ho Chi Minh; the other Bauhaus great, Mies van der Rohe. There were many Harvard deaths: Woody Woodworth (from whom he'd taken a course in The Sonata), Lem Cleveland, Bob McCloskey. Almost every obituary section contained such loss for him. It was as if he were receiving piecemeal a devastating message.

Against this drear subtraction surged the foam of the street, the—what could he call them?—kids, the young, girls, boys, the hippies, freaks, heads, the beauties and transfigured uglies from all over the world in every state of dress and undress. There were tonsured Buddhists in saffron saris, tinkling bells and chanting "Hare Krishna" on quarter-hour strolls through crowds; blonde Cherokees, fringed, feathered, dyed, pounding drums and playing flutes in Forbes Plaza; there were pubescent Mennonites, Shakers in flat hats and long dresses, Bowery bums, angelic longshoremen, Georgia belles in Leghorn hats, Hells Angels in leather vests. Thicker than bugs in a cornfield, the International Young, bare-chested, bare-legged, barefoot, walking, dragging, dancing, jogging, lying against the Coop pillars, sitting on the benches of the Mass Transit island while curly-headed Lenins hawked "underground" newspapers. A living museum of the self-possessed dispossessed.

"What is it all about?" puzzled Dr. Merriwether, walking, absorbed, toward class, lab, home, or Holyoke Center. What is this terrific need to look special? Is it so hard to be anyone now? Why so much noise? Why were the demands on others so huge? Was it that there was so much expression in the world that one had to go further and further out to even think of oneself as a person? How he wished, how he wished.

Poor Merriwether could not even get so simple a need to his lips—such simple physiology—he just drew them tight and peered in the bookstores at the bare-legged girls, stared at the flopping breasts, the bare bellies, and went home to puzzle the meaning of it all.

"Truth comes as lightning strikes." He read this gnomic splinter in the middle of the Charles, his smooth arms supported on the oar shafts, holding a paperback anthology of Greek poems. It was his only morning on the river that summer. He had stopped for breath and to rummage among the ancients. But though he was ready, Capital T "Truth" did not strike.

Four, sometimes five mornings a week, he worked in the lab. Mostly out of the old discipline he'd begun thinking of as another propping habit. ("Habits get you through life, not into it.") It had been two years since he'd published a paper, four or five since he'd done work that absorbed him. Yet research had been near the center of his life.

He'd begun as a student of thirst, a dipsologist. "Funny name for a serious pursuit," he told his graduate students. Like all drives which were called instinctive, thirst was a dense complex of chemistry and mentality. Dr. Merriwether had investigated its relationship to lactation, hemmorhaging, drugs (atropine, epinephrine, metallic oxides, opium), x-ray irradiations, inferior vena cava congestion, snake bites, salinity, fear, various exertions (including copulation), suggestibility and dreams. In twenty-one post-doctoral years, he'd published almost a hundred papers. He had believed that what Wolf called "the dipsologic triad," thirst, drinking, satiety, was a primeval life pattern, that life, a sum of tropisms organized by the basic "drive" of self-preserving, could itself be regarded as a gigantic thirst. He'd even speculated that what he referred to in class as "cytologic *coups d'état,* the cancers," could profitably be studied with dipsologic models.

Yet he did not really buckle down to his research. His mice withered around the electrodes, he noted the salinity of carcinomic cells, he glimpsed certain interesting recurrences, but, in essence, he drifted.

Of course, he was doing other things. The "doctoring" —his protective term for the moonlighting—took up nine hours a week.

Even as a part-time doctor, he'd seen almost everything in the way of flesh and its common disorders, but he enjoyed the work as a form of theater, the encounters with students, the skill or clumsiness with which they described their ills, the emotional guises assumed in examination, and, occasionally, the surprise of a body.

Even when he'd been most absorbed in research, Dr. Merriwether had liked at least the idea of being a physician. There was of course the real pleasure of relieving pain, but more, he'd long ago sensed an important relationship between the practice of medicine and that of the poets and sages whom even the most commercially minded Merriwethers respected. Many poets had been physicians or the children of physicians. Dr. Merriwether supposed the connection had to do with the importance of human crisis in both occupations. Doctors and poets had to do with essentials; they knew the confusion and mystery of suffering, the disproportion between the human being as complex chemistry and the human being unmade by death.

The week before the astronauts took off for the first human touchdown on the moon, a stirring girl came up to

Merriwether's office for examination. In the magic suggestiveness of certain times, she had a lunar name, Cynthia. Her surname was Ryder.

Dr. Merriwether rose for every entrant, an old courtesy learned early, but impressive to many patients, even those who, like him, had been raised amidst rituals and formalities. Miss Ryder was golden-haired but almost Indian dark, slimly full, tall, slightly prognathous, brown-eyed. Her hair waterfalled to the top thoracic vertebra, her tanned flesh issued from a laundered yellow corolla. A human sunflower. Dr. Merriwether said, "How do you do? Miss Ryder, isn't it?"

"Yes, sir."

"Are you feeling ill?"

"No, sir."

Drawer Three, he thought. The Pill.

"But you want to talk with a doctor."

"I want a prescription, sir." A distant speech of soft vowels, southern, a speech restrained by shyness and courtesy, a pleasure for Merriwether whose own speech had almost Bostonian "a's" and other piquancies of New England, derived perhaps from the tight mouth of skeptic reserve, the residue of generations of legal and theological hair-splitting. Or, perhaps, from the endemic New England constipation, the holding back as long as possible before going out to the icy latrine.

"Please sit down." The yellow skirt drew up, just concealing that for which she sought prescription. "As you know, a doctor can't prescribe before he examines."

"Yes, sir. I want a prescription for the contraceptive pill."

"Have you had a prescription before?"

"At school, but I didn't get it renewed last time. I thought I could get it here in Student Health."

"Have you had a Pap test recently?"

"In April."

"We make a point of talking a bit about these chemical contraceptives."

"Yes, sir. I've had some talks about them."

"That's fine. Have you noticed anything unusual since you've taken them?"

"I think my breasts got bigger." A wonderful smile, slow, the face finely engraved with parentheses outside the lips, a smile of intelligence and humor.

" 'Expel Nature through the door, she'll come back through the window,' " said Dr. Merriwether. Miss Ryder's smile flowed into laughter, her face creased beautifully. An intelligent face. "For many girls it's like simultaneously dieting and feasting. There's an awful lot of nonsense about The Pill's side effects. Some are serious, but researchers tend to stuff a mouse with a dose that's a tenth its body weight, record the ensuing miseries, and then wave red flags. For the *Reader's Digest*. You could kill someone with water on such an experimental base. My own view is that the chief side effects have to do with the new orderliness it introduces. As the white pills leave the blue dial, people chart their monthly psychophysical changes."

The lecture was directed to the sheared stone pipes of Memorial Hall. He looked back to Miss Ryder. Or, at least, to her yellow dress rising over a fine mesomorphic body, the bra less breasts, full, finely nippled, whitely isolated by bikinied sun-tan sessions. He had seen many girls' bodies and was habituated even to their surprises. Beauty would stream from what had appeared sheer adiposity; a slim virgin would simmer in dermal poison; another would unclothe a venereal monument, so munificent and warm that he had to force constraint into his palms on her chest and back.

"I see you don't have time to waste, Miss Ryder. But I

think I won't bother examining you today. I won't even ask you the state of your feelings. Don't report me." And he turned from the perhaps-offering, perhaps-display and wrote the prescription.

The dress was on one arm. Now it resumed its place, the golden hair disappeared and, reappearing, was tossed aside. The long, Indian-hued head hoisted, arched, tossed, an athlete's movement. "Thank you, Doctor. It's very nice of you."

"I hope everything works out well, Miss Ryder."

"It'll be ok. Thank you. For everything."

Wolf's book on thirst had an epigraph from *Psalms:* "My strength was dried up like a potsherd; and my tongue cleaveth to my jaws; thou hast brought me into the dust of death."

After Miss Ryder left, Dr. Merriwether felt a little dust in his own body. "Foolish," he thought. He found his eyes on themselves; in the small mirror over the sink. For a man of forty the face was remarkably ungrooved. Did the smoothness stand for emotional triviality? Shouldn't forty years of New England snow and sun have ground the flesh against its bones? What had he avoided? The hair too was a younger man's, dark gold, with silver grain. The eyes, blue-green, smallish.

A long, ordinary, blue-eyed face. Younger than its years. Had it been left aside for engagements with a later crop of faces? As if it were being given a second human trial?

Dr. Merriwether's life was surrounded if not filled with women. A distant, formal husband, a loving, distant father of two daughters. As for women lab assistants and graduate students, he was seldom aware of them except as amiable auxiliaries. Many such women felt their position depended on masculine style, which had meant brusqueness, cropped hair, white smocks, low shoes, little or no make-up. Fine with him. No woman was so despised here as the occasional student who strutted her secondary sexual characteristics. (The buried axiom was, "Don't foul your professional nest.") Though the women's movement had begun to touch the biology labs, it went slowly, perhaps because there was a greater awareness of the complex spectrum of sexuality, the hundred components of sexual differentia.

As for women encountered in doctoring, they were clearly more outside the emotional pale. Even part-time doctors know the danger of patients' sexual invitations. The act of disrobing turns many a woman into her idea of a vamp. Miss Ryder's quick strip was a familiar variation. Yet a gleam was with her; and left with her. Dr. Merriwether wished the day were over.

There was another hour to go, a fractured rib, a case of jaundice—which he rushed into the hospital—and another Drawer Three, a fat, hypomanic girl from Davenport, Iowa, who had discovered her sexual potential in the infamous Interpersonal Relations Seminar in William James Hall. Dr. Merriwether understood—or misunderstood—that the routine included LSD on weekdays, penile massages on the weekends. "You feel that you are prepared to deal with the emotional consequences of this grave step, Miss Wongerman?"

"I certainly do."

"Good luck then." And God pity the ambitious lad who tried those alpic gorges.

He saw Miss Ryder twice before he realized it was because she wanted him to see her. In a great straw hat ringed with blue and gold flowers, she stood in front of the old

Wadsworth House across from Forbes Plaza. She wore blue levis and a flowered blouse, and was eating an ice cream cone. She might have been waiting for a bus.

The third time he saw her, she waved. If she'd waved the first times, he hadn't noticed. (Though who knows. Stu Benson had found that courtship activity continued in the decorticate cat with no observable alteration.) At any rate, he saw her this time, and instead of turning left and crossing the street at Billings and Stover, he crossed toward her. "Hi there."

"Hi, Doctor. How are you?"

That modest southern speech, the least chiseled American speech, though in Miss Ryder's mouth, exceptionally clear. He put his left hand to his right pulse. "I seem ok."

"Want a lick?"

Dry as dust, Merriwether licked. "Thank you."

"You off to operate?"

"I'm off to shower and play tennis."

"Can I walk with you?"

"Glad to have company, Miss Ryder. I'm all alone this summer." This small excess hung between them for a bit.

Close as his house was to the Square, it was out of sight to all but Cambridge initiates. Once past the Loeb Theater, Cynthia Ryder was in strange territory. The country quiet of Ash Street, the romantic old moss of Cambridge, surrounded them.

Dr. Merriwether's uncle, Griswold Tipton, had been Professor of Geology, a pupil and successor of Alexander Agassiz, son of the great Louis. He'd built and died in the Acorn Street house. When Aunt Aggie's son, Griswold III, was killed on Guadalcanal Island in the Second World War, Merriwether, an undergraduate then, left Eliot House and moved in with his widowed aunt, partly as caretaker, partly as companion. Mr. Stonesifer's installation on the third floor relieved him of both chores. By then he was a graduate student and spending most of his time in the labs. In 1950, he married Sarah Wainwright, a graduate student in Romance Languages. They moved into an apartment on Ellery Street. When Aunt Aggie died in 1954—she'd left him the house—they moved in with three-year-old Albie and one-year-old Priscilla. (Mr. Stonesifer dismantled his electric toys and went off to New Hampshire.)

Acorn Street was eleven houses each of whose windows were part of Dr. Merriwether's inner landscape. The neighbors knew him, his gait, his clothes, his habits. When the *Times* mentioned his election to the National Academy of Arts and Sciences, they congratulated him. He could borrow lawn mowers from these houses, perhaps even money —if there were no real need of it. The houses were his scene, what was permanent for him. Walking there with a twenty-year-old beauty, the familiarity became accusation.

Merriwether talked fast, against the puerility of his feeling. He told Miss Ryder of the houses and their owners. This summer the street was a center of anti-ABM activity. His neighbors, George Bowen and Warren Defries, testified in Washington about the expensive futility of the system; in the *Times* letters columns, they countered the arguments of weapon-lovers; at night, walking dogs, they met under acacia trees to discuss interceptor rings, recognition patterns, megatonnage, silo costs. Defries, huge and bulbous as a parade balloon, spread over chain-smoking little Bowen. "It looked as if he were knighting him. He was just pushing off the smoke."

Miss Ryder asked him what ABM was.

Summies.

This was the affectionately contemptuous term for the Summer School Students. Miss Ryder was a Summie, not Harvard, not Radcliffe. The Summie Myth is that the girls are beautiful, ignorant, available. (The summer catalogue advanced the fiction.) Dr. Merriwether found Summies no different from what weren't called Wintries; only barer. (The real Cambridge shift came when December released the gloom of New England's winter.)

Miss Ryder's ignorance was easily repairable: Dr. Merriwether said, "It's the acronym for anti-ballistic missile. It's not a millionth as important as *Macbeth*. Though I suppose it could wipe out every copy and every reader of *Macbeth*."

"I do know *Macbeth*," said Miss Ryder.

They were in front of the little oval lawn, under the acacia tree. Miss Ryder had enormous, almost-black eyes, rounder and denser than Sarah's. He put out his hand and thanked her for walking him home. No facial subtlety hid her disappointment.

Dr. Merriwether felt a jolt of pleasure: he counted with this lovely person. Of course, students love to come into faculty homes, any faculty member, any home.

"Can I come watch you play tennis?"

"If I were good. Or even gracefully bad, yes. But I'm a hacker. Do you play?"

A little. She'd been junior doubles champ of Eastern Carolina.

"You certainly can't watch. It would hurt your game and my vanity."

"You're such a nice man, Doctor." She leaned and kissed his mostly unprepared mouth, spun on her hard-to-spin-on sandals and walked off. A stunning sight in her flared blue pants, the only sight of that sort on Acorn Street since Priscilla went off to Maine.

Dr. Merriwether's tennis opponent, John Davison, was one of those fellows who come late to Harvard and can't forget what it was like in the non-Harvard world. Half their life's satisfaction came from the ever-astonished self-gratulation of being in Cambridge. Dr. Merriwether had watched a television "special" on the Royal Family of England. What amazed him was that most of the Royal Conversation had to do with royalty, with stories of Queen Victoria or of the surprise at other people's surprise at the humanness of royal persons. He compared this odd provincialism with Davison's.

Dr. Merriwether had "discovered" Davison in the *Journal of Experimental Physiology*. A first-rate microscopist, Davison had worked out a scope which resolved features 2000 angstroms apart. His aim was to edit the genetic ribbon, and he was now working on the hemophiliac determinant. It was a job fit for a scientific Lancelot. It should carry its dignity to every part of a man's life. It didn't. Outside of the laboratory, Davison was childish. His only other modes of affection were tennis and Harvard. Harvard was his wife—though he had a fattish official specimen—and children—the world had been spared a junior Davison. Dr. Merriwether had thought of inquiring if there were a gene for Harvard-mania. (Its linkage would be with repressant narrowness. Perhaps Davison could edit it out of any future Davisons.)

Davison was bald, thin, taller than Merriwether and a few years younger. He had an open, quizzical face. Puzzlement seemed its permanent set. When he aced Merriwether, or when he'd done something especially fine in the lab, the face spread into childish triumph. Merriwether felt a gap of attendance in Davison; but that afternoon he needed someone to talk with and Davison was the only one around.

There were very few people anywhere with whom he could talk. Formerly, there was Sarah, and, for a few years, Albie and Priscilla (though the talk was mostly of Albie and Priscilla). There was Thomas Fischer, a pal of twenty years, but Fischer tended to fix their relationship as it had once been, that of wise senior to Merriwether's amusing but respectful attendant; that did not always make for ease. There were Stu Benson and Maxim Schneider, but they were off for the summer. Which left Davison.

Dr. Merriwether offered him his case. "Johnny," he said, as they were putting their rackets into canvas covers, "you ever fooled around with a student?"

"Fooled around with a student?"

"Yes."

"I try to be completely straight with them. I don't see your point."

He was tempted to say, "Davison, old prince, didn't you ever tell yourself, 'This girl is driving me wild,' think of taking down her pants and popping her on the lab table?" The response would probably have been, "What for?"

The physicist Wigner wished there were studies of the diversity of intelligence, plants to Shakespeare. He said that when he talked with John Von Neuman, he felt that he was asleep and Neuman awake. High I.Q. or not, Davison was asleep to the world beyond his microscope.

More than sex, more than drink, it might be company that human beings needed. Conferences, faculty meetings, towns, churches, sex itself might be ways of satisfying it.

The most hermetic hermit had the company of those he feared or hated, the company of the absent. At Walden, Thoreau walked into Concord every few days, his chairs were set for visitors. Company was the true human climate. Socrates returned to the cave prematurely from loneliness, not compassion. "Why hast Thou deserted me?" means "Why have you left me alone?"

Or so thought Merriwether, home, in the bathtub, soaping his right foot, knee to chin, the fleshed antebrachium rubbing his genitals. Then, into mind, came the faceless body of the boy for whom Miss Ryder was preparing herself. Why? One kiss? Lips together amidst the old symbolic perfume. Plus one view of a tanned, mesomorphic body, a few hundred words, a sense of fifty traits and ten or twelve accomplishments (junior doubles champ, student, *Macbeth* reader, ice-cream eater, hat-wearer).

Two days later, he looked across Mass Avenue and, seeing no Miss Ryder, felt sick. "So," he thought, *"disappointment."*

But its roots were shallow, there was oblivion in the walk home. "I should do the lawn." Davison couldn't play today, maybe Fischer was in town, maybe they could have supper.

He walked toward nothing, so walked slowly, vacating himself to heat, looks in windows, the customers in Zum-Zum's, the pleasant half-image of breakfast—bacon rolls, the small, fruity tear-segments of the orange juice, the first inroad on the *Times,* the sweet shock of the obituaries—round the bend, the grocer, the wine shop, the Brattle Theater—a Marx Brothers Festival, neither camp, amusement nor nostalgia for him—the grilled fretwork of the Loeb Theater.

And there she was.

Ahead of him, walking slowly, golden head bent, long,

dark, bare legs out of scarlet mini-skirt, an odd slowness in the spreadfoot, springy, unusual gait; awkward and athletic both. Dr. Merriwether doubled his pace, came abreast and touched her elbow. "Miss Ryder."

"You."

"Hi." And into her deep, unsmiling relief—his happiness—another "Hi."

"I'm so glad to see you. I was trying to find your house. I couldn't remember how to get to it."

"You were doing pretty well."

They walked by the Graduate Center, down Ash, past Acacia, into Acorn Street, up to his house across from the Japanese urns and the gingkos of his millionaire neighbors, around his little oval lawn, up the squeaky, red steps and in through the door where Miss Ryder said, "I like you so much. I feel so foolish, but I like you so much."

Not looking at her. "I like you too, Miss Ryder. And I am ten times as foolish, without the license you have." Meaning neither young—though inexperienced—nor free—though freed by intellect, will, abandonment.

Miss Ryder twirled from sun parlor to dusk parlor, dining room, kitchen, stairwell, touching chairs, old mirrors, oil lamps (feebly bulbed, pathetic conversion). Ill at ease, he remembered the modern innocent's "thing to do," went into the kitchen and made drinks, Dubonnet, lemon juice, soda, ice; new combination—awful—for new combination.

Miss Ryder was glad to hold a cold glass. Her hand was very soft—he did not then know the hours and hours of care that went into every inch of her body—touching it was sharp delight.

He sipped, sat in the least menacing of the chairs, and said that much as he would like it, no relationship was possible for them, every relationship between heterosexual man and woman could only progress and what progress was possible for them? None at all. Their feelings were of course natural. As far as biologic and even psychic structures went, the feelings made perfect sense, but against even the reordered social structures of this affluent, long-living west—people living a life doubled over the social structures which supported the old half-lives—the young girl and middle-aged man being one of the most familiar bond-pairs of the new age, even so, even so . . .

"Dear . . . Doctor, whatever. I love to hear you speak. But it is, isn't it, just you and me here. Isn't it?"

"I hope so."

"I mean, I know we represent male and female, young and less-young and all, but it's just you and me. Now. Here."

"Yes, Miss Ryder. But to understand something helps overcome it. There really should be no chance for us."

"Chance? For what?"

Headshake.

"Let me stay."

"Stay?" He could feel Davison in his voice. Was dull interrogation the easiest form of evasion?

"Yes."

"Ok. We'll play the radio, maybe have supper, I'll wish I were twenty-one and you can wish what you want to wish. And we can kiss goodby."

"We didn't kiss hello," said Cynthia, who bent over, and this time was kissed as much as kisser.

Weeks later, she said, "I was so surprised." Which surprised him, for people think the curve of their feeling is apparent to all whom they don't wish to deceive. Still, he was kissing in part for her sake (for therapy, for common humanity). So he could still feel himself Man of Principle, Man of Years, Doctor to Confused Patient, Professor to Easily Enchanted Student.

In short, the Decorticate Dipsologist. Courting.

2

In the parlor, he'd managed with talk. "I'm too old for such love. You know I like you enormously, you're a terrific pull on me." Any twentieth-century western parent, doctor, teacher, knew the importance of self-confidence. "But a man gets on, he relies more on what he's done himself. Whatever love is, it's not an accomplishment."

"There are plenty of people incapable of it."

"Not the same. I don't think the love system functions usefully after thirty. Real love comes at your age. I mean the early, parent-child structure of love is matched in the late teens or early twenties by the great transference. By the time you're my age, it's but a combination of lust and nostalgia. There's no real room for new roots."

"Bertrand Russell says he only found true passion when he was ninety."

"Was he honest?"

"If you can even lie like that at ninety, it might mean it was true at seventy."

"Russell remained adolescent. Didn't he lose his mother very early? He had the schizoid's passion for abstraction. His late amorousness was neurotic. He was a schizoid adolescent for seventy-five years."

She'd wanted him to hear a record and went off to buy it. He went off too, to buy wine, and then, in the Square, a bouquet of yellow jonquils, and, for her remembrance, a large book of Vermeers which, at home again, waiting for her, he inscribed "To my most charmingly impatient patient, in this loony summer."

The minutes of separation deepened his sense of the uniqueness of what was happening. This primary human illusion. As if human beings were as empty-headed as goldfish, swimming round the commonplace, astonished at perpetual novelty. Columbuses of the Bathtub. In a way, it really was that way. The neural complex was so staggering, a statistical case could be made for the absolute uniqueness of every human feeling and event. It was not true—as the Harvard poet Eliot said—that humans were most alike in their moments of passion. Everything was *more or less* like something else; but just considering the fantastic number of synapses involved, passionate moments corresponded to the greatest acts of intellection. Words might be displaced by grunts, but this did not mean the simplification of sensitivity. How much of his own system right now was alerted to Cynthia's absence. Her absence was a tremendous presence in him. She was off somewhere in his town. The *dakka-dakka* of the MTA escalator, the beaded chests, the saris, the billboards, the witch hat of Christ's (where he and Sarah were married about the time Cynthia looked more fish than woman), fifty thousand small gleams, noises. There, now, but here, part of his *milieu interieur*.

Home, the *Graves* in the freezer, the flowers in a blue Wedgewood vase he'd bought in London for Sarah's thirtieth birthday, the Vermeer on the arm of his chair. Absence soaked the room. Weight. Waiting. Had something happened to her? Lovesick, dizzy, maybe she hadn't seen an open manhole, a car. No one would notify him. Or, seeing him in his house, had she come to (out of?) her senses? Something said or not said, a gesture flicking the illusion, so that she suddenly saw the grotesqueness of their relationship and was now working up the phone call which would get her out of it.

Dr. Merriwether suffered in classic fashion; self-consciousness was no relief. He suffered, he knew the foolishness of suffering, he suffered more. "This is the fault of indolence. Acedia. Moping around, waiting for something to happen to me."

He changed into a Harvard sportshirt, did knee-bends, strummed the bookshelves, took down and put back tiny-print Victorian editions of Romantic poets, a medical school text (*The Etiology of Rheumatic Fever*), Aunt Agatha's Greek lexicon. Cynthia. *Kyneo,* to kiss. *Kynegetis,* a hunt ress. *Kynedon,* doggily, greedily. *Kynthos,* mountain in Delos, birthplace of Apollo and Artemis. *Kyniske,* bitch puppy. *Kynopes,* dog-eyed or shameless one. He picked up the Vermeer, sat on the sofa's barest fang, and studied the interiors within which bemused women read letters, poured milk, weighed gold, adjusted bobbins, stared into golden window light. The radiance of their absorption absorbed him. Then, clip-clopping on the porch, a buzzer, and, dress changed, face charged with prospect, browned and golden, Cynthia.

"I had to go back and change. I was so sticky." A whirl

inside, showing her dress, autumn leaves on a red base, high on her athlete's legs—slightly knock-kneed—long, child-soft feet in wooden sandals.

She had the record, could she play it for him, could she dance for him, would he think it silly?

No, surely not. He'd find it charming. But where?

"Where's the record player?"

He had to think. His own music came from the FM stations. "In Priscilla's room." He led her upstairs.

Into the family innards. Which was less easy for him. But he could not refuse what was so patently harmless. If slightly goofy. He looked away from the master bedroom, led her down the cluttered hall to Priscilla's room. Cynthia gawked, assessed, admired cabinets of Merriwether trinkets, marine prints, old beds, Stonesifer's abandoned communications board, Priscilla's wooden-pegged armoire. "It's so quaint. So sweet, so historic-hysteric."

He found the record player.

Cynthia took over, adjusted the bar, the tone arm, the speed.

To his surprise, the music was lovely, quiet, full of clear, steely plucks over which singers half-sighed a lyric about riding the wind. Cynthia spun, bent, shifted stiffly, intensely and then in large sweeps. Subtle and serious. Too large for this small room, too much. Yet oddly beautiful, touching, personal. A dance of love.

Too much for him. He was of a time that thought of the beautiful in a frame. Performance. A spectator had to be one of a crowd. Only Hitler sat alone in auditoriums. (Or did the television generation accept personal performance for personal declaration?)

Then too, there was his own body. Not flabby, but stiff with gravity; he felt sluggish, slow. God knows he couldn't dance like this. Had anyone ever danced like this here? Priscilla danced, so did Albie and Esmé, but theirs was home-dancing. Priscilla was lively, but she had more strength and beauty than grace; she was no dancer. Perhaps—and this brought the smile Cynthia wanted—Aunt Agatha had twirled here for Louden Stonesifer.

"Am I silly?" Stopping.

"It's beautiful. Thank you. Who are the artists?" after weighing "singers" and "musicians."

"The Youngbloods. Aren't they good?"

"I hope they don't feel out of place."

She'd stepped out of her sandals for the dance. Now she stepped not into them but into a pair of Priscilla's moccasins. "Are these your daughter's?"

"Yes."

"Her feet are fatter than mine." Cynthia's reading in women's magazines had given her a physiologist's index of proportions, the relation of feet to hands, of joint-space to body weight. Fat foot with thick waist, long fingers, long toes, long legs. Merriwether saw this forensic physiologist working out Priscilla's appearance. He felt a surge of loyalty to his daughter's feet. "Priscilla is a beauty." The belle of Acorn Street. A fine figure, a little squat, a strong, sweet face lit by his own blue-green eyes. He assumed a lovely body, he had not seen her nude for ten years, had no desire to, remained New England where it counted, in distance, privacy, the sacred space of one's own body, every person's zone of repose.

"I know. I'm jealous. Here's a picture in her yearbook."

This golden beauty, this sugared child from the Carolina beaches was doing what he'd never thought of doing, going through his daughter's things. A moral homunculus leapt in his chest. "Do you think?"

"Oh please forgive me." The long face tightened—in fear, not shame. Too much reaction. "I'm so awful. It's just —I want to know everything about you. Please forgive me."

"Nothing to forgive."

Though his discomfort would disappear more in forgetting than forgiving, and he just kept from saying "I think it's gone as far as it will go."

She could feel the need to get her out of this place. "All right."

"Do you know Boston?"

She did but said, "Hardly at all. I'd love to see it with you."

He drove the old burgundy Dodge down Boylston to the Drive and then along the river filled with kayaks, rowing shells, sailboats. In Boston, they parked near the wharves behind the Statehouse, worked their way through shoppers down Freedom Trail, the cemetery, the churches, the Georgian meeting houses tucked like Monopoly pieces into the cement bloat of the new city. Walking with Cynthia stirred Merriwether, not to ancestor-worship—for, moralist, as well as physiologist, he knew neither physiology nor morality had altered in the human centuries. Give or take a few gestures, a few resolves, heroic times differed little from others, and heroes hardly at all. (This was Merriwether's counter to his father's ancestral inflation. The old insurance man had spent his last years writing *The Memoirs of a Harvard Man* on unused ledger books.) Still, the black bumps in the Granary Burial Ground covered Merriwether dust. He showed Cynthia the grave of the first American Merriwether, Andrew. She read out the only readable date, 1674, and two lines of verse.

> No season's harshnesse was his Wether
> The godlie Andrew Merriwether.

Odd to hear them in the soft speech, the beautiful girl kneeling, the rear's interrogating curve pointed his way, while index finger moved in the black grooves of the seventeenth-century letters. Ah well. "We Merriwethers weren't any great shakes. Artisans, farmers, tradesmen. A few legislative types." The two best-known had been a Samuel who'd argued the Dartmouth College Case against Webster and an Albert who'd made a speech against American interference in Yucatán. (Albie had disinterred it from a diplomatic history and submitted it to the Boston *Herald* with a commentary on the restraint America had once shown in "Vietnam-type" situations.) Cynthia said, "To think you're part of this." Stones, old brick, steeples.

"I suppose so." With or against the grain, he was part of what lay under the automotive stink of this Black-Irish-Italian city.

In a tourist's bar, he ate steak, she oysters. (Full of health bulletins, she ate no red meat but veal.) They drank red wine and drove back in the dusk along the river.

"May I come home with you?"

They were by Dunster, headed up Boylston.

"I don't think you should."

"Please."

"For a bit, then. A drink."

"All right."

Downstairs, she sipped apple cider, sat beside him,

touched him, then went upstairs and waited till he followed. She was in Priscilla's room; her clothes were off. "Please," she said.

"Almost everything I know keeps me from this."

"Just lie down with me."

He did, talking. "There's a *déjà vu,* a *déjà lu* about this. It's so . . . typical: the good old innocent prof who's never even called an undergraduate by his Christian name. And the undergraduate taking him by the hand, leading him where she thinks she knows he wants to go."

"Does there have to be an echo in everything? Is it so shameful?"

"I don't like living other people's lives."

"People eat, sleep, love. You can't get away from that."

Silence. She lay still, pretended sleep, then fell asleep. He got up and went into his own bed. Where in the morning, he woke to find her naked, drawing his pajama pants off around the matutinal erection. "Oh Jesus."

And they became, biologically and legally, lovers.

Dr. Merriwether thought about aging. Not much was known about it. Buffon thought longevity had to do with growth. Flourens held that life duration was five times the period of growth. Bunge related mammal duration to ratios of weight increase in the new-born. Metchnikoff thought putrefaction the agent of degeneration. (The hindgut was crucial; he advocated a diet of culture-soured milk for lactic acid.) Weismann related duration to fertility: birds of prey produced breeds of one or two and lived longer than flies and rabbits.

These days, the talk was of platelets and "genetic noise," DNA errors caused by overheating, background radiation, chemical agents. The new jargon said that one source of aging was improper handling of input: the most efficient intelligence eventually succumbed to the silt of data.

The physiological chatter covered Dr. Merriwether's confusion. He took up his rowing on the Charles, ate "correctly"—no whiskey, no butter, no steaks, and yoghurt, in case Metchnikoff had something. It was for Cynthia. At night, he walked with her along the river, arm around her waist, happy at the sight of other lovers a quarter of a century younger, lying on the banks, "making"—as the chilling expression had it—"out." In another foul label of the day, he was "a dirty old man," the usurper of a trusting young beauty who should, in classic propriety, be the partner of a hairless-chested, sex-tormented, draft-eligible poet-in-the-egg. Instead, here he was, the well—happy, if nervous, quarry of this southern beauty.

And no longer sexually evasive. They went into the creaky old marriage bed and, after a few awkward sessions, learned how to please each other.

For a week, they met at night, walked at night, and went to bed without being at least publicly recognized.

But the Summer Session was ending; their time was over. "We can meet weekends," said Cynthia. "I'll come up every weekend."

"Impossible."

"Why?"

"Summer is special. Life starts again in fall. Everyone is here. Every inch of life is mapped out. There's no room. Anyway, Cynthia, you're going to forget it all within a week of getting home."

"I don't think so."

"Tell you what. You go home, no letters, no calls. You go back to school in a month. Wait another week. Ten days.

Wait ten days. If absence, time and the Swarthmore boys haven't diverted you from this"—shoulder shrug—"of ours, then write me. Or write anyway. Just say what you feel. We'll both be relieved. We'll have had a strange, fine time. We'll have been temporary outlaws. It's everybody's fantasy. We'll have had this time. It'll help us endure the Usual. It'll be stuff for memoirs. For getting to sleep on."

Their farewell was full of that strongest romantic glue, amorous torment. Cynthia left Acorn Street, Dr. Merriwether watched her out the window. The long, gold hair, badge of the young, of summer, of the end of romantic love and its paranoiac radiance.

A week later, he, Sarah and the children were in Vermont woods. They spent two weeks with the Schneiders in the geodesic dome Maxim had built with his sons.

The Schneiders were The Happily Married Couple of Dr. Merriwether's experience. Most couples could be mapped on the graph of marital wither (which often shows revival in aging couples who become each other's thermometers and medicine chests). Not the Schneiders.

They endured amorously. Merriwether studied them. They looked alike, large-headed, big-eyed, round-faced, Jeanne taller, a bigger smiler, Maxim, eye-glassed, rapid, full of gesture, of theatric flash. They'd met in high school, were lovers before Maxim knew what a clitoris was. They remained lovers. Of the two sorts of marriage, the partner-centered and the child-centered, the Schneiders were the former. Jeanne was her husband's center, her intelligence flowed only as far as unquestioned support for him. Dr. Merriwether thought her a marvelous woman, had thought she must be marvelous to sleep with. (This was speculation, not desire; he censored even mental treason.) He liked or even loved her as part of a couple; he cared for them both this way.

Maxim had begun in biology, but in his thirties, he'd sat in on George Sarton's seminars and one summer decided to become an historian of science. Now, in his forties, he thought of himself as an historian; he'd learned Greek, Tamil and Chinese, and had worked out a poly-lingual glossary for herbals. He had the comparatist's lust for analogies, unexpected symmetries, historical metaphors. It went beyond medicine. The return of Vietnam veterans *reminded* him of fifth-century Greek tradesmen coming from summer naval battles with the Persians to demand new power in the state. "War does even more for democracy than it does for technology." Such overstatements ignited most of their discussions. With no one did Merriwether relax more.

The families too relaxed with each other. The children were almost exactly paired. It made for jokes, mutual support, ease.

In the woods, near a beautiful pond full of fallen birches, with loons and hawks surfacing up or down, Schneiders and Merriwethers sailed, shot popguns at cans, walked trails, picked berries. At night, within the heat of the stove, they played recorders, flutes, piano. Sarah and Tommy Schneider sang lieder, the rest Gershwin, Porter, Kern, those lyric mendacities which had sealed their domesticity. Merriwether felt part of a human burrow. Nude against the plasticene skin, the pine boards spelled the logic of habitation. The construction point was how little one needed.

The queer, displaced, luxury needs of his Cambridge summer passed into air, movement, family gabble; the bitterness which made life with Sarah claustrophobic faded.

He thought of Cynthia only three or four times. Indeed, a month later, back in Cambridge, he was completely surprised by a postcard in his box. A postcard written in purple ink, the script clear and elegant, a calligraphy which called up summer, the obituaries, the solitude, her beauty.

But a postcard. In his box where Campus Mail and Miss Weeber could feast on it.

> I've been here a week. You asked for this. Here it is. Here I am. Thinking about it now, I must admit I love you madly. I'd like to see you and tell you back every word you've told me. Then I will ask you if you love me. If you smiled, I would understand.

And then, not wasting an inch, curled around "Edgar Degas (1834–1917) Dancers Adjusting Their Slippers-Pastel-Cleveland Museum of Art"

> Today was a day for waving hello to people you didn't know. The newest flavor here is called Awaawa Ukelele. I shouted & danced around the corner until I got one free. The flavors before that were Gullywasher, Fulla Bulla Olé, and Kiss Me Stupid. I got them all. Love to you.

How many other letters of his life counted as this one? One from Sarah on Duck Island saying she was pregnant, another from the *JEP* accepting his first article, one from Wolf congratulating him about the piece on serum osmalality. Not many.

What is it, he wondered. What is this feeling?

It used to be thought the body was more "sensitive" as it got deeper. But no, it's like the earth itself, the vividness is at the surface. You can crush an organ and get no pain, but look at the skin. One cm. of human skin contains two sensory machines for cold, twelve for heat, three million cells, ten hairs, fifteen sebaceous glands, a yard of blood vessels, a hundred sweat glands, three thousand sensory cells at the end of nerve fibers, four yards of nerves, twenty-five pressure apparatuses for tactile stimuli, two hundred nerve cells to record pain. This fantastic factory is our *surface*. No wonder our feeling is so exposed. Our hearts are on our sleeve.

At ten minutes to twelve, he'd stooped for his mail, low-keyed, middle-aged prof softened by American life and Harvard cream, and, at five minutes to twelve, he was once again the Burgher Outlaw gripped by passion for a girl a year older than his son, poeticized, transfigured, en route to restatements of the statements he'd lived by, a grotesque, a dirty old man, a standard character for story, a Jolyon Forsyte (Galsworthy's delicate, latherless soap opera had begun to dominate the Sunday evenings of university communities).

He answered the postcard on Department of Physiology stationery, a mistake from which New England propriety shrank. He rewrote it on plain bond, and bought a plain envelope for dispatch.

> Your card was the most beautiful of my life. This even as I trembled at the possibility the secretary would read it. In the *Essay on Human Understanding,* Locke writes, "Any one reflecting upon the thought he has of the delight which any present or absent thing is apt to produce in him has the idea we call love." I delight in you, I fear that delight, I fear what I fear, and *that* I fear, but who knows, maybe you are the way out of the prison of my feelings. Or

do I propose another prison for us both? I know nothing. You are my patient, and a pupil, I a doctor and professor, but here, in love, it may be that you will be more tutor than I. I foresee nothing for us. But, dear Cynthia, *je vous adore*. B.

3

Like half the college girls of America, Cynthia Ryder wanted to spend a summer in Cambridge. It was the new center of manageable excitement. Europe was back-packs, hostels, sore legs, sexist pinchers, museums. Berkeley—as Eastern talk had it—emptied in summer of all but freaks, heads and Panthers. The other choices were jobs-for-bread, resorts or family; these were for the needy or intimidated. No, Cambridge was it. Those that didn't settle there came through.

Cynthia told her father the Harvard Summer Session had a great program. That was enough; Mr. Ryder would subsidize an expedition to the Arctic if his daughters suggested there was a solid educational reason for it.

Cynthia and her friends, Weej and Dinah, took a semi-furnished apartment on Irving Street. Cynthia's boy friend, Jamie, lived with her and worked at an Amoco Station in Boston; the other girls changed guard every few weeks. Boys and girls on their way to and from the Cape, Maine, and Canada, were in and out of the place—the floor space was good and there were sleeping bags and old quilts for mattresses.

For a year, at Swarthmore, the girls had lived with boys in their dorm rooms, but none of them had lived as couples for weeks on end. Cambridge was domesticity without chains. It was great to come back to the apartment and never know who you'd see or in what state of undress. Everybody walked around half nude. There were always talk and music. If something clicked, you went into one of the bedrooms and made out.

Jamie had been Cynthia's boy friend for a year, but it was wearing thin. He was beautiful, he was sweet, but he was a baby. Besides he was always horny, she wasn't. She'd just about get to sleep on the quilted floor when he'd be tickling her for service at one end or another. She blew up, he turned infant, then asserted himself, said she was breaking him down, told her he was moving, then moved. She didn't miss him; she was already in love with the doctor.

Cynthia had grown up in a Xanadu house her father had built on the inland waterway below Shallot in Eastern North Carolina. It was an endless, golden house set amidst stables, courts, pools, gardens; outside and inside interlaced through glassed patios, boxwood corridors, rose gardens, game, gadget and play areas, photography rooms, machine shops. There was a runway for the plane the four girls learned to pilot when they reached sixteen, a pier for motorboats to draw them water-skiing, a five-hole golf course. There was a trophy room, each year fuller of silver shine as the girls won horse shows, tennis tournaments, Latin Competitions.

Much triumph, but not much gaiety, although the girls enjoyed family life, respected each other's wit, believed their father the most remarkable man in Eastern Carolina and their mother, although hickish, the best there was. There was, of course, much competition. Its source was need for Mr. Ryder's favor, fear of his disapproval. There was much of the last; the first was scarce.

Mr. Ryder was a driven man, a self-made son of a religious woman who owned Shallot's hardware store. He'd won a baseball scholarship to Elon College, then went on to Chapel Hill for his law degree. A great lawyer in a state renowned for great lawyers, he had, in his time, seen nearly everything in the way of domestic and institutional deformity. In a way, his house sheltered his disgust with the world which financed it.

Like many men of the late Sixties who derived general opinions from popular magazines and television, Mr. Ryder believed there was next to nothing bright American girls would not do. Sexually, politically, pharmaceutically. This even went for the four girls he'd raised in what he called "disciplined liberty." Like another nineteenth century phrase revived in the nineteen sixties, "benign neglect," Mr. Ryder's coupled apparent opposites in the interest of carefree policy. He had trained his daughters to question everything, to tolerate anything intellectually, even to try out anything that tested intelligence and physical skill; but not their morals. That area they could leave to the deprived and disordered. They should be content with mental and sportive adventure. His intelligence had created a special world for them. Their bodies were fine, their teeth straight, their clothes whatever they wanted; they went to the best Eastern preparatory schools and colleges, there was nowhere on earth they couldn't go. All he asked was that they should avoid the moronic license of their contemporaries who blew themselves up in revolutionary cells, fornicated with the casualness of gorillas, mindlessly advanced their mindlessness with crazing chemicals, and ululated into loudspeakers against the complex arrangements brilliant men had worked out over centuries.

Mr. Ryder was not unaware of tension in his daughters, even saw how competition for his favor created it; but he did not guess how deeply it had formed them. In his time he'd seen every sort of family mess, fathers and daughters at each other's throats or in each other's beds, brothers closer than man-and-wife or fixed in a hatred even murder couldn't appease; but these were disordered, untrained, miserably unfortunate people. His daughters' lives had been worked out as well as lives could be in such times.

"Let them alone," he frequently told his wife. "They know what they're doing."

They was the sacred pronoun. Cynthia's mother had learned to bear with it, as she had learned early how to bear or slide off, if not resist, her husband's petty tyranny and mockery. "What kind of a roast is this, Mary Jane? Somethin' you ordered from the Sears catalogue?" Her packs of cigarettes would be piled in the fireplace and publicly—daughters, Jimbo, the carpenter, and Emy, the cook—burned. Mrs. Ryder's humor bolstered her passivity. Her good spirit, decency and sweetness gave her daughters one sort of security, but subservience to her husband deprived them of another, a sense of equality. They fastened on their father's values: good looks, good bodies, winning; public distinction, private delight.

Cynthia's ambition was huge. She'd wanted to be the most beautiful, most renowned, most brilliant, most accomplished . . . whatever. Everything.

Boys were there to be used, to be loved, to be lost in, to be surmounted. Virginity was the first obstacle. Between that and marriage was the Era of Exploration: boys-men were to be explored, tested.

For Cynthia, the spring of Sixty-Nine had been a sexual pageant. Behind Jamie's back, she'd slept at least once with eight boys. Weej and Dinah claimed she wanted to sleep with every boy at Swarthmore, Penn and Haverford. "I'm no hick. Why stop there?" But it wasn't that interesting. She was curious about sex as she was about genetics and French poets; naturally, there was more. She loved her power to excite and the pleasure of excitement. For a girl who'd spent years in the shadow of a prettier older sister, who didn't wear a bra till the tenth grade and who periodically feared that she was ugly, the pleasure of being told she was beautiful (and occasionally seeing her own beauty) was finer than anything else in her life.

Alone in bed, she rolled out the names and bodies of her lovers; a Homeric catalogue. "Am I a whore?" Knew she wasn't, yet knew the curiosity of early sex, the variety of those concealed male tools. Jamie and Benjy, Tommy, Will, Chip and Petto, Doug, and Deny. It was Chip who'd raped her. Or tried. (He couldn't get in, she was so tiny then.) Two weeks before her seventeenth birthday, the summer before college. They'd made love every week; he never got in very far. He was huge like Gerald in *Women in Love,* but gentle, funny. They'd take his Volkswagen out to the airport, stick a surfboard through the back windows, drive out to the Shallot runway and radio in for take-off instructions. He sent her a poem a day her first year; awful poems. Then Jamie, a sculptor and dancer, nobody had a body like his, he wanted to make love every minute, any time, he walked around with a hard-on all day, he had to wear baggy pants, and she would have to help him beat off three or four times a day, taking it in her mouth, no great joy, though she loved him, still loved him a little. When he came home to Carolina with her, they made love all night. Within earshot of her father. Of course. She'd been using foam; she'd given up The Pill in March after she kept fainting. In the middle of July though, she was sick of the foam, it kept leaking out of her, she could never tell when it would. Which was when she went to Holyoke Center to get a prescription for The Pill.

4

Cynthia came up to Cambridge the last weekend of September and stayed in the apartment of Dr. Merriwether's friend, Thomas Fischer, who was, as usual, off somewhere.

The visit had been arranged in midnight telephone calls which, for Merriwether, had some of the excitement of love-making.

"So this is what the phone means to the girls." Once Sarah had taken the receiver from Esmé's hand as she poured school gossip into it. Esmé screamed. Merriwether came downstairs, pacified and dispatched her. "The phone's part of her flesh. Like a limb."

"She hasn't done her French, she hasn't begun her social studies report, she's been on that phone since seven-fifteen. I'm not going to live behind Esmé's Telephonic Chinese Wall." Sarah wore silvered eyeglasses which slipped down her nose; the rims made horizons in the black eyes.

"Perhaps we should get the children their own phone."

"I think that would be criminal indulgence. A phone is not a decent substitute for human intercourse."

Merriwether related an anecdote Thomas Fischer had told him about walking with Bohr in the woods near Copenhagen the year Fischer won his Nobel. "Bohr touched the trees with his cane and told Tom how odd it was one could *feel* the tree through the cane. There must be interactions that can be literally felt."

Sarah's head bobbed angrily, the glasses slipped down, she shoved them back. She could not bear his lectures; he stood over her as if she were an auditorium. "Esmé's indolence has nothing to do with subtle interactions."

"You're right as rain. I didn't mean she shouldn't do her homework. But I do think adolescents animate all sorts of things with their feelings. You know how the girls are with their little doo-dads. Telephoning is like that."

"I suppose you do know about telephoning."

Were the creaking backstairs significant for her? He got up. "I'm sorry, Sarah. If I call someone again at night, I'll try to talk more quietly."

Snort. Sarah had never been a facial actress, she didn't pout, didn't wink, but in recent months, she'd developed a variety of sub-verbal grunts, plus a few eye-narrowings and lip-pursings which broadcast her discontent. In the emotional husbandry of the Merriwethers, they were as telling as curses.

That night, Dr. Merriwether found himself checking her breathing before he went downstairs. Cynthia asked if she could bring some hash for the weekend.

"Hash?"

"Yes."

"I don't get it. Why?"

"Because it'd be nice."

"Oh. You mean hashish. *Cannabis*."

"Won't you take it with me?"

"I don't know."

Actually, he was astonished. He'd first thought Cynthia was talking about corned-beef hash. When he caught on, he felt as he'd felt when she'd danced for him, "out of it"; and then, depressed. Did the girl think their relationship needed this kind of bolstering? Couldn't she enjoy herself without it? "Yet it's their sign," he told himself (*their* assigning her to "The Young"). Was part of his feeling for her the joy of learning about a new species? Terrible idea. Had laboratory life so deformed him that even intimacy was heuristic? Though love and learning *were* old associates. (Maxim Schneider told him Sappho's love poems came at her pupils' graduations.) But he wanted Cynthia, not her bulletins.

At least not her hash.

"Don't bring it. If we need it, there's even less sense to all this than we know there is."

"I just thought it might relax us."

"I'm paranoiac about exposure here, Cynthia. You're a minor, this is my town. Your hash might, well, settle mine."

"All right. I won't."

"It's so easy for someone like me to subvert his pleasures. I'm such a proper, cautious type. You'll soon see what a swamp you're letting yourself into."

"I love you. I won't bring it. I'll just bring this little book I have for you."

"What's that?"

"Nineteen Ways to Sodomize a Minor."

The next day, Cynthia called him at the university to say she couldn't come that weekend; her father was coming to see her between legal meetings in Philadelphia.

"Can't you tell him you're going out of town? I fixed Tom Fischer's apartment for you." He'd put sheets on the bed and orange juice in the freezer.

"I just can't. You don't know him. He'd be deeply offended."

"I guess I'm not deeply offended."

It was worse than that. A week before, she'd canceled the trip because a photographer had invited her to a party in New York where she might meet people who could use her as a model. "I'd get all this money, then things would be easy for me. I could visit you whenever I wanted without dunning you or Daddy for money." Merriwether felt trapped by her whims. He was disappointed, jealous, anxious, enraged. "Let's just call it off," he'd told her. "Have a fine time in New York. We'll be in touch some day," and he'd hung up and left the office to avoid a return call.

The rest of that day was awful. There were no classes to distract him, no committee meetings, he couldn't work in the lab. He went home early and played one-on-one with George in the backyard, and that night went with Sarah to a movie, one of the few times in the year she'd been willing to go out with him anywhere. The movie was an unlucky choice, *The Prime of Miss Jean Brodie.* In it, a teenaged girl, after listening to her mad teacher's spiel about "middle-aged Dante" falling in love with "child Beatrice" ("they were both nine years old," said Sarah, edifying two rows of patrons), becomes the mistress of the teacher's own lover. Merriwether flushed. Here he was, exhibited in the cage of the film, listening to the audience laugh at the young girl telling her lover—five years younger than he—that he was over the hill. Was the situation so comic? Over and over, the same situations, the same warnings, the same conclusions.

He had to force himself not to telephone Cynthia. Instead, he wrote her a letter denouncing her frivolity, denouncing himself for being "taken in" by what he'd mistaken as a "deeper seriousness," for being so foolish to think any twenty-year-old girl could be anything more than briefly diverted by "an old laboratory grub."

"I shouldn't mail it." But he put on the stamp and walked to the mailbox. Yet he knew he would tear it up, knew it, almost knew, almost, and then, before he could let himself think, he'd opened the blue lid and tossed in the letter.

Why not? It was forcefully written; it would effectively *bar the door*.

Friday, Sarah drove Priscilla back to Oberlin. He planned to stay home with George and Esmé, then couldn't. Cynthia would be in Someone's Bed, he could not wait that out at home. Hanson, an epidemiologist, was lecturing on the degenerative disease, kuru. He'd go to it.

First, he took George and Esmé to dinner at the Wirthaus. They had a spat about who spilled the 7-Up, he was firm with them, and at home told them to stay apart, he had to go to a lecture. "Take any messages, sweetheart," he told Esmé. "Be sure you write them down. Don't forget. Put the messages on the bed-table."

"I always do, Dad." Esmé was very responsible, he kissed her, she stroked his cheek. "You didn't shave too well today."

"I'm only going out for a bit, darling. But don't worry if I'm not back at nine-thirty. Though maybe you ought to go to bed in our room, in case the phone rings."

Which puzzled but also delighted her.

"And please, children, be very good with each other. Don't let anyone in unless you know them. But don't use the chain, or I won't be able to get back in." He always repeated instructions when these two were left without a sitter. It was a recent arrangement, they enjoyed the independence and the run of the house.

The lecture was first-rate. Hanson was a youngish man from the Rockefeller Institute. He'd gone to New Guinea and encountered the Foré, a neolithic people of remarkable metabolism. Their potassium-sodium balance was incredible; lactating women suffered potassium poisoning, the urine output was as little as 200 ccs, yet there was no uremia. The Foré were cannibals, they had no numbers over ten, had no conception of themselves as a tribe or group, couldn't swim, had no boats or bridges, knew nothing of the world beyond a hill and thirty or forty other people. As for kuru, it was a virogenic, pre-senile dementia without inflammation and with a median incubation period of ten to fifteen years. After a year's work, Hanson realized it was a variation of the Creutzfeldt-Jacob disease: it derived from the Foré's cannibalism. (As a mark of endearment and respect, the Foré cooked, ate and ornamented themselves with the flesh of dead relatives; their "how do you do" was "I eat your buttocks.")

After the lecture, Merriwether joined Hanson and Fred Matthias, the department chairman, at Matthias's house on Kirkland Place. Mrs. Matthias had furnished this jewel of Cambridge Georgian like an office. Matthias was a genial emptiness. Merriwether thought that his wife, a smart neurotic woman, had set this Naugahyde stage to advertise the vacancy.

Hanson was hawk-faced, intense, knowledgeable about everything connected with his work, ethnography, epidemiology, genetics, medical history, even the politics and economy of the area. He had not only taught the Foré about kuru but about steel, swimming, boat-building, salt, arithmetic, and the great world outside their hills. "I felt Promethean."

Merriwether walked home through the Yard. What human variety there was. Was it only last night he'd been damning human sameness?

Back home, it was George not Esmé, asleep on the bed. The reading light was on, his son's little arm was over his eyes. On the telephone table was a note in George's unsteady script. "Sinthea called. Two times. She will call tomorow."

Relief foamed in him. His darling George. The taker of this message. Please God, may it not harm him.

The weekend went well. He told Sarah he had to stay in the lab with his rats. "I can't tell when they're going to pop off." He and Cynthia stayed in Fischer's room, watched television, played chess and read *Anna Karenina* to each other. Saturday night, they went to Boston, getting on the train at Central Square, sitting a few seats apart in case they met anyone he knew. A trial for both of them. Merriwether, in his tie and tweed jacket, Cynthia in her black stockings, mini-skirt and boy's sweater smiling nervously, foolishly over three seats. He moved next to her. "It's too silly." Yet he was so nervous in the restaurant, she said, "Let's just go home." They didn't feel at ease until they were back in Fischer's bed.

The next week Cynthia wrote him a letter in the love code of Kitty and Levin. "Bd," it went

i d of l f y
w y 1) l w m or 2) m m
C o

In the laboratory he worked it out to "Bobbie dear" or "darling" "I'm dying of love for you. Will you 1) live with me or 2) marry me." He had to get "C o" explained on the phone.

" 'Check one,' " she said.

As for "dying of love," it was hyperbolic, but he understood the feeling in it. Love-need was a crab-grip in the intestines. But if the grip was Cynthia, why did he scarcely think of her? At times, his sense of her was more her name than anything else. Not quite the name, but the idea of Cynthia within it. It made no physiological sense. The Love-Grip. Why not the Love Goddess? What did *missing her* mean? Costive tension? He missed her. He wanted her in bed. Ankle bones, hips, her—yes—all of it, moving, on, in, above, below. "I love you." Up in his study, head on his typewriter case. "I love you." The dark window beaded with drizzle. Books, note cards, goose-neck lamp, pictures of Albie, Pris, Esmé, George, of Sarah—he looked away. *Cynthia. Que je vous adore.*

> The grown-up who becomes neurotic on account of ungratified libido behaves in his anxiety like a child; he fears when he is alone, *i.e.* when he is without a person of whose love he feels sure, who can calm his fears by means of the most childish measures.

He had found this in Freud. Was it for him? Freud blamed the condition on excessively tender parents who "accelerated sexual maturity and spoiled the child, making him unfit to renounce love temporarily, or to be satisfied with a smaller amount of love in later life." His parents were, well, devoted, not, certainly not, *excessively* tender. What was *excessive?* Generous, sweet, courteous Mother. A little dreamy, a little distant, an intelligence that was not excessively nourished by Boston papers and Taylor Caldwell's novels. Love, Freud said, should awaken energies, not become their unique object. He was having a hard time concentrating, but his ideas seemed unusually interesting. As was his dream-life. It seldom had to do with Cynthia, though, surely, the dreams had Cynthian deposits. He dreamed he was the father of a psychotic daughter who, one day, couldn't see him; he watched himself fade away as she looked blindly his way. Waking, he found that the Love-Grip had relaxed; he had *no feeling* for Cynthia, no sense of her. In her place was a girl-sized rectangle. Blank. Nothing. Fantastic relief. It was over. Yet, what about her? What would she do? He tried to put her back in the rectangle. She appeared, but what was she? Nice-enough, pretty-enough, smart-enough, but nothing special, and childish, or anyway, too young, inappropriate. Relief. Tremendous relief. He was fully awake.

His thought was, "What am I going to do with her?" She was coming to Cambridge for the weekend. Perhaps she'd found the same blanked rectangle in her bed. "Oh no," he said out loud, and Sarah muttered on the other side of the bed. "What a see-saw." Later, walking past the Revolutionary War cannon in the Common, he felt the rectangular blank once more. The love song had stopped.

Yet.

Dr. Merriwether had not been around the unentanglers of biological mystery for nothing. The ethologist's Law of Heterogeneous Summation (simple quantity—not quality—of stimuli accounts for behavior) applied. Given the long abstinence and present opportunity, no single dream of blankness could dispel Cynthia.

Merriwether's assistant, Cy McTier, almost sang about the "beautiful reflex mechanism" of the mantises. "The female eats any insect she can catch. The male moves toward her, love in his beak. She eats him, head first." McTier was tiny, fiercely good-humored, an endless go-getter. "When she devours the sub-oesophageal ganglion, it no longer inhibits the copulatory center in the last abdominal ganglion. So our headless male can begin fucking. Eighty percent of the time, he makes it just before he's devoured."

Perfume glands on the moth's wings, music from the stridulating files of grasshopper legs, magnets in the budgerigar's painted feathers, tactile excitement as the orchid's nub mimics the bee. True or false, real or unreal, insect, mammal or physiologist, heterogeneous stimuli bring the genetic transmitter into heat.

Beside the unfriendly body of his formerly dear spouse, Dr. Merriwether lies awake. Mind, recently astonished at its release from grotesque servitude, now *sees* Cynthia making love to Whoever, sees her undressing, facing the boy's body, climbing, wrestling, sees the hand in her cleft, feels her melt—the fluids, the breath, the motion, the cries—and here, in the sheets, mattress buttons against his bare legs—why was there no new mattress?—Merriwether's penis swells, Cynthia is with him, he is Whoever, up, down, the river's going to flood, oh, Lordie, he makes it out of bed, down the hall, up the creaky stairs, into the guest room, down upon the bed.

5

Clocks.

The orange face on City Hall, the ghost pallor of those on Independence Hall. At night the clock faces of Philadelphia moon above the town. Time's cages.

Hand in hand, fingers in fingers, Cynthia and Merriwether walk down Chestnut Street to the Delaware. He is in belted suede, she in leopard. Animals within animals, lovers within animals, walking after *La Bohème* at the Academy of Music; old cornball songs of tuberculosis and back rent, Mimi and Rodolfo. Cynthia's first opera, Merriwether's old favorite, aphrodisiacal stridulation in the old city of the Republic. They walk down to the restored Georgian world of Society Hill, rows of cockeyed houses with red shutters, green, white, blue, by St. Peter's, by the thin skyscrapers of I. M. Pei, the messy old city flung behind them. "This town's a morgue. Eleven, eleven-thirty, you can't buy a cup of coffee." Their cabbie, Merriwether's age, but twenty years his senior, patronizing these odd but unquestionable lovers, letting them out at the Benjamin Franklin after their chowder and lobster at Bookbinder's.

"I lost my watch the day you called me," said Cynthia. "I always keep it in a jewel box Grannie gave me. Or on my wrist. You called you were coming, and I can't remember where it is."

"I'll get you one."

"It's just strange. It's not like me. Maybe it's to say, 'Time' "—euphemism for age—" 'doesn't matter for love.' "

Merriwether had given a seminar at Penn on Pauling's protein clocks and other biological rhythms, circadian, hebdomadarian, mensual, annual. He'd arranged it through his old student, George Nyswunder, a professor there, and flown down Thursday night. Cynthia had taxied to the airport and they'd met at the Eastern Airlines counter.

They were fixing up the airport. You came off the plane to a backdoor, climbed backstairs by sandbags, went along corridors of iron intestines until you hit the ticket counters. Across from Eastern was a girl in a huge-brimmed flop hat which shadowed half her face.

Cynthia.

Panic. What was he doing here meeting a strange girl?

Something similar showed in her face. He too was desummered. He wore a dark fedora, a topcoat, he carried a briefcase. Another salesman getting off a plane.

To cover the panic of non-recognition, they rushed to each other, touched cheek with cheek, then, feeling the warmth, getting the other's signals, the stimuli, felt familiarity drift back into them.

"Darling."

"Cynthia."

Not quite believed in, but crutches which supported them till they walked on their own. In the taxi, they embraced like teenagers.

He hadn't been to Philadelphia since a boyhood trip with the Latin School to see the Liberty Bell. "Excuse me, sir, you've sold me a cracked one," eight years old, handing the quarter souvenir to the vendor—his only memory of the trip. So he wanted to see the way the city looked. "What river's that?" She didn't know.

"Skookul," said the cabbie.

Cynthia was an urban, older version of her summer self, plucked, perfumed—*Je Reviens* (the odorous wingtips)—warm in a leopard fur, carrying a many-pocketed leather bag. (His own was ersatz.)

The hotel had an enormous, gloomy lobby full of Temple of Karnak pillars, rubber plants, Naugahyde couches; it was rimmed with luminous cigar stores, haberdashers, coffee shops; Muzak drugged it. At the desk, a knowing clerk awaited them. It is Modern Times. No identity cards, no atmosphere of "tryst," just the familiar shack-up of any two ordinaries coming together from any earth spot, arranged by phone, assembled by plane. No village tension to modern love. They registered for the first time as Mr. and Mrs.; he signed his own name and gave the right city.

An old bear coming out of the strawberry patch, muzzle bloody with juice, trailing vines. Grizzled, glittering Merriwether, eyes bright with novelty, leaked awkwardness. The ease of modern love was not ease for him. No sense of "interlude," no relaxation. Of the ninety thousand American males signing in at ninety thousand registers over the country, could more than a dozen have been as awkwardly illicit?

In the next half hour, Cynthia got her first orgasm. (So this was what the cheering was about.) In Cambridge, she'd come close, but twice, their first night and on her weekend, she'd had her period. It was painful for Merriwether—"the endometrium's shedding its lining." There was also the shedding of what she called his "hang-ups." Now in this

"T" of a room, their bed in the cross bar, the window full of room lights spattered down the adjacent wall, in a pell-mell plunge of relief, they made it; quite satisfactorily, then kleenexed up, washed, pajamaed, talked, ordered wine and turkey sandwiches from telephone Button 7—and received the silvered dishes and Greek waiter like hotel kings. Splendid American stuff.

At the seminar, Cynthia sat against the wall. She'd been presented to George Nyswunder with Merriwether's new boldness. "My friend, Cynthia Ryder."

Nyswunder had known a Merriwether whose highest spirits were reserved for scientific argument and tennis court triumphs; Cynthia Ryder was a large surprise.

"Are you a physiologist?"

Nyswunder was a more social man than many in the academy, but, used to academic catechism, his social intercourse was heavily interrogative. A lusty little man, he was still pink-cheeked, wide-eyed. Loyal, a scrapper, he was timid about himself. His strength came from following leading physiological lights. Merriwether was his first, but since, he had fastened himself to one of physiology's giants, Pulvermacher; he'd wasted years editing the man's lesser papers. Nyswunder did have a nose for "quality"; Cynthia fit his bill, and Merriwether took on a glow because of her. How did Merriwether bring it off? Nyswunder himself had a thousand erotic reveries, but was a quick self-censor; booze reinforced suppression.

"Just a physiologist's specimen," said Cynthia. Which won Nyswunder.

In the rim of class seats beyond the seminar table, Cynthia watched Merriwether in a role new to her. He felt her reassessment, saw himself as he thought she saw him. Why did he have her come? He did not manage the discussion with his usual ease. A serious, handsome graduate student countered an assertion with a report Merriwether hadn't read in a recent *JEP*. There was a bad moment. For Cynthia, he redeemed himself with authentic curiosity: "That does upset the cart. Can you tell me about it?" It was the student's glory moment. After Merriwether got the gist of the article, he saw—without looking—Cynthia's eyes on the student's Tartar mustache. He gaped, dry-mouthed, he lost connection. The Tartar's exposition dragged. Nyswunder interrupted. "Thanks, Jimmy, let's let Professor Merriwether finish off. Those results only speak to a special case anyway."

This grace revived Merriwether. He discovered a tunnel, crawled through, and, happy day, there was a flood of new light. On the spot, he suggested a chemical chain which had the students gasping. And, by God, they applauded.

Cynthia blushed. She loved him more in defeat than triumph; but triumph was also sweet. She had suffered years of authoritative maleness; to see it come back after discomfort was something she hadn't seen in her unbent father.

Nyswunder took them off to lunch in a fish place near the University. He was excited by Merriwether's final burst. "Pulvermacher's going to be knocked out, Bob. He's found the pituitary releases the antidiuretic hormone when the molar concentration is raised."

"Isn't that Verney's work?"

"Yes, of course, but Harry's done the analysis."

"Will you get it for me?" Merriwether was flushed himself. He was on to something; Philadelphia looked like an exceptionally lucky trip for him.

"I couldn't follow most of it," said Cynthia.

Nyswunder apologized, blushed, smiled, a child in the face of this girl, twenty years his junior. Still, she was a kind of stepmother, his guru's companion; he would go brush his teeth if she suggested it.

Lunch talk ducked intimacy; mostly there was reminiscence by old pupil and teacher. Cynthia stewed in her chowder, said she didn't feel well, she'd taxi to the hotel.

"Excuse us, darling," said Merriwether. Nyswunder too apologized. "This is bad. Forgive us. It's my fault."

Pardons streamed. Nyswunder's hand was grasped by Merriwether with conspiratorial gratitude. The pupil had helped his old teacher with his new girl. (Nyswunder was now a part of their lives.)

They returned to the room, feathers smoothed, and made love. Not for years has Merriwether made love in the afternoon, or more than once in a day. He kissed her shoulders; pushed the hair away, kissed her neck. Self-reinforcing system: hormones produced by the act for which they're needed. "Think love." (Short of heart-attacks, dry-mouth, cankersores, and general weariness, love created love-making power.)

Cynthia's body was still innocent as a volleyball, belly, hips, gold curls of pubic triangle, breasts. The oddest, finest thing, a laugh which somehow went from lips, cheeks, eyes into the body; so playful after *Sturm und Drang*.

Lying beside sleeping Cynthia, Merriwether imagined Nyswunder's routine. Lab-class-bar-home-to-Joan. Where were the Nyswunders on the spectrum of coupleness? Was theirs a marriage which supplied the delights of old home week? Like the Schneiders? God knows George was not one of those pioneers struck with the miracle that every skirt hid the paradisiacal lips. Not like the geneticist, Sharpe-Cairns. That aristocratic hoodlum looked like a human hassock, but was a sexual Magellan. He and Merriwether would be swamped in argument, when boom, silence, pause, Sharpe-Cairns had smelled something, and, sure enough, walking across the room, a woman going to the bathroom. "Take a look at that ass. It's Japanese." Fair little face concentrated like a pistol. Breath altered, cornea widened. No inscrutability. It would be minutes before he could recover enough to talk; he never recovered all the way. From now until he "scored"—it was from his Oxford lips that Merriwether learned this uncharming participle—he could not function above mechanics. His mind was on that bepanted rear-end and its tender verso. What was marriage to such hunger? The difference between unscheduled gorges in the street and three meals a day. "Time for lunch, George. Time for dinner."

Sunday was difficult for Merriwether. Tomorrow he'd be back in his own rectangle: home-class-lab-club. The boxed life. Though not an empty box. A box which held his children, his house, his books, his work, and, like prizes in Crackerjacks, dinner parties, jokes, music, movies. A good, steady, lucky life.

Cynthia was preparing for school, thinking of papers she had to write, of "waitressing"—she earned money in the dorm so she could dress for him and taxi to the airport.

"Can't you stay an extra day?" Not that he could.

"I've got to get this Vergil paper in. I can't write a line when I'm with you." She suggested a solution: he should come back and live in her room. "When I'm finished with classes, we can make love."

Splendid sight: lining up with the twenty-year-olds in the john. "Thank you."

"I've got to have some independence."

From him? Ok. A relief. The mania was over. In this city independence meant more than "give me room." Cynthia's meant freedom to have a lover and be unhampered by him. His meant freedom to get out. Be independent. You're free. But he only said, "I understand."

The next time they saw each other was a week before Thanksgiving. Merriwether spoke at Columbia, then met Cynthia at the Plaza (which offered educator-discounts in its smaller rooms).

It was not the sort of hotel Merriwether usually stayed in. A burlesque of high style, it made capital of its own creakiness. Ozark motels had more efficient comforts. The Plaza had marble corridors spooked with funereal light globes, massy, groaning radiators and toilets, brocade on stiff chairs, fresh roses in finger vases, gold-wrapped chocolate circlets on the dresser, and, out the Fifth Avenue windows, the waterless fountain with Diana bare-rumped to November. Breakfast came to the bed at seven dollars; corky wine and dessicated turkey sandwiches closed out the day at thirteen-fifty. Cramped, stale, leaking phony *luxe*. But in Cynthia and Merriwether's gonadal flush, neither absurdity, discomfort, nor wild prices subtracted from net pleasure. Anything short of humiliation was grist for the sexual mill. In their love, like Stendhal's Italy, anything went because *somewhere it gave pleasure*.

Merriwether and Cynthia roamed Central Park, checked out the zoo, the Frick, the Metropolitan, walked the east-west streets, read the bronze markers (where Grant wrote the *Memoirs* and died, where Franklin Roosevelt lived house-by-house with his mother). Three days filling in the sketch of *coupleness* which isolation, flattery, need, and boredom had drawn in Cambridge. Familiarity was as pleasing as novelty: they knew the look of each other's toothbrushes, each other's sleeping habits (Merriwether snored, Cynthia slept on the bed's diagonal so that he, yielding to the sleeper's *force majeure,* curled into one of the triangles).

Cynthia looked terrific. She wore fun furs bought in thrift shops, soft scarves, great-brimmed hats, thigh-length boots of kid and leather. And, as if some effluent of the gentled beasts which clothed her seeped into her system, she gamboled on the avenues with her foot-out walk. In an area where women gave each other the most critical eyes in America, Cynthia's beauty, inventiveness and flare went into a thousand envious inventories. Walking with the trim, middle-aged juvescent who held her arm, pulled out her chairs, brought her trays in bed, played her games, and even adopted her comic voices and obscenities, she felt absolutely terrific.

Their last evening, they were coming back from seeing *The Blue Angel* at the Thalia when a compact man in a tweed cap and checked suit walked toward them and said, "Bobbie."

Merriwether, discovered, flushed. "Timmy. What a surprise. Cynthia, this is my cousin. Timmy Hellman."

Timmy Hellman was actually Sarah's cousin; his father had married Sarah's aunt. Timmy had been Merriwether's roommate in Eliot House, had introduced him to Sarah. He'd studied geology at Harvard, then gone into scientific journalism, worked for UPI, then the New York *Herald-Tribune.* The year it folded, he went to Basic Books as a science editor. Knowledgeable, sympathetic, careful, he was one of the finest scientific editors in the world. He'd persuaded Merriwether to do a semi-popular book on thirst and had helped him make it a good one. For ten years, Merriwether had received small royalty checks for it.

Merriwether had always found it hard to fuse Timmy's

editorial meticulousness with his terrific vivacity. Timmy was a musician, an athlete, a gourmet cook; he was crazy for painting—he couldn't live a week without a few hours in a gallery—he was an adventurer who dove for Spanish gold; he'd spent a month with a tribe of Paraguayan headhunters. Yet he once told Merriwether that he had more energy than personality. "I'm not much of anyone. It's what makes it easy for me to take what other people call 'risks.' I feel danger, even fear, but I don't feel protective about whatever it is I am or have."

Timmy lived with a series of terrific girls who showed up on lists in *Harper's Bazaar* and *Town and Country* ("New York's Fifty Most Beautiful Women"), yet he had none of the strut or wariness of the sexual showman. Charm and decency animated him. He had a wonderful smile, one without presumption, suspicion or curiosity. His face was squarish, rosy without being boyish. The features were large, he would have been a natural for caricature except that caricature fixes, and the distinction of his face was expressive fluency. The eyes had a blue density that suggested mental power, as the rest of his features, the great nose and ears, suggested sensuous power.

"Can you have dinner with me?"

He always took people to dinner. This was not an extension of his editorial habit; if anything, he was an editor because over the old board of intake / output, food-and-ideas, he functioned so well. Merriwether was delighted to serve him up to Cynthia. Hellman would meet them in an hour. He was on his way to the Palm Court Lounge to have tea with "an old woman of genius," an accountant for Hallmark Greeting Cards in Kansas City who'd written a brilliant work on the perception of curves. (Timmy's world was mined with such hidden gold.)

"He's the happiest man I know," said Merriwether.

"It radiates from him."

They were warm from the minute's encounter. "He always has this effect. It's so clear life entrances him. I don't know why I didn't call him. Maybe I was afraid you wouldn't like me once you'd seen him."

"The only thing he can do for me is to take you to his tailor."

"Oh, what's wrong?" Merriwether had bought a suit especially for the New York trip. Daltonic, he didn't trust his color sense. For years, Sarah picked out his suits. It was only in the last year that he realized that the dull blues and raw liver browns were the register of unconscious animosity. He'd let the salesman at Stonestreet's guide him into this modest tan. Surely it was an improvement.

"You're perfect. Only a little staid."

"I'm too gray to be a peacock."

"You're crazy as a loon. You should see how Daddy's bloomed since men got color. And he's at least as stiff as you."

"Nobody is. I just want to look like this room." They sat in the Oak Bar, which, at dusk, was a place of dim sedation. "Quiet background for you. You're the tropical fish. Color's great for you. I'm just a rocky coast. Old New England anfractuosity."

"Whatever that means. Where do I look fishy?"

"From *ambi* and *frangere*, "broken" and "around." Tortuous. In the feet."

"And the New England coast is beautiful."

"But it doesn't doll up like the Pacific. That's a young coast, quaky, mountainy, a showboat coast."

"You are one anfractuous loon."

Timmy took them to Lutèce. "The best for the best."

They sat under the greenhouse glass; it was like being in a garden. A marvelous meal, a marvelous evening. Cynthia had never heard such a talker. In Timmy's talk, the somberest detail glittered. Yet he never tyrannized, never interrupted, never corrected. His talk fed on itself, he enjoyed it, was surprised at what came out of himself. The talk was driven by the desire to connect things: Indochina linked with the lost fortune of Franklin Roosevelt's grandfather, the nineteenth century's search for energy, the chemical nature of energy substance, the colonial nature of men, animals, plants, with a wind-up about a Vermont farmer who ran his cars and farm machines on gas from dung and created—except for "a small perfume problem"—the perfect eco-systematic day, rising, teeth-brushing, emptying intestines into the fuel tank.

When Cynthia went off to the bathroom, Hellman changed gear. "She's a fine girl, Bobbie. May I ask if she's your vacation? Or are you and Sarah finished?"

Merriwether said he hoped not, although for years he and Sarah had little but an address in common. "I hope this won't compromise your feelings toward me, Timmy."

"I am loyal to those I like. I like you both, I'll care for you both. I'm not a family necrophiliac."

"Sarah's just had too much Merriwether. She feels like the caretaker of a museum nobody visits. And she doesn't like the chief exhibit. I suppose I'm responding."

"No defense necessary, Bobbie. In New York, monogamists have to defend themselves. You were thirsty, and you went to the well."

"I was thirsty and someone delivered a case of champagne to the door. I hardly knew I was thirsty till it came."

"She's lovely, modest, doesn't advertise her youth, doesn't conceal it. A winner. And you look years younger, happier." Timmy put his hand on Merriwether's arm; a felicitation.

"Except for the fear of hurting the children and Sarah—I still care for the part of her that doesn't detest me—I feel all right."

Timmy looked to see if Cynthia was coming. "Will you let me say something, though? About young girls?"

"A warning?"

"In a way. I know the danger of classifying human beings, but I've known a lot of these girls. That's been my companionship. Sex and tenderness. Nothing more, not even friendship. So I have to meet many women. The last few years I've felt a terrific drive in them. They want, they want, and it's we not-quite-graybeards who give them the most the quickest. We teach them, we spend on them, we show them off, we tell them what everything means. We're their Graduate School. Which means they're closer to graduation through us. And that means there can be lots of tears when Graduation Day rolls around."

The next day, back in Cambridge, Merriwether got a call from Timmy. "I may have let myself go on too long and far, Bobbie. I'm so used to spinning off I sometimes make a case just for the drama of the talk."

"I appreciate it, Timmy. The call too. I haven't had anyone to talk to."

"I really meant to talk with you about doing another book. I never got around to it."

Merriwether said he was having a hard enough time keeping up his research. Nonsense, said Timmy, he should do a book in the summer instead of his medical work. "Do a theoretical book, one that would force you to think through a number of things. It would help your research."

Merriwether knew the invitation was Timmy's attempt to divert him from his "diversion." He wasn't ungrateful for it. "I like to be asked, Timmy. Especially by such a decent judge as you. But I just don't know."

Timmy talked about the books of Dubos, Monod, Rostand. "They do very well; and they're valuable. Why not think about it?"

Why not?

Now and then, Merriwether had felt the impulse to vault the laboratory world, to do something that would get written up in the medical, even the news sections of magazines. It was, perhaps, a vulgar impulse, but there it was. The children would enjoy seeing him better-known. They grew up with children whose parents' pictures were in the *Times*. It was a special security for children; maybe he owed them something like that.

He was not the first Merriwether to *thirst for fame*. The day after his grandfather retired from the family insurance firm he'd gone out and bought a typewriter, ten pounds of onionskin, a thesaurus and a rhyming dictionary. He'd begun putting in the same number of hours at poetry that he'd put into the firm. He wrote about anything, the "grand men of wisdom" who had "instructed my youth" (Lowell and William James had been his teachers), the opening of the Mass Transit Station in Harvard Square—"Oh Swift Tempter of Young Harvard's Blood"—about Cuba, about McKinley's funeral. In his last years he'd worked on an epic poem about marine insurance, *The Riskiad*.

Sing, American Muse, of those who backed the sea,
And guaranteed our vessels through its watery threat.

Sing of those Heros of the Everyday
Whose schooners were their desks, whose 'poons their pens.

Merriwether had often been summoned to "the Muse's Seat," his father's unfilial characterization of his grandfather's study. His ivory-headed, thin, unsmiling grandfather counted out the lines he had written that week. In his second year, he'd exceeded the combined production of Vergil and Homer. "I'll be up to Dante by Christmas." His grandfather's will enjoined his heirs to see if "there might not be some matter of public interest in his verse" and "to take steps toward modest publication of what was so deemed." Merriwether's father had taken *The Riskiad* to a friend at the Harvard University Press who said that scholars interested in the development of marine insurance might find it of some interest and that Mr. Merriwether should see about depositing a copy of the work with the Massachusetts Historical Society.

When Mr. Merriwether himself retired, he also "took to the pen." *The Memoirs of a Harvard Man* began with an epigraph from Lowell's poem on the Harvard dead,

> Those love her best who to themselves are true,
> And what they dare to dream of, dare to do. . .

and finished with the amalgamation of the family firm with the Traveller's Insurance Company of Hartford. For some reason, the memoirs were written in red ink and on the left-hand pages of six ledger books. The stiff, upright, scarlet script rolled on like a healthy cardiogram. No blots, no cross-hatched words. Merriwether had read the ledgers in the weeks after his father's death. Or read at them, for they were tedious; though remarkable, considering that his father had never written an article, let alone a book. The chronicle was as regular as the script. And all uphill: tragedies were exercises in fortitude, triumphs exemplifications of principle.

One night in Cambridge, he read Cynthia his father's account of his own birth day.

> On that frosted March morning, after twenty-one-and-one-half hours of what even a coal miner might agree was labor, our son Robert entered this life. If strength of character be measured by the endurance of pain, my Hattie must be regarded as a veritable Gibraltar; if it be measured by strength of lung, then my dearest Robert's first seconds in the world gave ample promise of what he has proved to be. Character is the tenacity with which a man fulfills what he knows is expected of him. Endurance does not suffice; strength does not suffice; ability does not suffice. Two things count: intelligence, which knows what is expected, and will, which moves to fulfill expectation.

"Family and duty," said Merriwether. "Do you wonder I'm such a cautious cookie?" (In the three months since Cynthia had moved to Cambridge, he had never gone shopping or seen a local movie with her.)

"That's your Merriwether *fourmisme*."

"Concern for good form?"

"No. Ant-ism. *La fourmi,* hoarding and hoarding against perpetual winters. I was hoping I'd convert you to *cigalisme*. Grass-hopperism. Motto: it's winter now. Live it up, and not behind shades. Accept yourself."

"When you've lived through as many New England winters as I, you'll change that tune."

" 'No season's harshness was his Wether, the godlie Robert Merriwether.' You've perverted the tradition."

On the phone to Timmy Hellman, Merriwether said he'd think hard about it, there was lots of undigested stuff in his head, he might be able to make sense of it in a book.

6

For years, Thomas Fischer's apartment on Ellery Street was little more than a storage bin for his few possessions. His real home was his overnight bag. *Chelonia cambridgiensis,* he called himself, the Cambridge turtle. Childless, abandoned by his second wife after a year of marriage, he made a virtue of solitude. "There's a certain wastage in solitude, but as Einstein said, if it's frightening at the beginning, it becomes delicious. Of course, Einstein didn't live alone."

Fischer's life was work, the first half in biochemistry, the second in scientific policy. In his twenties, he'd synthesized a pituitary hormone, and received a Nobel for it. When he was forty, he joined the National Science Foundation. The politics of science replaced the chemistry of macro-molecular synthesis at his center. In 1965, he formed an independent, international group of scientists whose aim was to designate crucial research areas. "It's like Wells's Open Conspiracy. The hope is to set policies which these ballot-Punchinellos will execute. Who are they to speak for national, let alone world needs? Tinkerers, liars, showmen, posturing crooks." But Fischer knew how to manipulate the tinkerers. "You do their work, then congratulate them for it."

In 1966, he resigned his Harvard professorship and lived on a small subsidy from the Rockefeller Foundation. His chief expense was air travel; he wore the same clothes year to year, ate little, drank inexpensive wine, and stayed in small rooms which bore the marks of permanent transience: the opened suitcase, empty refrigerator, a pile of 24-hour-service laundry. His Cambridge and Washington rooms were somewhat homier. He owned the books, the television sets, the beds; domestic leavings of his wives were in closets and cupboards.

Fischer was solid, red-faced, blue-eyed, handsome. Dr. Merriwether—who had been his only real friend for years—had seen him tender, grim, furious. He had a feared wit, he had grown conscious of other people's fear of—or delight in—it, his earlier directness was now frequently a performance of what had been "natural." As he became surer of his own powers and of other people's lesser ones, he indulged himself more and them less. He interrupted his friends when thoughts or jokes occurred to him; in front of them he seldom bothered to control his contempt or fury. Capable of extraordinary courtesy, responsive to fine work in ten or twelve areas of science, he also could be one of the finest of listeners and critics. Still, even here he had blind spots. He was excessively strict about scientific genres. He disapproved of Merriwether's recent interest in dipsologic models for certain cancers. "It's fanciful, trivial. You're wasting yourself, Robert. Leave cancer to virologists and geneticists. You've got plenty of important work in your own bailiwick." His own research had applied crystallography to hormone synthesis in what was then a totally new way, but Fischer was not one to see himself as a model. In rare moments of self-examination, he swung from modesty to manic conceit. Continuous work pushed aside self-doubt, increased self-absorption, narrowed his tolerance for innovation. Since most new work was unimportant, Fischer's self-righteousness increased; but the increase was more in density and narrow fierceness than in strength. His few friends moved away from his tyranny; regretfully, for they acknowledged his bravery, intelligence and basic dignity. They had the option of telling him to stop his egoistic poaching or to stop seeing him.

Merriwether was the only friend who cautioned him about his excesses; and he remained Fischer's closest friend. For years, he'd recognized and even suffered Fischer's growing narrowness, but he still treasured the intervals of thoughtfulness and responsive intelligence.

Merriwether was one of the few harbors in Fischer's life, his house the one in which he most relaxed, perhaps the only one he loved. The Merriwethers embodied his sense of family worth. The four children, the attentive parents, the fine old house seemed to him a domestic expression of noble intellectual and spiritual traditions.

Two days after Thanksgiving, Fischer stopped off in Cambridge. Thanksgiving Day he'd been in a plane. (He often traveled on the holidays, piecing over the emptiness of such times with the official convivialities of stewardesses.) He came to Acorn Street directly from Logan Airport. His suitcase was in the hall, the Merriwether children, seeing it, called "Hi, Tom," and went in for handshakes and shoulder squeezes. Priscilla kissed his cheek, the first lips that had been there since she'd last kissed him. The children were interrogated and joked with. When they left, Merriwether told Fischer about Cynthia.

Fischer was less innocent about international than personal complexity, but he had not been married twice without knowing something of human grit. It had been years since he had felt anything like love for anyone. Abstinence and activity had kept him from all but occasional twinges of need, but he met many men and women all over the world, and he saw that as many as one in three was kept from doing his best work because of emotional trouble. At least, such trouble *usually* incapacitated them; now and then, a new emotional involvement was connected to a burst of achievement. Fischer had shaken hands with many new loves shortly before or after extraordinary work was announced. He had enough evidence of this sort and had heard enough intimate talk to think of himself as "a scientific confessor."

In the familiar old parlor, with the glass-and-silver knickknacks deflecting the firelight in ways that stirred what sense of home he had, Fischer listened to his decent, thoughtful old friend speaking in the same voice with which they had for so many years talked of politics, enzymes and the NSF. Now, though, Merriwether spoke of a domestic aridity which Fischer had never suspected. This was the only household in the world in whose workings he took an interest comparable to his interest in the scientific policies of government, and he had known nothing about it. He watched his old friend's long face grooved by perplexity. "I had no idea, Robert. I knew Sarah suffered from not going on with her intellectual work; but I thought she had accommodated herself to it. There's so much of that. Danica"—Fischer's second wife—"complained of it. I don't know why. She never cooked a meal; we were out every night, except when I cooked. I certainly never suggested she leave the laboratory."

"I'm afraid we did," said Merriwether. The sidetrack was relief.

"Of course you did. I was always amazed that you admitted her. I'll never forget her little talk on membrane permeability. I think she thought the cell was made of cardboard. She never did find out what a lipid was, though I occasionally touched her at their cumulative points. Her permeability was as indifferent there as elsewhere."

"Sarah has not been a case for diffusion either."

"No, no I imagine not. Well, I'm older than you, Robert, and I've found the chief metabolic product of these years is callous. I simply don't feel anymore. I guess my hope for you would be the same. In a few years, you won't care about what disturbs you now. Your young girl or your troubles."

The friends had remarkably little experience of personal talk. There were always inquiries about health and progress, but neither man enjoyed confession. After Danica had run off with a technician in the Zoological Laboratories, Fischer opened up for the first and last time. "She doesn't know what she's doing. That clown's bewitched her. If she'll come back . . . I won't say anything." Danica was a surly, chesty talker, a clumsy, persistent flirt. Yet Merriwether had liked her for her doggedness and then pitied her for being left alone so often. Fischer was gone more than half the year. When he was around, he was tender and devoted, but he had an old Germanic contempt for women. He said he had married Danica because of her learning, sincerity and what he took for sweetness. "Camouflage," he'd said in his confusion and rage that day. "She was skittish, nervous, a troublemaker. Born to cheat and connive. I'm well rid of her," but for a year he wasn't. Then he dreamed one night that he'd smashed her face, and never again thought of her coming back to him.

"I've had sheaths on my feelings for years, Tom. An old Massachusetts man is taught to think old from age six."

Partially true. For conversational ease, for brevity, Merriwether, like most people, simplified himself. In the age of analysis, personal integrity is an antiquated term, Catos are shredded into pathology. Honest, modest men pretend to be something else. Merriwether was somewhat more innocent than most alert, modern men, but he was alert enough to his ploys and disguises; he could feel under his own sincerest moments other selves criticizing his omissions. He detested these simplifications, these posings, yet, to protect his special, deep, yet limited relationship with Fischer, he exaggerated his unhappiness. His wife and children read poems and novels full of comic self-abuse and hatred; they were so frankly narcissistic, he too enjoyed them; but to do it oneself was despicable. Yet, for Fischer, he found himself playing the minor poet, darkening the view in order to conceal the shame he would or could not shake that he had gone against the grain of good sense and decency. "It's better than thinking of yourself as a child," said Fischer. "I'm only sorry you couldn't have found a thirty-year-old widow who liked time to herself."

"Anesthesia would also solve my problems." He pressed the familiar lumps of the leather chair. So much of his life was habituated to discomfort. "I don't believe in fatal attractions, Tom. Isn't there a book called *Elective Affinities?* Cynthia was not elected by me. But like most of us around here, I haven't chased women since my teens. I don't know any. Children, work, the pleasant life here; you know it. Sarah, in many ways, was a marvelous wife." He spoke softly. She was upstairs. "Probably not suited for marriage with a scientist. I think she'd have been happier with someone whose work she could have affected. Or shared. She read at my articles, she read histories of science, God knows she's heard a lot of scientific talk over the years, but now it appears it's been something she suffered because of me. I'm not the narrowest of men, I read pretty widely, have always read. Perhaps more than she. This too became matter for resentment."

"I've seen so many men used up attempting to satisfy the insatiability of women."

"Better not let Priscilla hear that. Or even Esmé."

"The main problem is your friend. Does she leave you enough time for your life?"

Strange disjunction, thought Merriwether. So alert to some things, so childish about people. Yet it was good to talk. It put his troubles out there, where other people's troubles were. "I feel about her the way Galileo did about the telescope. My feelings for her enlarge my feelings for other things. I suppose that's a well-known phenomenon. As for the children, I don't know. I sense their worry. It's inchoate for the little ones, but it's there. Though Sarah and I don't argue around them. But it's in their air. I feel it so for them. Maybe I transfer my anxiety to them. They become more and more precious to me."

"You're not recommending your mode of life as a domestic vaccine?"

"I recommend nothing. I envy your insulation. Every step away from the familiar is damn lonely. At least, in our little society. These days every event has a new inflection for me. A kind of ionization. Letters, telephone calls, stray remarks. So little is casual now. As for Cynthia, she's my responsibility too."

Fischer said he thought that a serious mistake. "Everyone takes care of himself, Robert. You mustn't let this girl turn you into a parent or a doctor."

"That was something I might have thought about early. In fact, I did. Knowledge isn't always contraceptive."

Fischer said human relationships were mostly mess, one had to make up one's mind to amputate or suffer. "I'm sorry, Robert, but I think it will get worse. At least for a while. Then the girl will find something else. And fatigue will overtake your affection. I wish I could help you."

Merriwether fetched a drink for them. When he came back with two glasses of scotch, he told Fischer about Cynthia's using the apartment.

He was not entirely surprised that Fischer minded this. He said "fine," but it was clearly not fine. Fischer had felt a piece of grit under his shell. For a man who lived in suitcases, he was fanatic about clean dishes, spots on rugs, rings on his coffee table. Knowing this, Merriwether had gone around after Cynthia's visits and tidied up. Well, he might as well let him have everything. "Tom, I'm not capable of carrying on an affair. I mean long distance. Sneaking off for weekends, sneaking away to telephone. That consumes, it humiliates."

Fischer's rosy, big-nosed face took on once again the depth of a friend. He pushed off his annoyance. "Give it up, Robert. It will be painful for a bit. But you know as well as I how much easier everything else will be. There might even be another chance with Sarah."

"Even if I could, the girl is committed. She's deeply involved. And she's not the steadiest sort of person. Just imagine what could happen."

"Nothing will happen."

"This girl could do herself an injury."

"They say that. They feel that. But people can take a great deal more than they know. It will be hard for her, but then she'll feel the terrific relief of being out of something unsuitable. After all, she'll have had the experience of having known a superior person."

"She's at least my equal, Tom. I'm going to have her come here. She's tired of her school, she's exhausted the professors there. She's extremely intelligent, her record is superb, she'd benefit here academically. She wants to take up Japanese, they have next to nothing down there. She can do serious work here. I can do my work. She can get an apartment. Not yours. I am sorry about that."

Fischer shook his head, grimly, even angrily. "You're making a foolish mistake. For her, as well."

"If she comes here, I think it'll burn itself out. Maybe I'll have had my fill of whatever it is I've needed."

"Maybe."

"And she'll be with young people, first-rate young people. She'll leave me before I get tired of her. I can take that. It'll be the proper punishment for me. It'll be misery to see her around with others, but this is a big place. I don't have to see her. She doesn't have to flaunt her conquests."

"So you say."

"Maybe she can leave as soon as she gets her degree."

"Robert, I will do what I can. I wish I could dissuade you, but it's clear I can't. You want something, and your actions suit your want. Just consider this," and Fischer waved his arms around the old room, the chairs, the books, the fire, the couches, the upstairs noise of children. The paraphernalia of comfort. But there was a force here that destabilized everything. Fischer was no guide in these questions of feeling. "If this isn't enough, well, I pity you." Fischer had an odd smile, small teeth, small eyes. A cat's smile. He got up. "I hope you'll be in better shape when I come through again." He went to the stairwell and called goodby to Sarah, Priscilla, Esmé and George—Albie hadn't come home for Thanksgiving.

PART TWO

7

From Marseilles to Menton, the Midi is on fire. The Minister of Coasts and Forests proposes massive reforestation with less inflammable vegetables, but meanwhile, the coast blazes. Driving up the hill in his rented Peugeot, Dr. Merriwether sees flames and smoke in the Var Valley. A strange excitement for him. A student of one of the four elements, perhaps he has a feeling for the others. "You're a natural firebug," Cynthia tells him. "You'd better watch yourself. They arrested a creep yesterday up in Levens. A pharmacist from Genoa. Claimed he was satisfying *un besoin naturel.* Naturally. Everybody likes fires. So watch your step. I think Mademoiselle's got her eye on you already."

Mademoiselle Seville is their landlady. With her dogs, Julot and Zephyre, she lives below the little villa in a wooden storage cellar. The fires terrify her. Coming back from her shopping trips to Nice, she closes her eyes when the bus rounds the turn at Boule-sur-Mer. "If there is no excitement, I open them. But every night, I dream the bus will turn, I will hear *'Mon dieu.'* I will open, and see my *propriété* in smoke."

Mademoiselle is tiny, dark, always scurrying, her skin is the color of the dry ground, brown inlaid with olive and yellow. "She's like an exhausted gold mine," says Cynthia.

Twice a day, Mademoiselle drags a hose over to the stone cistern and waters the acre she gardens. "Though what can a single woman do?" Headshake, gloom, a crooked little arm sweeping overgrown fields. *"La terre reste inculte."*

Two weeks before, they drove up the stony path the first time. She'd stood on the terrace, grinning, holding a welcoming bowl of fresh raspberries, the seedballs glistening with sugar crystals. "What huge teeth you have," muttered Cynthia. The dogs jumped on the little *quatre chevaux* Peugeot they'd baptized "Screed." (After the Apostle's Creed: The first article of Screed's Credo was "I believe in regular gas.")

"Oh God," said Cynthia. She'd gotten out of Screed and looked around. Fruit trees, a grape arbor, the white villa gripped by red vines, roofed with blue clay tiles, and below, slope lapping green slope with shivery slices of the Mediterranean poked between. And in the air, country noises. In the school *cahier* he bought the next day in Nice, Dr. Merriwether wrote the first of his summer observations: *The air is one great motor: flies, midges, frogs, crickets, bees, humming birds. Plus scooters with musical horns ("Never on Sunday").*

Every morning, he sits on a beach lounger under the shredding timbers of the grape arbor, picking from a bowl of plums and writing away at sights, sounds, thoughts. He wears nothing but shorts Cynthia scissored from a pair of blue jeans.

Four days a week, he works in the laboratory of the *Faculté des Sciences* at the University of Nice; Tuesdays he takes part in the Conference on Motivation which the University and the *Fondation Rothschild* sponsor at the Rothschild villa in St. Jean. Early mornings, he writes in the notebook. *Poor Robert. Not enough flies in his joy ointment.* (The early entries were often self-indictments.) *I practice the golden mean: gold for me, meanness for others. Why do I suck the grape meat and complain about the bitterness of the skin?*

Every morning their eyes open on a bough of yellow plums. Says Cynthia, "It's as if they've been eating moonbeams all night." Cynthia lies on the other side of the great bed. Small jaw and coppery little nose peer out of the gold hair. Dr. Merriwether wakes up, puts on his blue shorts, a sport shirt, moccasins, washes up, and walks two hundred yards downhill to the *épicerie* for the morning loaf, butter, jam and cheese, then back up past church and post office (shut for July) for a pre-breakfast breakfast with his *cahier* in the grape arbor. The dogs nuzzle him; Zephyre, a police bitch shaved in ribs and belly, and Julot, a cataract-blinded terrier. Dr. Merriwether dislikes the two nuzzlers. They do everything in slow motion, even humping each other or hoisting legs to urinate on Screed's tires.

Merriwether watches a bee dive from flower to flower, nerve-rich threads sinking toward the sepal, body somersaulting in the ruby stamen. The bee scrapes, emerges, gold-dusted with pollen, dives next door, scrapes, returns to the ruby. *Only men lead double lives. The bee's decisions were made a million years ago. (Imagine a bee who didn't want to dance out the location of his honey. Impossible.) Lucky single-mindedness of animals.* The bee scrambles by a gold pistil, ascends it, then—an oddity—holds up. For rest? For goodby? Sunning itself? More likely getting a reading. *Their internal clocks synchronize with polarized light*. Dr. Merriwether dissolves in the joy of observation, speculating, remembering, lets himself become what he hears: gnats, ticks, blowflies, dragonflies, swoopsail butterflies, a trillion flying parts, marauding, raging, courting, laboring in flower mines; antenna, wings, tymbals, mandibles, whirring, crkkking, chrrrping, humming, buzzing. *Insect mind is insect action.*

A flash of yellow: Cynthia, with an armful of shirts and shorts. "Hot lavender," she calls, hoisting a pair of his undershorts. "Mint, savory, marjoram, posies of mid-summer; that's for my sweetie." Merriwether did the wash last time, agreeing, at times in theory, always in practice, that house chores be shared. The new age. "My shorts 'stand in the level of your dreams.' " They have read *Winter's Tale* out loud. "It's too crazy," says Cynthia; he found it magical. But no more servile Hermiones. No more Mademoiselles.

Every day they get more of her melancholy history, along with *petits cadeaux:* baskets of *tilleul* leaves for infusions, lavender stalks heavy with sachet, bowls of blue plums, raspberries, medlars. Tiny, toothy, lordotic, she peers into the kitchen through the plastic strips. "Tomatoes?" Hour after hour, comma turned caret, she picks the golden bloodballs hung from the propped plants.

"She looks like a mourner in an Indian village," says Merriwether. The plants are propped like wigwams.

"Like hell. That back comes from bending over Julot."

Cynthia and Merriwether have waked up to moaning. "Love calls." "*Elle fait le soixante-neuf avec le chien.* How do they say 'make the beast with two backs?' "

"You mean the table with five legs." Cynthia sketches that in his *cahier*. "I was going to leave my papers to Widener."

"This'll show you have heart."

For the most part, Merriwether is content. Now and then Cynthia suffered one of the depressions he'd first encountered in the spring after her move to Cambridge. He'd found what he thought was a safe apartment for her in the Commonwealth Apartments on Mellen Street, an apartment-hotel for old ladies run by old ladies. "Why didn't you stick me in a nursing home? Or a cemetery?"

It was his idea to get her out of the Harvard mainstream, though not too far from her classes. The place was clean, safe, hermetically proper. There was a maid to clean up and change sheets daily. "Are the old ladies so dirty?" It was—in its way—furnished: huge lamps squatted on flimsy end-tables by a coarse-grained, cigar-colored sofa and cigar-colored chairs. Part of a cigar-colored family whose cousins were in the lobby. Dr. Merriwether bought a used television set from the offerings on the Holyoke Bulletin Board, Cynthia put up her pictures, her jewelry tree, her books, laid shawls and Indian rugs over the chairs, stuck her bottles and statuettes on the tables. In a day she made it her own. But the circle of old ladies who sat day-in-and-out in the lobby rotted her patience. She passed under their eyes with trepidation and then hatred. "I thought suttee only came after death. Or is this some Merriwether rite of living burial we simple folk don't know about?" Dr. Merriwether had thought she'd feel more secure here. "You could have put me in your deposit vault," she said. "That's probably the heart of the matter." She sank from anger to silent misery.

In St. Vetry, it went better. Merriwether did not feel like Judas, nor Cynthia a pariah. They became easier and easier with each other. Her intelligence and wit delighted him. So many years he had been uncomfortable, sometimes miserable at Sarah's incomprehension. Partly, it was that Sarah played the fool. "You wanted it that way," she told him later. He hadn't. Yet he preferred the Old to the New Sarah who corrected everybody. The Universal Expert. "I have a right to an opinion."

"It's not a question of opinion."

"That's your opinion."

"You know the function of the liver or you don't."

"Everybody has common medical knowledge."

"But the liver does not filter waste products. Maybe you were thinking of the kidney."

"I said the kidney."

"Ah. I thought you'd said the liver. That's what I was talking about with Esmé."

"If you'd listen to me once in a while, you'd know I said the kidney."

"Mommy," said Esmé, "I think you said the liver."

"I meant the kidney. It's not worth this barrage. There is no point in acting smug about what one's been trained for." Exit in fury. His corrective calm infuriated her.

Cynthia too resented his calm in the face of her anger. "You're so cold." But somehow they were equals. They argued as equals. And they could argue about anything. Driving up from Nice, they debated Hilbert's postulates. "Connection, congruence, continuity and," she came up with "parallelism," he, "symmetry."

"Stoopid. You're sooo stoopid."

Nuggets of shore light below them in the mild air; at Boule-sur-Mer, perfume from a wall of jasmine.

"I may be stoopid, but you're wrong."

"You're stoopid and wrong. In you, they're congruent, connected, continuous and parallel."

"They can't be parallel *and* connected. But," as if remembering, "as a matter of fact, I am wrong."

"All right," she said. "You're just stoopid. Sometimes

you remember a fact or two. I mean if you've just read it in the noospaper or something. Not something you read too long ago, of course. Twenty-four hours is a long time for my sweetie."

She was so tan now, any twist of her face made flash points in her teeth and eyeballs. Within the bleaching hair, the small, flashing face was exceptionally lovely. Lots of ruffled feeling could be smoothed by that.

Their French day began at breakfast with the night's dreams. She was a beautiful dreamer. An electron was trying to get through the dusty layers of the moon, the moon was a proton, the proton a plane. The electron flew it.

"That's you flying me."

"Creep."

"You're one of those people who live to dream."

"At least I'm on my own there. Awake, I have to depend on you."

Sunday was a day to fill. Swimming was out. Cynthia was used to empty shore beaches. The Riviera beaches stank and were full of stones. (On every stone reposed a huge hunk of adipose tissue. The biggest deposits were American. In cafés, she and Merriwether guessed the nationalities of rear-ends. She was right. American girls, from fifteen on, had fat rear-ends. Her own, much worried about, was almost French in firmness.) They drove to Renoir's house in Cagnes, to a perfume factory in Grasse, to Vence to see Matisse's chapel. Mostly they walked in the hills, but of late Cynthia tired easily. For a girl who'd been a dancer, acrobat, tennis player, a rider of horses and motorcycles, it was unsettling. Her breath got choppy, her system sluggish; it was not just low blood pressure. He worried about her. *Is it a kind of imitative senility,* he asked his *cahier. To equalize us?*

He also worried about his children. Letters weren't

enough. He wanted to kiss them, talk with them. When he missed them like this, he grew numb with anxiety, the sun gave black light. He could be finishing up some terrific fish-stew in the old market of Nice, listening to one of the wandering musicians playing some heartbreaking Fritz Kreisler song, when the thought of George and Esmé, and then Priscilla and Albie would fix him where he sat. Cynthia would pick up the *bad vibes,* and within ten minutes there'd be an argument which was not playful. They would drive home in silence, his heart a rock, feelings anesthetized.

"You're an ice-man. You're inhuman."

"It's the way I am."

He'd sleep alone in the small bedroom. Or wouldn't sleep. One look, one word activated an arc of misery in her. "The way I am," the way she was. Which put them in separate beds. Knowing her state was rockier, deeper, more miserable than his, he forced himself over his coldness to kiss her, to say he loved her, to make funny noises. Five minutes, and she melted. The waters ran back, and he felt the love he had pretended.

The first day he drove down to the Zoological Laboratory, the Rector, Dieudonnet, showed him around.

"I wish we had more space for you," said Dieudonnet. He was stiff, dark-eyed, ironic. Square-feet-of-laboratory-space was a professional caste mark. "We do offer you an assistant who knows your work. And knows English as well. Though I see that is superfluous."

The ironic play in the Rector's face prevented Merriwether from knowing whether or not his French came up to snuff.

"You're extraordinarily generous," he said.

Merriwether's assistant was Georges Pecile, a solid, handsome, in-drawn man of twenty-three. Merriwether sat on a table and told him what his project was, what he needed, what he hoped to do. Pecile understood perfectly, even seemed interested in the work. They got along. Not perfectly, for there was the tension of two intelligent researchers, twenty years apart, one enjoying privileges, the other serving what he regarded as unnecessary apprenticeship.

Pecile was from Nice. He said he'd show Merriwether the city.

"That would be fine. I'm here with a friend." The "e" of *amie* is silent, but the look and tone were clear. "We would like to see what's going on." Though even saying it, he felt a constriction. Cynthia was Pecile's age, Pecile was attractive and intelligent. Merriwether wanted no strain. They drove down to a café near the old market, and sat talking for two hours over coffee. They talked in both languages, often in the same sentence. Shop talk. Very pleasant. "You claim maturation is there for the asking?" said Pecile.

"The baby girl has her 200,000 ova in her, the enzymes are all there. Who is to say that the physical theater of the chemical play isn't significant? If the theater's too small, the temperature, the actual velocity of command-response must differ."

Pecile is surprised by this American with the mild face. An alert type, yet filled with Anglo-Saxon wind. Hands expressed French disgust with metaphysics; Pecile knew the proper boundaries of discussion.

Merriwether did have a recent passion for the metaphysical. (And wondered if this meant his scientific menopause.) "It's my dessert," he said.

He drove up the hill.

The sun is boiling color out of the flowers. Cynthia was in the garden in her yellow bikini, reading *Fort Comme la Mort*. They kiss, he tells her about Pecile, she tells him that the painter has just fallen in love with his mistress's daughter. "Disgusting," says Dr. Merriwether.

He changes into his shorts, pours two glasses of white wine and reads *Nice-Matin:* Eddy Merckx is humiliating his Tour de France competitors; a firebug is arrested in Villefranche; there is trouble in Nigeria; new films. He goes for his *cahier* and sketches the villa, the flowers trained over the eaves, the bird-cage lamps, the wood strips glued on the stucco, the scalloped roof, the porcelain urns, Cynthia reading near the medlar tree, feet, ankles, knees, thighs, the strip of yellow cloth. He crosses out the sketch, takes up a *Que sais-je* book, *Sacred Scriptures of the East* (Cynthia's choice), and returns to a passage he thought of using as epigraph for his Conference paper. A Genesis story: The Primeval Being, Aditi, Thirst, which moved over No-thing until it created *ar-ka,* Sanskrit cousin of *aqua.* "What was neither existent nor inexistent, out of darkness concealed in darkness, born from the force of contemplation, out of which rose Kama (Desire), the Germ of Mind."

Amidst the tiger-colored bees, the humming birds, the blazing flowers, five yards from his beautiful companion, Merriwether melts with this antiquity. These beautiful texts survive by miracle. The Genesis story had been carved on a grindstone. Grains of millet were found in the cuneiform grooves. *The fragility of what's precious,* "Cynthia."

She looks up, sees him looking at her, smiles, stretches her legs, sticks out her tongue.

The other American at the Conference was John Brightsman of the University of North Dakota. A student of mosaic and regulatory propagation in molluscs, Brightsman did pioneer work that had been disregarded for many years. Soured to the point of mania, he showed up at conferences, but his papers were badly phrased and organized. Very few understood what he was getting at. He, in turn, sneered at men who went on doing work his own made redundant. He became more and more of a troublemaker, burst out during the presentation of papers, corralled authors in the lobbies and told them they ought to take up plumbing. On the other hand, he was generous about work which pleased him. Merriwether had once received a wonderful note from him, full of praise and useful suggestions.

After the first session of the Conference, he came up to Merriwether. "Remember me? Met you in Detroit." He wore a Palm Beach suit, rope-soled sandals, no socks.

"Glad to see you."

Brightsman suggested they have supper together.

Merriwether said he'd like to, but he was staying way back in the hills with a friend who expected him.

Brightsman's diction and syntax were irregular, even shattered, as if he were gathering thought bits in broken containers. "I get you," he said. "I guess I get you. Or maybe I got you."

One evening, eating with Cynthia at an Alsatian restaurant on the *Rue de Suisse,* Merriwether spotted him looking at them through the window. Caught, he smiled and waved. Brightsman came in. He was wearing a dark tweed suit, the only one in sight not in summer clothes. It was like a coffin coming through a circus. "You been hiding this," he said. "Where did you keep it?" The eyes, mottled and glittering, rolled back as if summoning Cynthia into his cranial cave. "Such a sly boats. Well, we gottcha."

"Have you eaten, John?"

"More more than less."

"We're finishing." There was coffee, cheese and fruit to come.

"I've got nothing better in the chute."

"Will you take a little of this?" Merriwether held up a bottle of Anjou rosé.

"No point drinking vinegar." He summoned the waiter like a dog. *"Y-a-t'il un Montrachat Soixante-Cinq?"* The waiter said he'd look. "That's *vino.* I hate this country." This was said in the decibels of his summons; half the patrons looked their way.

"I think these people understand English, John."

"I detest the south of any country. Southerners have the temperament of equatorial animals. Violent posturers." The speech was clear of twists. Maybe hatred was the right gear for his tongue.

"I'm from North Carolina," said Cynthia.

"That changes nothing. But you're a terrific looking person."

"Thank you."

An old man, carrying a violin case, came into the restaurant.

"What's with Heifetz?"

"He comes around at dinner and plays for money."

"He's wonderful," said Cynthia. "We've heard him before."

The violinist played Kreisler's *Liebesleid.*

"I do love chocolate syrup in my soup," said Brightsman. The piece wasn't over.

"Give him a break, John."

"I come to get fed, not to swallow chocolate schmaltz."

Merriwether and Cynthia clapped loudly, stimulating applause that was hard to come by from the experienced victims of these café artists. The violinist played at the Mendelssohn Concerto. Brightsman groaned, triple forte.

Said Merriwether, "I'd appreciate it if you'd stop groaning, John. I want to hear the music."

Brightsman sat up. "You're joking."

"I am not joking. This is a decent old man. This is his living. Even if it weren't, I enjoy his playing."

"You're a musical ass, Merriwether. A cocksman maybe, but an ass."

"Take yourself out of here, please."

"Says who."

"Get off now, or I'll take you out by the collar."

Brightsman said to Cynthia, "I pity you with this Harvard prick," and walked out.

Mademoiselle brought them the mail at breakfast, the standard prologue for an aria of despair. This morning, still shaky over Brightsman, they wanted peace, and said "*Merci*" and "*Au revoir,* Mademoiselle." "I can't face those red toes before three cups of coffee," muttered Cynthia. "Who's your letter from?"

"Priscilla. And one inside from Esmé. Excuse me." He read: Dear Dad,

> Missed you in the news pictures of the Baron de Villemorin's party. Expected to see my handsome père chiding Elizabeth Taylor for being forward with him.

He smiled and Cynthia, eyes up from her letter, asked him what was so funny.

"Priscilla has a pleasant style."

"Let's hear," she said.

"Dear Dad," read Merriwether aloud.

Missed you in the news pictures of the Baron de Villemorin's party. Expected to see my handsome père chiding Elizabeth Taylor for being forward with him. (Or were you that shadow in the corner handing Madame Onassis a glass of champagne?)

All quiet, desperately quiet, on the *"American Scene."* (I'm reading that book. Why does such a smart man have to use such fancy foil???!!!) Read it? Don't. Tho it is, I know, brillllliant.

Work is gross. The lab is steamy—who said it was air-conditioned?—and though Mr. Davison is very nice to me, I get the feeling he has trouble distinguishing me from his rats. I might do worse than share their fate. Occasionally I hear what can be called screams of rat pleasure.

No one is here. Only Dasha, Mark, Mark W. and Sally Okanobu. Fred left last week. A relief to me. I was becoming his nightly toddy. Did see *City Lights* at Carpenter the other night, and that lifted me up for hours. I would trade a year of my life to get a look like Charlie Chaplin's from someone.

Forgive the empty letter. Esmé was writing, and I thought I'd give the envelope some weight. Lightweight weight.

Have a good time (but not too good).

ooo and xxx,
Priscilla

Esmé's letter was written in purple ink.

Dear Dad,

Between-ugh-camps. Cheerleaders Camp was, believe it or not, great. Great people, great spirit, and you do learn a lot, though I'm ashamed to tell people I was in "Cheerleaders Camp." (It is, in a way. Boastful Esmé.) I am looking forward to riding camp, though I know I'll be the worst one there. Mom has been giving me pointers. Also a book called *Saddle Up* which tells you what the pastern is and how a horse can kick you to death, what to feed him (ugh) and how to dress and comb him (also what lipstick a she-horse likes), but between all this HELP and my tender whatsis, I dunno. Anyway, if you have to come home and treat a broken esmé-bone, don't hate me.

I miss you a lot. Not that I don't hope you're having a gooey time and wowing other people with your discoveries. But don't forget the land Columbus discovered. It contains your boastful, fearful, horselady daughter,

Esmé Tipton Merriwether
XXXXXXXX OOOOOOOO

"I prefer Esmé's," said Cynthia. "They both write well."

"Albie writes better than anyone in the family. When he writes. It's his one non-athletic gift. Unless you count refinements in time-passing."

Cynthia is in a man's shirt—not his—which covers what pants would cover. Her "face" is not on, she looks a bit snubby, but beautiful. She tells him the night's dream. She was a fly just getting out of a cocoon before the moth which belonged there grew and crushed her.

Merriwether told her how moths secrete an enzyme early enough so that they'll have just enough of it to dissolve the protein of the cocoon. "It's the same process in ovulation. Yours."

"And Priscilla's. Is she on The Pill?"

Merriwether felt the slightest of hooks. "I don't know. I'd guess not."

"She's rather pointed about old Fred."

"You should see Fred. He's very sweet and plump. Like a doughnut center."

"I'll bet they have a grand old time."

"Well, if so, I trust she's on The Pill. She's certainly known about it from Year One. Dr. Rock had a summer place near us."

"If you know Rock, does that mean you don't have to use The Pill?"

"I just meant the subject's been in the Merriwether house for a long time."

"Why don't you give her a prescription?"

"Why don't you ask your father to prepare the divorce papers for the ancient you're sleeping with?"

"I'm going to write your children letters," said Cynthia. " 'Dear Priscilla, Hi. You don't know me, but your name was given to me by a mutual acquaintance. He said we have much in common. We are both in college. I like college. Do you like college? Are you lonely? I am! I only have one good friend. Are you a virgin? I am not. Your loving stepmother, Cynthia Ryder.' You like it?"

Merriwether said it was very funny.

"Do you think I have a good epistolary style?"

Merriwether assured her she did. "Maybe I'll write one to your father. 'Dear Mr. Ryder. I want to introduce myself. I am the doctor who examined Cynthia last summer and found her in good health. I am also in good health. I weigh a hundred and fifty-two pounds. Your loving son, R. T. Merriwether, Ph.D., M.D.' "

"You have a crumby style."

"I thought it was businesslike but affectionate."

" 'Dear Albie,' " said Cynthia. " 'Hi. Maybe Priscilla has written you about me. I am a friend of a friend. Last year I was a junior at Swarthmore. Next year I may be a junior at Radcliffe. Aren't I making good progress? I hear you are a fine person too. Though I do not favor boys your age, maybe we could be friends. Are you a virgin? I am not. Try it on some time. Your loving stepmother, Cynthia.' Now that's a letter."

"Yes," said Dr. Merriwether, "that is a letter."

Under the grape arbor, with Julot growling curses at his feet, he wrote a real letter.

> Dear S, P, E, G and—if there, A,
>
> 'Spega': the Rumanian for an optimistic faucet? (Five cents for an etymology.)
>
> The Riviera is not what the posters say. Not even what it was when I worked here five years ago. Vallauris was a smallish town. You sat in the café by the Picasso statue of the Shepherd and Lamb, drank coffee, then ate a wonderful meal for two dollars. Now Vallauris is a suburban shopping center.
>
> It is so crowded here one doesn't dare take to the roads. Luckily, I travel a smallish back road down to the lab and the conference and can zoom back to good French bread, wine and cheese.
>
> Heat, yes, but not bad in the hills. Lonely? A bit for my spegalians. Though you seem to be prospering; at least those who take pen in hand.
>
> The landlady, an amiable crone named Mademoiselle Seville, is on the edge of the pepper grove below this arbor nervously waiting her chance to tell me her night's awful dream. This is my chief social pleasure, so I'd best sign off and get to it.
>
> Love, from the loving
> "Père des Spegalians," *id est*
> Dad

Merriwether's conference paper examined water and salt changes during congestive cardiac failure; the changes were correlated with the release of the anti-diuretic hormone by Verney's osmoreceptor. The technical presentation took thirty minutes. Then, for twenty, Merriwether speculated about "levels of" what he called "neuro-consciousness" in the "registration or certification" of the changes. "When is thirst *thirst?*"

The conference room was an enormous red salon filled with tapestried chairs and sofas, decorated with lunettes and ceilings full of seraphim. In the room's center were a rectangular table and thirty-five tubular chairs. By each chair were earphones for simultaneous translation, note pads, pencils, glasses of water, coffee mugs, and—left from a previous conference—logarithmic slide rules and calipers.

John Brightsman sat at the long end of the rectangle. The only one near him the day of Merriwether's presentation was an Italian biologist, a thirty-five-year-old *professoressa* from Turin with red hair and a spectacular figure. She and Brightsman exchanged frequent looks during Merriwether's presentation; when Brightsman made his comment, she nodded emphasis.

Brightsman's comment was that Merriwether's speculations were perfectly acceptable after-dinner musings for high school students, but out of place at a serious conference. There was, he said, such a disparity between the "at least professional standards of the research work of the gentleman from Cambridge" and "these out-loud musings" that it amounted to "a kind of schizophrenia which might be useful to investigate in itself," though that was, as far as he knew, not on the agenda.

The insults brought silence to the room. Merriwether felt as if he'd been pushed off a roof. The Chairman, a physiologist from Marseilles, looked around for the next comment, as if Brightsman's could be the ordinary basis for ordinary discussion. An old acquaintance of Merriwether's from Basel finally said that he was a bit surprised at "our friend Brightsman's comments, though we all know and enjoy his high spirit and wit. I suggest we focus on what to me were not 'high school musings,' if I heard correctly, but an interesting conceptual framework."

"Gentlemanly nonsense," called Brightsman.

"Please, *chers collègues,*" said the Chairman.

"I see no reason trivializing time," said Brightsman.

Merriwether replied, "I'm sorry that my little coda displeased the distinguished professor from North Dakota. However, I can't see making any reasonable response to his remarks."

"What the hell are you talking about, Merriwether? Why don't you go back to your child whore and let the rest of us do serious work?"

Merriwether got up, moved toward Brightsman, and then with one prolonged needle stare, left the room.

Driving up the hill, swerving at curves, pulling quickly away from trucks, cars, scooters, he finally recovered enough to stop in the café in St. Vetry.

On the little terrace, among the green vines, listening to the click of the *boules*, holding sips of red wine on his tongue, letting the sights—vanilla church, post office, the green slope—blot up what was left of his fury, Merriwether worked himself into sympathy for Brightsman. Uncertainty, isolation, terror, horrible envy, what else had that fellow suffered? How long had he been nuts? And yet, the attack on his paper was basically right. Merriwether had taken off on a theoretical fling. And Brightsman, in his crazy way, had sensed it as an equivalent of Cynthia.

Brightsman stayed in a pension on the lower Corniche west of Nice. His peculiarities had been the talk of the other pensioners. They had "observed his strange hours and his bizarre arrogance." In view of the "menace to the whole Riviera," they decided they should keep an eye on him. "The unstable are unnaturally excited by fire," reported one of them, an undertaker from Lyon who had—as he added to the reporter from *Nice-Matin*—"read much in psychological literature." He suggested they follow Brightsman. One morning, three of them trailed him into the hills and watched him walk off toward a clump of shrubs.

> He stooped and did something which we could not observe. We were a hundred meters distant. Seconds after he rose, there was a burst of flame. We were waiting behind our car, and when he approached, we jumped out, seized and then tied him up. He struggled like a madman. M. Pauncelot ran to extinguish the blaze and then we drove here to the Prefecture.

Above this front page story was a picture of Brightsman glaring at his three accusers.

"Fantastic," said Merriwether. "I don't know arson types, but I wouldn't put it past him. But it's pathetic, horrible. You can't imagine what extraordinary work the fellow does."

They followed *"l'affaire* Brightsman" in the papers every day. The Conference members discussed the situation and decided against doing anything other than offering a written statement about Brightsman's work. Merriwether thought it might be his duty to testify to the man's instability; but the fellow was in enough trouble. The *juge d'instruction* was calling in psychiatrists.

"I can understand his interest in fire," said Merriwether.

"Our lab work is small scale. There's something very exciting about tremendous changes. A sensible man, let alone a nut like Brightsman, might be tempted by all these fires to try and see what was what."

"Jesus Christ," said Cynthia. "Don't let anyone else hear you." They were sitting under the grape arbor. Cynthia had her bare legs in his lap. "They can hang Ph.Ds."

In *Le Monde*—for anti-Americanism and the anti-intellectual backlash of the years of university riot had made this a national story—Brightsman gave an interview about his "passion for all natural phenomena."

> No natural process is alien to me. I have rushed to the Missouri River during a flood to study its incredible force. Imagine, here is the same substance that in one's drinking glasses and faucets is so tame. In flood, this domestic pet tears oaks from the ground, turns forests into seas. So with fire. Here it is at the tip of our cigarette, jolly little thing. But there it is, the devourer of the earth. This is what I study. But I do not create the natural laboratories. I did not start the fire any more than I started the flood.

One day, Mademoiselle Seville met Merriwether and Cynthia as they drove up the path. "A journalist from Paris is here to question the Professor." She pointed to a handsome, thirtyish woman in a mini-skirt who smiled at them from the terrace. "Jill Chambliss," she said, coming up. "I'm from *Newsweek*." She wanted Professor Merriwether's thoughts about the Brightsman case.

Merriwether had had no experience with the charm of good reporters. Over wine, he talked about Brightsman, first with caution, then more and more freely. Miss Chambliss—"Jill, please"—was elegant, and very pretty.

Cynthia frowned, pouted, finally went inside. Merriwether told about the incident in the restaurant and "a crazy outburst" at the Conference. "Yet the man is close to being a top-notch physiologist. I haven't convinced myself that he's lost control to this extent."

The notebook, balanced on Jill's tan knees, filled, page after page, so, a week later, Dr. Merriwether was surprised that the entire *Newsweek* story was only a half page long, and then dismayed to find a sentence about "the Harvard physiologist, Robert Merriwether," who'd said that Brightsman had made a scene in a restaurant during which he'd insulted Merriwether and "his pretty, young assistant, Cynthia Ryder."

8

Cynthia had gone wild after the telegram from her father, and though she'd calmed down thinking up strategies—from moving out of the house to saying she and Merriwether were married—he couldn't guess from moment to moment how she'd be.

Not that he relished seeing the man. "Your father's not a caveman," he'd said to her, "and we're not rabid dogs," but he had fears about Mr. Ryder. Firstly, he had a notion that legal training emphasized sophistical distinctions which vaulted essential relationships. Lawyers dominated American life by creating divisive issues. They had a vested interest in complication and bullied clients into helplessness before it. Even lawyers he liked were often conversational bullies. Secondly, Mr. Ryder was a physical man, not like Merriwether himself, a sensible exerciser, but someone who needed activity to siphon off violent impulses. The man loved speed, he raced planes, motorcycles, boats, he was a hunter, Cynthia said there were guns all over the house.

Thirdly, he was top dog in a small southern town; that gave a man a lot of moral elbow room. Merriwether had never been south of Washington, but he had his own confident notions about the South's contempt for the law its lawyers used as shields for illegitimacy and violence. God knows if Ryder wouldn't gun them down in the grape arbor and go back home for his medals. Merriwether let himself exaggerate, but it didn't help him laugh off his discomfort. After all, from Ryder's viewpoint, he probably looked like an old lecher debauching his daughter. If the vocabulary was outmoded, so—according to Cynthia—was her father.

"You're out of your depths, Daddy."

Mr. Ryder was walking along Riverside Drive with his oldest daughter Lisa a few hours before taking the plane to Paris. New York was equatorial. The wind was out of a blast furnace; the golden filth of the Hudson shimmered. And across, the oxide red Palisades baked and steamed. Lisa, bare-shouldered, mini-skirted, short-haired, was drenched with sweat.

"I don't think French waters are that much deeper than ours, Lisa." He was going to keep his temper. Though he could not get used to this plain (no make-up, no flirtatiousness), long-legged beauty of his telling him what she called the score.

"The Pill's changed everything, Daddy. You have to get used to it."

Here was someone whose every atom he'd either created or subsidized, who only existed because he'd stirred out of a dream twenty-four years ago, and here she was mapping out the world for him. It was not easy to take. Not in this apoplectic heat with the old ladies and their ancient pugs staggering along the Drive with their tongues out. "I don't like to have my face rubbed in mud, Lisa, that's all. Not by my own children."

He'd called Lisa in New York after he'd read the *Newsweek* article. Did she want to go to France with him for a few days, he trusted her judgment, maybe she could help detach her sister from whatever mess she was in.

Lisa didn't want to go, she was the last person to budge Cynthia, the sibling war was over because they didn't see each other, but it would be years before they could talk easily. She still tried to help. "Maybe she is working with the professor. It said she was his assistant."

"She has a thousand dollars for eight weeks, she doesn't need to work. She's supposed to be seeing the Louvre and the Uffizi."

"All right, so she met someone she liked. Is that unnatural?"

"Nothing that happens is unnatural. I'm just going over to take a look and see how far she's gone."

Lisa stared toward but not into her father's eyes. It was very hard facing up to him, he just overwhelmed you; he was a bully with right on his side, and a bully without it. Every encounter with him was a struggle for survival. It was unfair. He weakened her, then bullied her. And the worst was she loved him.

"You'll scare her to death."

"I telegraphed I was coming."

"God warned Adam and Eve about the apple."

Such a burst of female mis-analogizing; so dear these intelligences but so fouled up. "Lisa, honey, your sister may be in deep water. Isn't that the point?"

"She seems to be doing all right. I just think you don't know the score."

They were the only ones in sight now, the only ones dumb enough to be on the street. Now and then a bus lumbered by, or a few cars, but this part of New York could have been a ghost city except for the two Ryders facing each other. "It's too hot to fight. I'll buy you dinner at the airport and send you back in a taxi."

Lisa said she'd better not go, she had a welding class. "Have a good time, Daddy. And don't," the bare shoulders lifted and fell.

"Don't worry about that." He took the check he'd made out for her from his wallet; she accepted it like defeat, and, head low, walked slowly to Broadway and waited till he flagged down a taxi.

Mademoiselle was watering when the Citroën drove up the path. When the regal gentleman descended, she almost curtsied. "Cynthia Ryder?" he asked.

Mademoiselle wiped her hands and chattered alien gibberish, while he repeated, "Cynthia Ryder" till Cynthia ran out and leaned against the white suit.

The first hour she kept off his questions with her own: how was the trip, how was Lisa, how was Momma, what were Jenny and San doing, they never wrote, wasn't it beautiful here, look at the apricots, the plums, the medlars, come see the tomato field, the church, isn't Mademoiselle grotesque, and those hounds, aren't they devils. Mr. Ryder had a diplomat's patience; and he enjoyed the charm and beauty of his daughter. The sun had bleached her hair, her legs—in denim shorts—were a woman's, there was no baby fat in the thighs. She spoke easily, listened well, without Lisa's shoulder-chip, without her mother's hickish clowning. Still, the evaded point was swelling. It was time to find out things. She wasn't renting this villa on the thousand he gave her. Finally she came to it and said her friend would be coming back from the lab before long.

"This is his house, I take it."

"He rents it from our red-toed friend here. Two hundred a month. I pay twenty."

"You're getting a good deal. I suppose he is too." Which went further than he'd meant. Cynthia blushed.

"He's a friend, a close friend."

Mr. Ryder said he'd seen that announced in *Newsweek*. Cynthia, small face aburst from its yellow wood, began talking, talking. It was at Harvard, such a summer, they met by chance, he was a distinguished doctor, professor, researcher, he was lonely, he'd been separated-in-spirit for years, she was lonely, she never got on with boys, she needed an older man, Merriwether was full of scruples, she overcame them, he had children—yes—some nearly as old as she, but there were millions of such couples, take Onassis, take Justice Douglas, Senator Thurmond, Dr. Barnard, it was difficult, but they loved each other so, please don't do anything, Daddy, please don't take it away, she did not know what would happen, they were making no plans, just trying to get through day by day hurting others as little as possible, that was why she hadn't said anything, who knows, by the time she'd written, it might have been all over.

So there it was. The word storm blew and Mr. Ryder stood in the sun looking at this blonde child he'd raised. In minutes he would be meeting a sag-bellied, lecherous graybeard, a father, a careless, oblivious professional man who'd taken leave of his senses and debauched this girl. Here they were, abandoned to their confused felicity in a French villa, thousands of miles away from their obligations.

"What a business, Cynthia."

He knew he should touch her, but did not want to. These old vines and fruit trees, the glistening urns, the stucco with red splints gashed across it, what a setting for this absurd amour.

"He doesn't know what to do," said Cynthia.

"Doesn't know. He doesn't know." Strong feelings turn people into machines; they go mechanical, repetitious, they sputter as the newer system of mentality tries to control the lava spurting out of the infantile fears. Mr. Ryder's face grew bloody, liverish, then pale, he walked the terrace, away from this suddenly detestable presence, this oddly unfamiliar daughter. He came back spouting his own marital story, how he had courted her mother for years until he'd finished law school and passed the bar exam, they had restrained their passions, they had not gone against the grain of their teaching. All right, the world was on a moral bender, things had changed somewhat, but mores were stored training as heredity was stored environment, and she had been trained, what did she mean by so going against the grain of her life?

Yellow shirt, maroon shorts, one-band sandals, Cynthia looked more waif than lecher's morsel. Mr. Ryder could have scooped her up and paddled her. But no, there was a woman's rear, and under the yellow shirt, there were woman's breasts. His daughter was not only capable of having a grand affair, she would be a lucky man's treat. What madness to waste her sexual noontime with an antique.

"I haven't gone against anything," she said. "You wait till you meet Robert, he'll be here any minute. He's the dearest, finest man. Not unlike you. In many ways. It's probably how I found him."

"Don't spread that jam on this stale bread, Cynthia."

"It's not stale. It's the good old bread of compatible human beings. It's common sense, it's truth." This was laced with hysteria, she felt the unsteadiness, the unloosening of something she knew she didn't want to release. She managed to hold on. "Yours and Momma's story's lovely. I don't even care that people today would think it unnatural. For me, it's something out of Jane Austen. Out of Camelot. It's lovely. Only it's not mine, Daddy. My life is different."

Mr. Ryder had lots of legal acreage on all sides of his feelings. With words, discussion, debate, argument, he settled in. "I know times change, Cynthia, and I know you can't live anyone else's life. The cliché is I can't live your life nor you mine. I don't accept that. If something happens to you, that becomes my life. I hope the same is true for you. If only to the extent that I still support you."

The nausea of authority, the old claw, the male threat in the male throat, affection quantified to death. "Your daughters don't need those reminders, Daddy."

"Knowing's one thing, doing's another."

She shook her head. "I have to sit down." She sat where she stood, on the cement. "I'm not here to hurt you," he said, looking down. He touched her head. That was better. His daughter's head. Her father's hand. The shuttles between rage and bafflement slowed up. He knelt and stroked her head. "Do you have a cup of tea?"

They went inside, she boiled water, Mr. Ryder sat at the table. He kept his coat on, a uniform of paternity. When the Peugeot bounced up the path, he took a long swig of tea and followed Cynthia outside.

Merriwether was clearly no chicken, but to Mr. Ryder's

large relief, no Grandpa Lecher. Middle-sized, nice-looking, sporty without flamboyance (he wore sneakers, slacks, a sport shirt); his hair was a bit shaggy—"professorial," thought Mr. Ryder—but conventional. He had a pleasant smile, and his speech—"So glad to see you"—a blend of Kennedy and England. A decent-looking fellow. And, it turned out, direct. "This secrecy has been burdensome to both of us. We have difficulties enough without that," and right there on the terrace he launched into them—his family situation, his love for his children, his "deep feeling" for Cynthia. "Nothing in my life prepared me for this."

It overwhelmed Mr. Ryder. Too much, too quick. The garden noise, the flowers, the silken heat, the tiny lady in long dress and sandals hoisting water arcs over a tomato field, the fluent doctor, his daughter, even his own displacement (a condition as real as these other things), all of it worked against meaning. Mr. Ryder was used to thinking clearly, feeling strongly, deciding quickly. Now cloth seemed as much a part of flower as of the shirt it composed, the shirt had as much to do with the heat as with the body it clothed, and Merriwether—name, voice, sport shirt, trouble—was but part of the scene, a speaking vine, not something that menaced the happiness of a daughter. What was a daughter anyway? Something visible, glinting fibers, dark spheres, a triangle. This disorientation passed in a second, but it was a deep, unique, strange second in Mr. Ryder's life. Meaning, decisiveness, movement: useless, that was what that visual disintegrity spelled for him, and as it passed, and as a giddy ease it brought passed too, Mr. Ryder fought back for what he knew: settlements, breakage, families, homes, plans, the order of the world whose threats he'd faced down so many years in the courts of Shallot and New Bern, Durham and Raleigh. "How could you let it happen?" he said to Dr. Merriwether. "How could you let it continue?"

Something between sigh and groan came out of Cynthia. There was her father, dark, small-chinned face drawn in like an inquisitor's, standing over Bobbie in his white suit, his face like a thuggish prince's, glowering with regal menace. "What are you saying, Daddy?"

"I understand, Mr. Ryder," said Merriwether. He was holding onto himself. *You owe him,* was his control. *You owe it.* "Life surprised me. That's about it. Now I go back with the not-easy job of telling my wife and children."

"I suppose too much milk is spilled," was Mr. Ryder's odd response.

"The marriage part of my life was spilled long ago."

"And you and Cynthia, that isn't spillage?"

"I'm going inside, Daddy."

"Cynthia," said Merriwether. "Maybe we can drink a little wine in the grape arbor."

"You drink," said Cynthia. "I have to lie down."

Merriwether went inside—what relief—and opened a bottle of white wine. He and Mr. Ryder sat and drank in the arbor. Their clothing made them seem like adult and child, but now they talked as contemporaries.

"Have you thought about breaking up? With Cynthia?"

"Yes. But every day we're together makes it more difficult. Not that it's all wine and roses."

"I can imagine," said Mr. Ryder. This wine was augmenting his vertigo. And suddenly he knew and simultaneously felt the strain of it all. What did it all have to do with his life? "I've come close to divorce myself—may I call you Robert?"

"Of course."

"My wife is a good person, but we couldn't be more unlike. The years haven't made us more alike. But we both saw where our center was, so we stayed together. There are so many things in life."

Merriwether said he came from a family where there was no divorce, the idea of doing anything to hurt his children was an agony to him, but he believed his married life might be poisoning them; as for leaving Cynthia, though he believed he would almost enjoy the pain as a kind of martyrdom of reparation, he feared for her. "She's not the steadiest young woman in the world."

"You think she might do something to herself?"

"Such threats are common, but I believe they're genuine. There's an enormous amount of sheer lack of will to live in people. It's very hard for people like me—or you, I should think—to understand. I don't believe psychiatrists generally accept Freud's notion of the death wish, but he surely felt it himself and saw it in other people. I think Cynthia could yield to it, yes."

Mr. Ryder had no close friends at home. His life was activity. He'd had intimate talk from clients, they were fond of him and he of them, but the intimacy was one way: their troubles, his advice. He did not open himself to anyone. What was the point of stirring up emotional subtleties? He was no artist, no psychologist and, as far as he could tell, not particularly neurotic. But talking with this intelligent man was unusually pleasant. He enjoyed the talk, he enjoyed his stake in the man, and he enjoyed something that he wouldn't have acknowledged, the marks of privilege he himself lacked. This man had twenty years' advantage over him, he'd grown up with people who'd talked quietly about all sorts of things, he felt assured about his family, he had a place that existed before he was born. Mr. Ryder had made everything he had. His father had been a drunkard, his mother had worked hard, a decent woman who ran the hardware store and went to church, he loved her, but as soon as he could, he'd gone off on his own. As early as he remembered, he'd made up his mind to drive the hick out of himself, bit by bit. He'd done it. He still lived where he was comfortable, in Shallot, but he took no value, southern or northern, on face value. When he was concerned, he looked into things. He'd taught himself a thousand things, he designed a house, built a car, learned to play the flute, to fly a plane, and enough about market procedures, animal husbandry and oil geology to make far shrewder investments than he would have made through most brokers. He was proud of his skills and proud of his methods, but there was also a grain of innocent dazzlement at what could not be achieved, for those skills and that knowledge which one "breathed in," which one was born to. The way Merriwether held himself, the stretched legs linked above the white sneakers, the lift of the head, the dramaless quiet of the voice, the courtesy and attentiveness, the naïveté of the look. Maybe none of it expressed a truth about the man, but it did express what was beyond him, and Mr. Ryder found it valuable, as he had when he was nine years old listening to northern voices on his radio, watching Tyrone Power, Gary Cooper (in civilian, not cowboy clothes) and William Powell in the Shallot Paramount.

"Robert," he said. "Maybe we should save the rest of this. I better go take a nap back at the hotel, or I'm not going to be up to much. I only have five days here in Europe, and I'm planning to see a few things. Maybe you and Cynthia will come down to the hotel"—the accent was on "ho," one of the few remnants of his family speech—"and have dinner with me."

They said goodby using, a bit self-consciously, first

names—"William," "Robert"—Merriwether pulled the Peugeot out of the Citroën's way and pointed it down the road to Nice.

They met Mr. Ryder on the dining terrace of the Negresco. Cynthia wore a scarlet dress with brocade collar, Mr. Ryder a navy blazer and white tie; Merriwether was slightly askew in olive turtleneck and tan polo coat. Thirty yards away, cars whirred Cannes-or-Menton-ward, six or seven yachts lit up in the bay, a band of red moon glowed on the palms, there was glitter, mildness, poly-lingual babble, and then lobster stuffed with crab meat, a *salade Niçoise, crêpes flambés,* showtunes of the American Thirties and floods of anecdote, Harvard, Carolina, legal and medical cases, travel stories, family jokes. Mr. Ryder was now completely at ease with Dr. Merriwether. He even had the added pleasure of being a proprietor: this was almost a son-in-law.

Cynthia felt excluded. "They have me here like those flowers," but, after all, this was the solution to her worst fear, that her father would hurt Bobbie or take her away.

Mr. Ryder was going off to Rome, Paris and London, and he felt much better than he had hours ago. "I want to help," he said, at the end. "I'm afraid you're going to have bad times. I'll do my best to stick with you." He wasn't at all drunk, but the remark came out of a general, blurred delight to which a few glasses of wine had contributed. Mostly, though, it was the beauty of the place, the beauty of his daughter, and the distinction of the man who was a kind of brotherly son-in-law, a man who, almost as inexperienced as himself, had somehow fallen into a new life.

Driving up the St. Vetry road at eleven o'clock, Cynthia

could barely believe that what she'd so dreaded had come and passed, that her father and lover had met and somehow gotten on and that she was going back not with her father but—with his implied consent—to her lover's house.

It was a lovely night; once they'd left Nice, the air was fresh.

"Did you like him?" asked Cynthia.

"I liked his control. I liked the way he treated me, I liked his courtesy, his manner. I don't know that we'd ever be friends."

"You looked like old pals to me. I felt like a stain on the tablecloth."

"You're a gorgeous stain," said Merriwether. "If we'd looked at you too much, there might have been knifeplay."

"We'll have to introduce him to Priscilla."

Merriwether drove on the wrong side of the road until she said she was sorry.

"*Chaque homme porte la forme entière de L'humaine condition,*" Merriwether copies from a *Livre du Poche* Montaigne. His last day in France, he's walked down to the *épicerie* for rolls (they wouldn't use up a whole loaf of bread), shaken the *patron's* hand (Yes, he and Madame will return some day), and said his goodby to church and state (the reopened post office). The morning is like almost every other here: a sun burst—jots of which star the timbers of the arbor—the morning tune-up of the bugs and birds, the snuffling, prowling, micturating hounds, the raking Mademoiselle, the sleeping Cynthia. This afternoon, London, a week later New York, then he flies north, she south, and in a month his shuttle-life begins again. Somewhere in the schedule sits life. Yesterday, a letter came from Mr. Ryder.

"About the third I've had from him my whole life. I don't know why he hates to write."

"Lawyers are word-cautious. Letters are potential traps."

"No. He just feels he's wasting them on me. He loves all of us to call though. Every week. Maybe not the calls themselves, but the fact of the call."

"You're too sensitive for social life."

She was too sensitive for Mr. Ryder's letter. He suggested she get some psychiatric therapy in the fall.

> Not because their version of the world is foolproof, but because you shouldn't build a long relationship without using everything available to drain the foundation land. No matter how strong your *feeling,* if it's feeling that seeps out of old fears, it will poison any relationship based on it. You and Robert are splendid people. And together you seem to have a special splendor, but so does an apple tree on the edge of a desert. It's set apart and glows, but the soil is in danger of baking out, and when it does, the tree dies. The difficulties in your relationship are the desert. You need extra strength. I say this to help, not to test you. I love you, and I send you and Robert warmest greetings. Though where the warmth comes from I don't know: there's a chill rain in Paris that's like December at home. Still, I'm off to walk in the Tuileries.

Cynthia put the letter down and her arms around herself —she was in the yellow bikini. "Why can't he just trust me? It's not as if you were something inhuman. A horse. A turnip. Should Jackie Kennedy go to a shrink for marrying Onassis?"

"Every rich American's entitled to mental clarity."

The privileges of the *forme entière*. Mademoiselle shuffled up the path, humming the day's dirge—its ground bass the departure of her tenants. Merriwether scribbled the final entry in his French journal: *fathers, gardeners, rectors, therapists, scientist-arsonists, all of us deluded with our "improvements" of each other. Fantasists posing as realists.*

"Quel cauchemar, monsieur," said Mademoiselle. In her nightmare, she was alone in the house all winter, tenantless, penniless, without food. "You could cook the dogs and live for months," thought wicked Merriwether. *"Vous trouverez quelqu'un, mademoiselle. N'inquitiez-vous pas."* He tossed a merri-witticism into his final entry: *My rod can't comfort her.*

PART THREE

9

Dr. Merriwether had written home his probable New York-Boston arrival time but didn't expect anyone to meet him; every Merriwether ran his own circus. He was surprised to spot Albie waiting at the gate. They shook hands, still, after some years of no kissing, an artificial chore for the affectionate father. "How well you look."

"You too." Albie took his father's bag, patted his elbow for reinforced affection and unnecessary guidance. (Merriwether was not unpleased by this filial paternalism.) "The others are buying school clothes." They walked through the esophagal plaster corridors.

"This gives us time together. I only see you about two days a year." Merriwether, looking at Albie with his note-taking care, saw, if not a stranger, another metamorphosis. There was an intense finery about Albie. His color was theatrical, a sun tan that made a leather case for his dark eyes and brought out maple-gold stains in his hair. The hair fell thickly toward his man's neck and over his forehead. A luxuriant, compact human tree. But an athletic one. Albie walked springily, his steps almost hops. It relieved the stockiness which he carried as if it were a public nuisance, sufferable only until it came to use in a football game. But Albie had a look of reserved power, like a president on vacation. Merriwether who enjoyed a chameleon's unobtrusiveness for himself, also enjoyed his son's vividness. It was an assertion of independence, a signal to parents they'd done a good job.

Albie also looked expensive: the vents of the red sport shirt showed not flesh but underwefts of red; thin leather thongs criss-crossed the v-neck. Double-knit slacks, soft leather shoes. He cost himself a fortune. Merriwether studied his son's squareness, his tan, the broad forehead covered with fox-hair, the narrow shoulders, surprising on such a powerful thorax. Hard to think he had held other metamorphoses of this a thousand times, baby, child, boy. (The mystery of development; not just its process but its *why*.) Five years ago, no, six now, sitting in the stands with Sarah and the other children, he'd watched Albie playing football. Stands, cheerleaders, benches, a PA system, and there was his Albie built-up like a blue bunker in helmet, padded sweater, gold kneepants. The students cheering like lunatics, a band, *his* Albie, part of a public occasion, kneeling on a line, shoving at a bigger boy, tackling a runner, the public voice announcing "Tackle by 37, Merriwether." He'd watched with tears—he didn't know why. What was a father's stake in a son? His dissociating head flashed a bloody, literal version of this phrase. Odd. (Optical agnosia, momentary 'fatigue' in the stellate cells?) His feelings were *proper,* love, surprise, admiration, but he was thinking as an experienced tourist: "Don't be taken in."

"What was summer like, Alb?"

"Ten thousand two-by-fours." He'd worked with a master carpenter in Williamstown.

"No fun?"

"I met a girl. We put up her father's garage."

"Are you good friends?"

"We haven't slept together."

Dr. Merriwether didn't like this. He had never talked to his children about this sort of thing. Even when it came up indirectly, theoretically, it overburdened domestic discretion.

"It's not necessary to sleep with every girl friend, is it?" They'd just pulled out of the lot—Albie had paid the parking fee before Merriwether got his hand to his wallet.

"I'm not intimidated by this statistical crapola, if that's what you mean. Though Ann had a terrible time freshman year. Half the girls talking her into bed with the first available cock." Another parental twinge. "She thinks she's ugly and doesn't have much choice. Which made it worse. She's still a virgin. I'm the first boy she's confessed that to. Imagine having to *confess the sin* of not being autographed by a sexual pencil. It's disgusting."

"*D'accord*. But we don't have to live like our neighbors."

"Saints don't."

"I hope Priscilla isn't intimidated. One way or another."

"Don't worry about Priscilla. She's got the nervous system of a computer." Albie and Priscilla were close but competitive. "And better not ask me about her virginity. I have no idea, and don't care."

"I feel as you do, Albie. Still, fathers worry about their children's happiness."

"You used to tell us happiness wasn't the human goal."

"Did I? I meant pleasure."

"What you said always meant more than anything."

"I wish I'd said better things then."

"They were good things. I wish I lived up to more of them."

This was almost too much of a good thing; Merriwether felt the skeptic's fibrillations. Against his will. Keep to the surface. That's what makes social peace. You have a fine son. Hold to that. For years, Merriwether had felt Albie's stony opposition. Necessary springboard, he'd told himself, but it was painful. Albie had gone around with a group of what Merriwether thought of as "displaced boys." Many dropped out of colleges or never went. They drifted over the United States, coming back to Cambridge to see their fellow drifters. They took odd jobs at the post office or Jordan Marsh's. They pursued neither careers nor official learning. Life was an extended summer for them. They took up such things as scientology, Hopi culture, stained glass windows. When they lived at home, they got high, went to movies, and, above all, played games and watched them on television. Football, basketball, hockey. The Merriwether house was a center for them: the comparative merits of the Bruins' slap-shots and the subtleties of first-round draft choices were great topics. Passing themselves off as Harvard students, they used the Harvard gym. None of them played on teams; training was repugnant to them. In the long pauses between jobs or returns to school, they stayed up late and slept late. Sleep was their refuge, sports was a refuge, life itself was a campaign of refuge from the insistence of their fathers and mothers *to do something worthwhile*. Meanwhile their old classmates went through college and readied themselves for professions; each year separated the two groups more. Albie's friends collected the complaints of the other boys ("What else is there to do?"; "I'll suffer a few years, and then it's a hundred thousand a year just spreading butter") and worked them into their ideology of contempt for the ordinary, running world. They were not going to be corporate sucker-ups, legal toads, hating their wives, their lives, their towns, they were going to take things slowly, in the world's rhythm, they weren't going to be ironed by the System. Touch them anywhere —clothes, music, anarchic politics—*laissez-moi* poured out: "You're so hung up with production and rut-greasing, you don't even know the idea of spontaneity."

Albie had felt with them, he sometimes talked as they did, he played poker and basketball with them, but from inside he'd learned their fear and their sadness. Even when he agreed with articles of their contempt, he wasn't part of it. He had a big hunk of conventional ambition. Which Merriwether, without verbal evidence, somehow knew; and was relieved by.

"I'm really glad you came alone, Alb. I'd like to talk to you about something."

Albie was an excellent driver, cool, careful, with excellent reflexes and driving manners. He kept his eyes on the road but his head, the Sarah-ish head, bent politely fatherward.

"It's something difficult for me to talk about."

"Is it about you and Mother?"

"Yes. I don't know quite how to go about it." Ahead, Merriwether saw the insurance skyscrapers. Mineral lint on the old splendor of his child's memory. But it was a grand day, one of those designer's preview shows of autumn that New England stages around Labor Day. The air's polleny white and gold had a holophotal intensity. An urban migraine, yet beautiful, the sky's dense chemical blue.

"Ann showed me a squib about you in *Newsweek*. Did you see it?"

"Yes, I did. Did it upset you?"

"I don't know. It looked harmless enough. I guess we'd guessed you were with a girl." Merriwether grabbed at the manful equality but missed the effort under it. "Is it something serious?"

"I don't know, Albie. What counts, I'm afraid, is that Mother and I have been having trouble for years. I guess you know that."

"I guess so. You didn't let it out, but Pris and I have talked about it. It must be very hard. For both of you."

"People become machine-like about trouble. The other parts of life take over. Though you pay a toll. Usually without knowing."

"Mother knows."

"Yes, she does. And she started remaking her life. I admire her. Terrifically. But she needs more than my admiration. And I need more. More than the laboratory, more than you and Pris and George and Esmé. In some ways, you're the center of my emotional life, but there was a big empty place there too. Now someone's there." Merriwether kept his eyes on the road.

"Are you going to divorce Mom?"

Merriwether breathed heavily. "I don't want to, Alb. I hate the idea of it, hate the fact of it. Nobody ever divorced in our family. The word's like barbed wire to me. I know it's silly; but I don't want to take anything from those I love. The girl doesn't care about marrying. But if Mother saw the thing in *Newsweek*—"

"She saw it. Mrs. Bowen showed it to her."

"That's what friends are for. I'm going to tell her anyway."

"Maybe it'd be better not to. Maybe it'll all pass away."

"Maybe. But we've not been *really* married for so long

now. And now there's this." What a fossil he felt. Yet he *felt,* and feeling was not fossilate. "We separated emotionally years ago. Probably my fault. Without meaning to I dominated her. That was the way of things. *My* schedule, *my* friends, and though it's hard for young people to understand—"

"I understand."

"—*my* money, even. And the house, she didn't get the chance, or didn't make the opportunity, to make the house into whatever she wanted. The house was an expression of the life. For women especially, the house is like part of their body. Like a fiddler's violin. Mother doesn't think too much of me anymore."

"Mother respects you. I know she does."

"I respect her. Very much. For all our differences. And you know how different we are."

"I'm different from Ann, too. And I'm like you, I guess. I dominate her, tell her off. She takes my guff."

Dr. Merriwether was rather annoyed to get shoved off center stage. Albie, however, had had as much of his father's confession as he could take. He did not want to hear any more. He drove over the bridge and swung into Memorial Drive. Sailboats filled the basin, blue, red, ivory. The summer gestures of Boston: the Esplanade, the grass banks, the cyclists, the patches of old meadow, the shells with bare-chested strokers in the Charles; cars, boats, trees, highrises afloat in the particled glitter. They drove by Hinham, Akron, Peabody Terrace, swung past the white-belled redbrick Georgian strut of Dunster, the glassy rise of new Leverett, up Boylston. Thought Merriwether, why hadn't Albie come here? Why hadn't he tried a little harder? Wouldn't he have been more at ease with himself, less distrustful of the world? No, that sort of view was out of date.

Strong, solid, red-gold, wheeling the car, talking of their comparative problems with women—one his mother—Albie was someone who understood the world. Maybe too much. If that was possible.

They were into Ash Street. The old stillness, the emerald heaviness of the trees.

"Thank you, Albie." In the driveway, Merriwether shook his son's hand.

Albie blushed.

Sarah Merriwether's bad time was before supper. The blood sugar was low, the demands on her were high. And then he would come home—unless there were a call at five-thirty saying he would not be home—and after a loud hello into this dust-magnet of a house (in which he'd embalmed her for twenty years without a glimmer of feeling for her feeling about—and without one single attention to—its headlong disintegration), he would strut upstairs to the news, stopping in the sun parlor for a glass of red wine, or the kitchen for some Gorgonzola and cold white wine. The classic lord's life, which for years she had not minded. He had worked, and worked hard, winters, summers, weekends, and she had gone along with his work, tried to follow it, tried reading the offprints in the technical journals, tried hard to read the little book he'd done for Timmy Hellman, tried harder and often succeeded in enjoying the departmental gossip, the international gossip about the great figures, Haldane, Linus, René, Jacques, Francis, Josh; shc could have passed an exam in the biographical history of modern biology. An apparently quiet man, he was really a teacher to his bones, instructing, pointing out, "clarifying"; and it was she he mostly clarified. How many thousands of clarifications had she undergone, and in the presence of every friend they had, let alone the children. She must look like Moron Numero Uno. And she went on cooking suppers and doing the cleaning, and the wash, and the children grew up and out, and his frugality leashed them to his desires for them, so that Albie could not take it any longer, and though still polite, even respectful and affectionate, paid absolutely no attention to the quiet directives, the "eyes to the future," the hints about hard work, about reading this, or staying summers in the lab.

She had one year of course work beyond the M.A., and, for almost twenty years, she'd forgotten that she too was a person of expert training. Then, before she broke down she'd converted a few of those credits and was doing her Master of Arts in Teaching; within a year she'd be qualified to teach French and Spanish in the schools. She would have her place and that meant new life. He had apparently approved, there were speeches about her excellence, her good grades, her fine study habits; he sometimes read her texts, and for a few months, she'd sensed a revival of sympathy, she almost felt she could not only endure life with him, but that if this Merriwether mausoleum were sold and they were installed in a manageable apartment, it might be a good life.

And then what? He took off for Europe, and his disgusting affair. *Advertised* in a national magazine. Madness. All spring, night after night he had gone out, she could hear the door clicking despite his care. He would be off, the secret prowler. While she kept the home fires burning.

And he blamed her. As if her body could be purchased by three daily meals, and this leaky hutch which she alone kept up. (He couldn't hammer a nail.) As if he really cared to make love to her. Frigid? No, no more than any woman with a husband who saw her as an interior broom. By no means frigid. Despite her weight, the wrinkling belly, the veins showing through the flesh he had cursed with contempt and now infidelity—though God knows he'd been unfaithful, at least in thought, with half a dozen other women, some who claimed to be her friends. (She could see him look at Jeanne Schneider.) Despite all she'd gone through, anemia, bad teeth, a D. and C., a lustrum of disinterest, she had her desires; and no outlet for them. Men had flirted with her for years. Despite her chunkiness she was in better shape than most women her age. But she wasn't capable of being unfaithful; and besides it was the husbands of her friends she cared for—who else did she see?—Max, with his devotedness, his decency, his political force—he was the first of their friends to see what the war really was—and he cared for her. When he kissed her in front of Jeanne with the usual flourishes of academic passion which denied passion, she knew there was more there, he cared for her as a person, he respected her. And Dev Calender, severe, ugly ("a gargoyle looking for a cathedral," said Stu Benson, "a stain without a glass"), decent Dev, one of their few non-scientist friends, Professor of American History, husband of her closest friend, Tina. Another profound sympathy which had no physical expression but the goodby kiss. A kind man, a man who did things, who was neither mastered by his work nor his ambition, yet who was first-rate. She'd sat in a course of his on the New England Mind; the names of her own family and childhood worked in mind-boggling debates on governance and church; too much, but somehow something that belonged to her. She'd given him some letters her grandmother had left her, and he had done a piece for the Massachusetts Historical Society Bulletin on a Wainwright who had fought Jonathan

Edwards's heresies in Western Massachusetts. Not that ancestral piety was a piety for her. God knows, part of Bobbie's weakness was that New England tightness and secretiveness which came out in such things as this affair. There'd been little real affection in his family. The Merriwethers had come out of New Bedford, they'd been insurance tabulators, penny-counters, there was no real joy of life in them. Joy was something done out of sight, in the dark. They were really made for sin. Morton, who'd practiced the black mass, had been in their family. Then there was German blood and maybe Indian. Racial nonsense, yes, but somewhere were the fuses for their repressed English rage. Bobbie had a *mestizo*'s uneasiness; if he'd been surer, more patient, maybe his scientific work would have been what he'd hoped it would be; but he could only buckle down when fired up. God knows he had a high enough I.Q. Why didn't he become top rank? There was something deeply unsettled and unhappy there, some profound indolence took hold of him.

It was no longer her business or concern. What concerned her now was destruction. She was being destroyed, this life could not go on, she was not a mat, she was not a maid, she was not going to clear up his messes, she was finished. She didn't need Kate Millett and Germaine Greer for strength. This was simple recognition of humanity. She'd done a paper on the *droits de la femme* of 1793 passed after the Convention had proclaimed the *droits de l'homme*. She was no revolutionary, she did not believe it demeaning to raise children or stay at home. There was dignity there too. But she was not going to be made a human vacuum cleaner. She would not live five years this way, she could not live two years like this. Not for the children. No, she'd lived so much for children, and happily, but she was not going to die for them. She was only forty-two, she had twenty-three years of official working life, and if she lived like her parents, she would live beyond eighty; that was half a life.

"H'loo everybody." The steps, the voice. Please don't come out here.

But here he was, the European traveler. "How are you, Sarah?" Kiss on the cheek. "How good to see you."

"So the traveler returns. I missed the arrival. It wasn't in *Time*."

"Oh," he said. "That was a foolishness. How's everything?"

"Just fine, thank you. Everything ran smoothly. I see by the magazines you had a fine time too."

Did he think he could walk in from the French stews and have her trumpeting "Welcome Home"? What perversity. He had left her chewed bones for years. No more. This was it.

Shaking, then shaking off this frozen greeting, Dr. Merriwether went up to his room, washed up, and went up to the third floor to talk with Priscilla. They had kissed and talked a bit at the door, he'd given her perfume and a handful of postcards, and gone out to the kitchen. She'd gone upstairs and talked with Albie.

When her father knocked and came into her room, she was flushed and scared.

For years, she had loved talking with him. He so clearly wanted her to be something special and believed she was. When she and Albie were younger, he would read over paragraphs of Thoreau or Spinoza to them and ask what they made of them. Then they went over them word for word. Years after, she decided things on the basis of those sessions.

She was in shorts and blouse. She'd put on a little weight this summer, but she was still lovely. Merriwether felt an almost illicit pride in being her father. She had a purer, a simpler beauty than Cynthia, more familiar, more natural, less intense, less dramatic. Despite the dressing table and bathroom crammed with beauty aids, the rigor of Cynthia's concentration on beautification wasn't here. Perhaps because there was no imminent battle. Priscilla had boy friends, but she seemed untroubled by them. Now and then she went with one boy for months, but what they did together was not much concern of Merriwether's. He imagined that when Priscilla was ready for sexual love, she would have it without much fuss. At least, it helped him to think so. He guessed she was still a virgin; that too didn't displease him, though he believed he had no moral scruples on that score. At least, she knew about contraceptives—he had talked to her about their mechanisms and chemistry—she had enough money to buy them and, he supposed, at Oberlin, as at most schools, she could get a prescription when she needed it. Merriwether examined Priscilla medically only when she had something like a sore throat; if anything, he was less medically sensitive to his children than non-medical fathers to theirs.

"I talked with Albie about something on the way in, Pris. I thought I'd say something to you too."

"He told me, Daddy." The stereo was on, a girl's clear voice over a guitar.

"May I turn down the stereo?"

"Are you sure you want to talk with me?"

He saw now that Priscilla was pale and trembly. "I think it's better, dear."

"For you or me, Dad?"

Whew, thought Merriwether. "As long as you know, I want you to hear what you also know, but still hear it from me. You and the other children are the most important things in my life. That's all. If you want to talk with me about"—a hand tossed into the air, a sound that stood for "this thing"—"this or anything else, please do. As for now, maybe you're right. I may be easing myself rather than you." Priscilla picked up a book, which made Merriwether shiver. Was she trying to hurt him, or to show him he'd hurt her? He turned to leave, and she said, "One thing, Dad."

"Yes, Pris?"

"Does Mom know? About, what's her name?"

"She saw the thing in *Newsweek*. Anyway, I was going to speak with her shortly."

"Do you think that's wise?" Priscilla's voice slipped out of its groove. "Or necessary?" She hadn't cried in front of him for years.

Merriwether turned away from her. "I don't know, darling. Mom knows better than anyone how far apart we've been. I think she's thought I've had much more elsewhere than I have. She suspects a good deal now. I think it's time to say something."

"All right, Dad," said Priscilla. He left quickly, to miss what she wanted to do by herself.

Sarah was sitting up in the double bed.

"It's about time one of us slept upstairs," she said. "Preferably you."

She wore a long cotton nightgown. Her face was matted with fury, the cheeks scraped with a kind of whitish scurf—had she been using an astringent soap?—her black eyes were especially, unpleasantly brilliant. "You're a terrible person," she said. "You're a terrible, miserable man."

This was it.

"I'm not much, Sarah," he said quietly, "but I couldn't

go on the way we've been going on. It was just too hard. All these years I've lived on sexual fantasies. You've seen the embarrassing marks. I found something else. I'm too timid for whores. I tried once or twice. It was absurd."

"You've found something. Aren't you fortunate?"

"It became impossible for me, Sarah. I'm not a cactus. I couldn't endure without intimacy. You know I don't just mean intercourse. I may be incapable of having an adolescent affair, but I'm not going to shrivel away. I've been driven to the wall."

"Everybody in Cambridge knows. You couldn't even keep it from reporters. You reek with your cradle-theft. You preen, you sneak, you connive, you perfume yourself. You're pathetic and grotesque. You join the notorious, except you have no excuse. You've been 'driven to the wall'! You drove for the wall, your ego drove you, your emotional failure drove you. You need some soft girl who'll croon to you how marvelous you are. Who is the lucky what's-her-name? I should write her a note of warning."

He got his pajamas from his drawer. "I thought we were civilized enough to be straight with each other."

"Straight? You straight? You don't know what straight is. Get out." Sarah was shouting.

"The children. Lower your voice."

"The children. The children. How about ME?"

He had never in his life wanted to hurt her, but he felt something close to it rising in him. Before it went further, he left, closed the door behind him, and went upstairs to the third floor guest room.

10

From that first night home until he went out to Colorado the next summer, Dr. Merriwether had very few full night sleeps. Until he moved out of the house in spring, he lived on the third floor. He and Sarah seldom talked to each other, except when the children were around. When they did talk, fillets of lightning fury broke from her; and often drew corresponding flashes from him.

"When are you going to see a lawyer?"

"Isn't it best if you go?"

"Isn't it best? Naturally. For you. If it's something unpleasant, *isn't it best* for me to do it."

"Go to hell, Sarah."

They would pass each other on the stairs and exchange grunts. Two adult Americans trained in one of the centers of human fluency, grunting. Twenty years in one bed, and the contrafaction of their lives issued in grunts.

The children had long ago stopped expecting their parents to kiss or even touch each other. Their parents no longer went out together, and there were almost no adult guests. The contrast between the comedies they watched on television while eating supper—for Sarah could not bear to hear his dinner talk—and the polar divisions in the room brought awkward silence when the taped laughter was loudest.

A year ago, George had asked Merriwether, "Do you and Mommy love each other?"

"Love is complicated, George. Mommy and I are very different sorts of people, we disagree about many things. We've been married a long time, and people change. It isn't the same as it was ten years ago, when you were born, or twenty when Albie was. Human beings—"

"I see, I see," said George and left the room.

One night Merriwether came home at nine after supper with Cynthia. Sarah caught him in the living room and said she had put the house up for sale. "I should have done it years ago. I never wanted to live here. This was your house."

"I always thought you thought it one of the nicest in Cambridge."

"It could have been. If you'd helped care for it. If the whole weight of it hadn't been on me. Nobody lives in a house like this without servants unless the husband's willing to lift a finger every now and then."

"I've always wanted you to get people in, Sarah. I wanted the cleaning woman to come more often, wanted you to get carpenters in to do what you wanted."

"You didn't want an inch of it altered. If there'd been outdoor privies here when we'd moved in, they'd be here now."

They hadn't heard George come in. Blue eyes wide, red-faced, forcing a smile, he stood at the door of the living room. "You two better get a divorce if you have to argue."

Merriwether heard himself say, "We're not there quite yet, George."

George ran out. Merriwether followed him to his room. The door was shut. Merriwether knocked. There was no response. He went in anyway. George was crying on the bed.

"I don't think it will happen, George. But you know the way Mom and I have been. It hasn't been all roses for us lately."

George shook his head, wouldn't let his father approach, picked up one of his sports magazines and put it in front of his face. "It's all right," he said.

Merriwether looked at the little room, the walls plastered with the elongated cartoon figures of the *Yellow Submarine* and posters of football players. The tool bench, the games, the books. George. What in this world was worth bringing misery to this precious person?

Sometimes Merriwether could not bear the thought that the children were sinking into the bewitched passivity of television-watchers. In the commercial intervals of the suppertime comedies, he'd try to interest them in something, tell them about "a colleague"—Sarah grimacing, you could never tell if his "colleague" were at the adjacent lab bench or in Tokyo—who had trained a house cat out of killing, stalking and capturing mice. "Could they do it with humans?" asked George. Tiny snort from Sarah.

"Yes, they can. Our colleague Skinner had some famous results. And Delgado in New Haven. But the instincts are tough. They can be revived like that," snapping fingers. "There's a permanent battle readiness. It's like the Pentagon. No matter how serene the world, they're always stirring with belligerence. Making contingency war plans."

"Shh," said Sarah. The program had started again.

It was not undeviating misery. Now and then, to his enormous relief, Sarah talked kindly, reasonably. It was inexplicable. Perhaps she'd just run out of the chemical fuel. Or did she believe it was worth another try? He wasn't sure, but usually these gentle intervals seemed to come after he hadn't gone out for two or three evenings (he'd seen Cynthia before supper or she was busy, studying for an exam).

Cynthia had moved out of the Commonwealth Apartments into a little apartment on Cambridge Street. "What a relief to get away from that morgue."

"I miss those old ladies."

"Visit them. They always said what a nice young man you were. There's no other place in Cambridge you could hear that remark."

Cynthia also found out that Radcliffe was giving her less credit for her Swarthmore work than she'd understood. It meant still another half year for her B.A. She was furious. "My G.E.T.s are as high as you can get. My I.Q. is a million, I have close to an A-minus record, what do they want? And not giving me credit for all that French and Sociology. I'll graduate and be eligible for social security the same year."

"All for love."

"For a piece of sheepskin. Do they call it B.A. because it sounds like baaa? I want an S.A. I'm going to write Gloria Steinem."

"Sheep of Arts?"

"Sister of Arts. Creep."

Cynthia feels the high costs of her love for Merriwether. She spends hours and hours alone in her little apartment.

On permanent tap. He tells her to go out with people in her class. "I know you don't mean that. If they're boys, you're jealous, and the girls are creepy."

"I do mean it. I don't want you to be alone. I won't be jealous. You know how to act."

"They're creeps. Anyway, I can't stand young boys."

They start out for a movie, he sees an old professor coming down the street and holds her back in the doorway. She tears her arm away and goes back upstairs.

"I'm sorry, Cynthia. That's Tryptiades, an old teacher of Sarah's. There's no point in shoving ourselves in people's faces. No point in gratuitous humiliation of Sarah."

"Sarah? What about me? Have I no presence at all? Aren't I a person?"

It is misery. He doesn't introduce her to anyone. Once Tom Fischer comes through town, they go to dinner at Japan Gardens. After perfunctory questions about her "studies," he and Merriwether talk about the cuts in the National Science Foundation grants. She feels like a misplaced comma. It is a human wasteland, a one-person concentration camp. Except the guard is her lover and usually there's nothing but him she wants.

Merriwether agonizes with her. Sometimes he feels his life is little more than holding her together, salving, bandaging, amusing. There are ups-and-downs in his love. Sometimes it's a gaping ache for her, her intelligence, her alertness, her charm, her beauty, her taste, her sadness. They do get along marvelously, joking, confiding, and their time in bed is usually wonderful.

When he comes in the evening, they read, often aloud, or watch television programs. In the fall, they read Colette; male-dominating, male-charming, male-resenting Colette; earthy, Dionysian, inventive; perfect female poetry. Cynthia feels Colette's freedom, she'd give anything to be like her.

"I have erotic dreams with her."

"You have them with everyone. You're healthy. To have them and to talk of them."

"I'm more voluptuary in dreams than in bed. No, I'm not. There's nothing like this. But it's so brief. I could go on forever."

"That's my fault," he said. "You need one of Master's vibrators."

"Lovely." Playfully, truthfully.

He finds a passage in Colette: " 'Women allow us to be their master in the sex act, but never their equal.' "

"Let's see. Sure, she's quoting a man. Baloney. Men don't realize sincerity isn't spontaneous. It's only after women master 'passionate dupery' that we strip to sincerity."

"*Toi? Sincere?* You don't know the difference between 'fall for' and 'tumble to.' "

They lie naked under the patchwork quilt he has brought her from home, "Granny Merriwether's lust-cover," she calls it. Their shoulders touch, their legs, their feet. Colette's book, *The Pure and the Impure*—a Penguin bought at Heathrow and begun on their flight to New York—passes between them. "Where's that part about the woman for whom other women were too salacious. 'They never allow you to stop.' "

" 'Cause we're not genitally fixated. I heard a whore on Dick Cavett say she reserved a place between her shoulders for her real lover."

"A woman?"

"What's that matter, creep?"

" 'O indiscreet little breast, can you now allow us to hover over you, calling up visions of pulpy fruit, rosy dawns, snowy landscapes?' Who's fixated?" He opens the quilt, he loves the look of her, the boy waist, short full breasts, the *centime* navel. Small scream, "I'm frizzing." He rolls over on her, rolls her back over him. Pillows and Colette are pushed to and over the edges of the double bed she has inherited (along with a dresser, chairs, kitchen equipment and assorted junk) with the lease of this students' apartment.

She keeps talking. "I read in *Mademoiselle*—huff—emission rates are *très modestes en France.*"

"Très modiques, tu veux dire."

"French uninterested if—yes—you—oh—can't put book jackets on it."

"What's that mean? Yes?"

"Wait. Yes." Pause. "Fewer pens, more penises. Jiggle. Preserve—hff—the trees. Ohh. Soo sweet. I love you."

Two days a week, Cynthia goes into Boston to the therapist, Dr. Monahan, a severe little woman she doesn't "take to."

"I don't think there'll ever be a transference. Whatever that is."

"You've just started," said Merriwether. "There's tons of crud to come off before you even see the surface of the mine."

"How would you like to have to spill your insides twice a week?"

"Too late for me," he said. "My trouble's calcified. I'd need a million volts just to get started."

"What defenses."

"Granted. Anyway, I can't afford it."

"The main thing is you want me to fit around you. I'm the one who has to change."

"You're still malleable."

"Just less sure of what I am."

It may be. Merriwether feels the evidence of his rigid imperfections: Sarah, Cynthia. Yet he cannot see his way to a Monahan. Even at night, alone and baffled on the third floor, he feels things will somehow work out.

Cynthia fills her days with routines, rituals. Many have to do with making up or maintaining her person: hair-washing, exercising, eyebrow-plucking, self-inspections; many are study habits: bottles of soda water and lemon juice by the bed, notecards and colored pencils on the table, a special pair of red and green woolen socks up to her knees, her Teddy bear, one-eyed, earless Muggsy, set between Japanese-English dictionaries in the bookshelf. Preparation for sleep is also complicated: the alarm clock has to be set and placed, a regiment of pills to swallow—Gelusil, Andrux, multi-vitamins, tons of rose hips (vitamin C) when colds threaten; even the method of taking pills (the pill put halfway down the tongue, a swig of lemon juice, a gargle of soda water, a grimace).

Cynthia is a magnificent preparer. She will not be tested without preparation. This has led to triumphs all her life. She is too smart, too competitive, too fearful for off-the-cuff engagement. Yet most of what she enjoys comes from spontaneity: love, charm, gaiety. For examinations or paperwriting, she goes into St. Anthony-like solitude, the notecards in piles, the marked books assembled; the night hours become the fortress from within which she attacks the enemy, the paper, tomorrow's exam.

For love too, there is preparation. She sees Merriwether's need (sometimes before he has it), she strips, she softens the entryway with lotion, flops mockingly, open-armed-and-legged, and awaits the mechanics of arousal. (Even these times of obligation can lead to pleasing climax.) Sometimes

Merriwether's mind drifts, he labors not over Cynthia but other bodies, sometimes in multiple junction. He has never bought a pornographic book, but Cy McTier has a shelf-full in the laboratory and Merriwether has taken one—the first act of theft since childhood swipes from a candy store—brought it home and stuck it behind medical texts in the study where, now and then, he takes it out for embarrassed peeks. The picture-excitement doesn't last; couplings become as familiar as the wall paper. Cynthia cannot bring herself to think of anyone but Merriwether. In reveries, yes, she imagines others, men, women, relatives, classmates. She has recently—a late discovery—learned to masturbate to climax; she also has multiple orgasms, some lightning-fast and radiant over the surface, some rumbling and revolving deep within her, almost unendurable. Now when she hears or reads of women who have no orgasm, she tells Merriwether she'll write and tell them how—"Cynthia's Guide to Sexual Bliss"—or send him on a mission of mercy. "I don't like that, Cynthia." Actually he does. (Though he and Sarah were happy sexually, their mode was never low comedy. It had been quiet, loving gratitude in the first years, a form of aggression—not unexciting—in the last.)

"Sexual street repairs, that's all. Creep." Kiss on his limp parts.

But he feels the hook even in comedy. Not that sex is sacred ground, but it is not easy for him to think of Cynthia doing her own repairs. "You're not a sexual drug store."

"If someone I like is desperate, why should I hold back?" Comedy, but a corner of truth, and it keeps Merriwether's love up to snuff. Yet she knows how tight he is about it and avoids what will turn his ever-ready worry into fury.

Still, now and then, they quarrel; they grow numb to

each other, or work love's see-saw, one up, the other down. Around exam time, anything can set them off. He can correct a pronunciation—"I believe it's *har'-ass,"*—or make a joke about lawyers—she wants no one but herself to hint of imperfection in her father—"I wasn't thinking of him." "That's what you think." He stupidly responds to her anger, and they inch toward, then slide into rages of exchange. Cynthia's intelligence challenges him, he's always liked argument. A foolishness. For her, argument with him is rejection, hatred. Her face turns stony, her lips curl wolfishly from the gums. If she could see herself, he thinks, vanity would push her from the edge. But she doesn't, she can't. The whole world is rock, she feels herself a rock of ugliness. Fury, hatred, despair. It's prison. She screams, she shrinks into a fetal ball. "I hate you. Don't you see what you do to me?"

If they're in the car, she kicks at his legs, at the windshield, she hits out at him. She can hurt, he flinches, he drives toward a parking place.

He turns furious, he cannot bear her like this, pulling, spoiled, miserable, self-pitying. He thinks. "You can control yourself. Stop this now." (She can't. She won't. He will not feel with her, he is glacial, he cannot wait to leave her.)

He starts the car. They drive and drive, down the Avenue, along the river, back the other side, down again, sometimes into Boston, or toward Concord, toward Lincoln, Cynthia weeping, screaming, until "Take me home. Now." Coldly, he does. "Go away," she says, but she knows no one she can call, she's alone, he is her only human contact. There's nothing she can do. She doesn't even have an errand today—sometimes she can buy groceries or take the MTA to Dr. Monahan—there is nothing but bed.

Half an hour later, from his office, he phones. Her voice

is rigid with hatred. "What dyawant?" His voice is twisted by artifice, false, sweet, a horrible voice, persuading, talking. Words. She hates him, but she can't hang up, she won't. There are long silences. He'll say, "I can't say anything to help you, you hate the words, you hate the silences, you hate me."

Silence.

"I'd better hang up," and hangs up.

He comes to her place. Usually she unlocks the door, then runs to bed; already self-hatred is replacing hatred of him, but what she needs is touch. He kisses her. In the days before he understood her weakness and need, he didn't know this formula. She told him all she wanted was to hear "I love you" said right, with kisses. Against his glacial disinclination, he has learned to do this.

In this second year, their quarrels are fewer; they are more an equilibrium of love. He does not turn as cold, though he still fears and hates the unreason of her bad times and what he calls her "*Glamour Mag* rhetoric." "Don't fit me into your *Glamour Mag* vocabulary. Stop this shit about 'wanting to be a complete person' or 'You are treating me like a walking cunt.' "

She has her own vocabulary of abuse: "You and your mean little burgher life."

"You know nothing of its sweetness."

"Well, go back to it. You're so smart, you know every fucking thing. You're so damn wise, and I'm nothing."

"Get off, will you. Quit telling yourself these *Glamour Mag* fables."

"I hate you. You are the absolute worst."

Silence. He is emptied, or looks it; or tries to look it.

"Quit making me feel sorry for you. I'm sorry, Bobbie,

but I just can't manage to work up any sympathy for you at this moment."

They have each other's number, and, in bad times, dial frequently. She talks about handsome men, about boys with large, hairless chests, though, days later, praises his hairy one, praises his body, and believes it.

The fear of losing her sometimes overcomes him. He will not easily find someone who can laugh right, see right, remember so well, be so precise, so amusing, also so fine-looking, though he already finds many other girls pleasing in his sight now, and a few words exchanged with a graduate assistant in a lab will show him how many fine girls there are in the world. He had hardly noticed them before. (Cynthia feels the same, but has been careful to censor temptation.) "Cynthia, this is where age tells. I'm not interested in this hunting and pecking. I've learned to type. I just want a fine girl, the same one forever. You, in fact." And she feels and says the same thing. "I only want to be yours. I'll never love anyone else."

"Do we seem like ones who lose or ones who win?" (They have read at Dante together in the little gold and blue Temple Classics edition he'd bought himself for an eighteenth birthday present, three years before her birth.) They didn't know. Up and down, these two oddballs of love drag their own channels of habit.

He sometimes comes by for her in the old Dodge, lets her off, watches her run across to the Yard. She wears flopping hats, old furs, blue jeans. Head down, her beautiful face cleared of the tiniest "imperfection," she is off, "not like one who wins." Even when there is little but stone in his heart, this view of her, leopard and blue under the great hat, carrying her satchel of texts toward the seminar room, softens him into love. The melancholia, the fears, the tantrums, the hatred for life, for doing anything but huddling in her room begging for proofs of love—"Please, write me a letter."—these are gone as she runs through the lace of falling leaves, through the iron gates with the Latin mottos, along Boylston's gray wall into the Yard.

"When is a person most himself?" The Dodge starting up, no trouble except when the battery clots with acidic discharge around contacts. (*"Comme nous, comme nous,"* said Cynthia.)

What a burden the self was. Jesus was the great therapist: Bury the self, and begin to live. Didn't he, Merriwether, secular Jesus, do his best work when he was self-oblivious, say helping students, *discipuli*. Not worrying that they were going to steal his discoveries, his data. Stu Benson hardly opened up to his students, only pointed here, hinted there: "They'll steal me blind, look at Chambers." (One of the brilliant rodents, a rumor of greatness for forty years, "passed by" because his students published all his results.) Prodded by Sarah's harshness, Dr. Merriwether sometimes felt he had to cut himself off from his students on the one hand, from competitive or dominating scientific intelligence on the other. But that boy's competitiveness which shone so comically in Jim Watson's book was just that, boys' stuff. It carried a man in the early years, but the great workers were those who kept on for twenty, thirty years, often better working out other men's notions than thinking up their own. Rutherford, Bohr, the Oppenheimer of Los Alamos, the Fermi of Chicago, and now Jim himself on Long Island would count as much for that as for what put the laurels on their heads.

The same with Cynthia. To worry that he was being done in by her, mastered by her ups-and-downs, was terrible, New England narrowness. Fear of the Indians which led to killing them. And what Lasswell called "self-fulfilling prophecy." Think small, become small.

Falling in the old Yard, the leaves arthritic with color. Age's rending beauty. Somehow an easement in his own bafflement.

II

Within the small system of Dr. Merriwether's life, almost everything altered. The ac-and-decelerations were not those anticipated, his life-schedule shifted, his awareness, his feelings for places, objects, people. A year ago, the schedules of love-by-phone-and-letter and love-on-the-wing dominated his life; then, with Cynthia in Cambridge, the day's clock changed, he discovered the world of late night and early morning. Out of Acorn Street at ten or eleven, he returned—comfortable in his home, wanting to breakfast with his children—at three and four A.M. In the cemetery stillness, his was sometimes the only moving car. Sometimes a police car approached, whirl-light dazzling, sinister. He rehearsed menacing interrogations: "Something wrong there, buddy?" "Just taking a little drive, officer. Couldn't sleep." He was careful to wear his sartorial visa to safety, coat, tie, fedora, and the ID which, at worst—he hoped—would label him *professorial kook,* restless after battling theories the long day. Merriwether was one of many people who'd never had anything to do with police, lawyers, courts; he'd never even had a traffic ticket. He'd heard and understood stories of police harassment, but knew less of them than he did the interior of his salted rats. Nor did he realize police views of normality were not his own: few would have failed to place this midnight cruiser.

Leaving Cynthia's place was terrific relief: out of "the love nest," safe, in the cold air, and what joy to be in his old Dodge, driving the streets he'd walked in light or civilized dark for forty years. The glittering civic jewelry was put away, only here and there a student's night light, a lover's. By the high iron paling of the Yard, the spook lights of the Square—the cafeteria open for the night people—into the depths of country stillness, Ash Street, where, turning into Acorn, he doused the car lights and glided into his driveway. He entered his house with a quiet meant to erase the hour, as if he'd come back after a walk. Up the stairs, each creak a lash, till in the cold guest room, safety, peace, a kind he'd never known. The night noise of the house was precious now, the stirrings below, the children's breath which collected in the halls and made the atmosphere of his home. He was there, if something happened, fire, burglary, sickness, he was there to help. His own breath met his children's.

One morning, coming back with his mind full of ache for Cynthia, her loneliness, her sweetness—he often spent the last minutes talking her away from fears into sleep—he found the house door chained. He went around to the back door. Latched. Locked out of his own house. Should he throw a stone at Sarah's window? He remembered the cellar window, went around, got it open and forced himself through like a load of coal.

"Don't ever do that again, Sarah."

She was in the breakfast room, eating Cheerios, reading the *Times,* wearing one of her school outfits, a long-sleeved blouse, a blue smock. There was desolation, ice in her face. The black eyes glittered at him, outraged. "How dare you?"

"This is still my house. I don't lock you out. Don't lock me out."

Even in his fury, he could see the valiance of her overcoming her fear of his severity, but, this morning, it was not enough for words. She slammed the paper, the coffee jounced in her green GOOD MORNING mug and wet James Reston, she threw one imperial stare at his exploitative leisure—he left half an hour after she—and took off to drive the children to school on her way to Boston.

Even strung on the barbs of her hatred, he could pity her. She had no Cynthia. She spoke about her life to the Calenders and the Bowens, but she was not a woman who opened up to people. She would be ashamed to tell the whole story. (Of course, he didn't either.) He pitied her, yet felt she was stronger than he, that she'd been boiled hard by her hatred for him. She remade herself using hatred of him for strength. She needed the hatred. Who knows if that wasn't the source of everything? (The greatest theories showed wider gaps between effects and causes.)

Even now, Dr. Merriwether could see the jetsam of the decent, honorable, good-humored woman he'd married; never, really never complaining, never asking; exceptionally virtuous. He'd loved her decency, her looks, her gifts, the French poems twirling in her mouth. She'd made a literary space for him; never had he enjoyed poems as much as when she read them aloud. Or music. No virtuoso, she played with taste and feeling. Upstairs, marking his journals, something she played below would break in his heart with loveliness. Nights on Duck Isle, when rain thumped the panes and timbers of the house, she played Bach and Schubert. Had he ever been happier than those nights, the children asleep upstairs, when over the rain and fire noises, she'd played something that melted the difference between out-and-inside. Sublimity. What was anything else in life next to it? He owed that to her. Fine little stump of a wife, lifting fingers up and down on the sea-stained keys, round back, square flanks—no hourglass there—rocking, arcing, evoking that sublimity.

As French country families still keep the *pot-au-feu* simmering, always adding, taking out, adding more, so Merriwether somehow or other always kept up his mental life, and took in, day after day, the journals, the books, the reports which came in with the mail. At home or in the office, they came in, the technical journals, the general magazines whose subscriptions he alternated year by year, the *New Yorker* with *Harper's* or the *Atlantic, Time* with *Newsweek, Encounter* with *Commentary*. The world simmered away. In a single Rockefeller Foundation report, he read of reversals of the agricultural crisis by "multiple cropping," of new methods of financing ghetto business, of brave new theaters, of conferences in which doctors, lawyers and philosophers worked out new meanings of death and life—what was prosthesis? what was death? who should decide about "termination," who about genetic engineering (the social peril of the XYY male with the criminal valence in his cells). Intricate human activities that were, Merriwether believed, the proper activity of such privileged humans as himself. Sometimes, he gorged on this authentic news of the world. Along with love for his children, and his own soundings in the cells of his rats, it seemed the essence of proper earth-time; the rest was lotophagous indulgence.

Not living in a vase, the world leaked through a hundred thousand pores; and what he called *essence* was made up of thousands of components. Esmé sat on his lap, asking for a backrub; he rubbed her small shoulders, fingers on the vertebral signal nodes. They talked of an elephant hunt she'd seen on *Wild Kingdom,* the pacifying darts, the little plaques of identification to chart the elephant movements. "What's the point of knowing where they go?" He told her of the inherent fascination in movement and grouping, the animal sense of "home ground," its definition by food, drink, safety, love.

"What would they learn if they charted our movements?"

"Plenty." Hand on his daughter's hair, golden rivers in brown banks. He'd read a piece about a Chicago executive who took a panoramic movie shot of the city from his penthouse window every hour of the day. "I suppose he's registering traffic flow, or light changes, you know, the way Whozit—Manet? Monet—did with Rouen Cathedral. I suppose he could enlarge the pictures and discover a million stories. You know, the messenger gets his package at ten, and instead of delivering it, goes to a bookie. I bet Mayor Daley's police would eat it up."

"Oh, Daddy, that's absurd. Who cares? Who'd want to find out about me going to Miss Bonney's room, the john, phys. ed., waiting for a bus. Who cares?"

"I care."

"You do not. You care about me, not my movements," with a little laugh, thinking of the variety of movements.

He thought it would be the reverse with Sarah: she doesn't care about anything but my movements. Now and then she'd tell him where he and "your friend" had been seen, oh, she knew what he was about, what he was doing.

"You're right, sweetie. It's these overall views of the world that make the most trouble. Cheers for close-ups."

"Here's to us near-sighted ones."

With Sarah, now, there was nothing but short views. The Foundation reports stayed in his lap, his head filled with their quarrels. No matter what he'd done, how could she think as she did. Usurpers hired historians to rewrite history, but why did Sarah have to rewrite their life? "It was rotten from the first year. I saw it before Albie was born."

"Saw what?"

"What a tyrant you were inside that quiet."

"Why did you stay? Why did we keep on having children?"

"There was always hope you'd change."

After such an exchange, he sometimes checked her birth control pills (taken not for him but to stabilize her system); no, it was not her period. Maybe it was a glycogenic dysfunction. Or early menopause. But no, it went deeper. She had a nose for "tyranny." She detested authority. She'd never been able to work under anyone. Almost meek to people's faces, she could rage against women who ran charity drives, or senior teachers in the part-time teaching jobs she'd occasionally had. Merriwether, ranging over Sarah like a research problem, wondered if it might not have been the Wainwright family maid, Vera, a brilliant black woman who dominated the house and pulled the children around by the ears. He'd gotten along wonderfully with her, sitting for hours analyzing the family and its habits. She was the most literate and amusing member of the household, a domestic genius; she cooked like a great chef, she could have had a doctorate in the chemistry of filth. "Given" as a wedding present by Mrs. Wainwright's mother, she'd stayed thirty years, the indispensable tyrant.

"Why didn't you speak up?"

"You wouldn't have listened to me. Everyone knows you despised my intelligence."

"I know I was wickedly stupid sometimes."

"Easy to say now. Admission is so easy. After you brought me to my knees. Or tried to. Because I'm not there now. Nor ever again."

"I wonder if you know how glad that makes me?"

"You think you think that way."

He retreated to wine and the evening news: people on the roads of Africa and Asia carrying kettles, hoes, straw mats. Human tornadoes—acting out some subtle policy of devilment—had smashed them. But their misery deflected his.

That double vision of the mind which *knows* but cannot feel or act its knowledge, which squats behind its own bones and measures everything from within those slats, which, at five o'clock, takes the long view of its own troubles like a surveying god, and at five-fifteen shrivels into a nut of egotism; human duplicity with its sparkling outer and inner crepuscular brains, cortical light dazzling over opaque old fear.

One evening, a week before Thanksgiving, Sarah went up to Merriwether as he poured his evening glass of wine. (He no longer asked her if she wanted any; she made herself a nightly martini.) "Bob." It was a not unkindly voice. "My lawyer is going to call you in the next half hour or so."

"What?"

"I finally went. You wouldn't go. Everything is ready. He'll tell you everything. He's a very good man. You'll get along with him. Tina told me about him. He's helped someone she knew."

Merriwether went up to his old room and sat on the bed by the phone. When the phone rang, he did not pick it up. As it began its third ring, Sarah called up, "You getting it, Bob?"

"Yes." He picked up the black handle, steadying everything by gripping hard.

"Dr. Merriwether." A cold voice, a hint of roll in the "r's." "This is Donald Sullivan. Mrs. Merriwether has spoken to you, I think." Sitting on the bed he'd slept in so many years, not daring to put his feet up as he used to, Merriwether felt the plastic handle contain his future, his children's future. Why had she? The Moby Dick wallpaper, the mushroom-white gauze curtains veiling the Japanese urns across the street: this room was going, the whole bit was going. "I'd like to see you in my office tomorrow morning." The handle spoke an address.

"You couldn't make it out to Cambridge, Mr. Sullivan?" There were still things retainable, his lab work, his lecture preparation, his lunch.

"That's impossible. Is ten o'clock all right?"

"All right, Mr. Sullivan, I'll be there."

The rest of that evening Sarah spoke to him almost with the tenderness of years ago. Under the stone of their last years were thousands of moments which were not stony. So much of their lives were each other's; for months, years, she'd thought only of the stone parts; now some of the others bloodied the stone. Not just children, birthdays, vacations, but looks, jokes, meals, a rewound movie blur (rated G, passion was censored). His promotions, his discoveries, his papers, his "recognition." Not even the pronominal bulk —*his, his, his*—was bitterness tonight. She felt as if she were looking in the rearview mirror at an accident; their own life cracked up there.

On Merriwether's trip to Boston the next morning, everything was dense with significance. There was a power failure on the MTA, he had to get off at Boylston, a stop early. Hating to be late—and hating what made him hate it—he rushed through crowds, huffing, charging. He passed DeVane's where he'd had his grandmother's diamond set for Sarah's engagement ring. Sullivan's building turned out to be the same one Sarah's Uncle Barton worked in. (Barton, an auto-didact, had had Merriwether down to the building for lunch to pump psychological lore out of him for a client's survey on soda pop.)

Sullivan was a squarish, elderly, odd-looking man. "Maybe it's a requirement for tenancy here," thought Merriwether. (Barton looked like a duck.) His charcoal suit covered a complicated body, huge arms, a smallish box of a torso, long legs that stretched under his desk to Merriwether's side. Sullivan's accent was a two-tiered cake of Irish lilt and Harvard vowels. Very pleasing. He spoke softly, firmly, but the eye bulge had metal in it, the face sharpened, as if the business at hand turned it into a revolver. Innocuous and open at first sight, the face in action seemed the skeptic registry of a million connivances.

Merriwether sat in a low chair by the window. They were on the twelfth floor. Merriwether had the sense that above and below him, counterparts of Sullivan and himself spelled out similar options of termination.

That was their subject. First, coldly, then, seeing he had a legal patsy, intimately. Sullivan said, "Sarah has had a terrible time. Her physical condition is poor. She's got blood sugar, her blood pressure is low, she's anemic. This relationship has worn her down." The *ow* in "down" rang mournfully. "This woman friend of yours has caused Sarah a lot of anguish. In a community like Harvard, it is especially humiliating." The *a* of "Harvard" was pure Boston, the *a* in "humiliating" was drawn out of Ireland. Merriwether was taken by the speech, he was taken by the view out the window, the roofs of Tremont, the pyrite fire of slate. He said, "I know, it's been terrible for her." A brilliant day; from here it could be summer.

"So there are these options, Doctor." Sullivan leaned forward, thin hands flat on the leather rims of the Florentine blotter. Merriwether swung fully around to him. The revolver pointed, then discharged, gently. "There can be legal separation, or divorce. If the divorce is contested, there is no doubt in the world that Mrs. Merriwether has evidence to secure everything she needs. If the divorce is amicable, then you and she, being two reasonable human beings, will be able to work out arrangements. I have the papers filled out now. In fact, I'm going to walk over to the courthouse as soon as we finish and file. If you come along, it'll save you the serving officer's fee. There is, of course, the possibility of reconciliation—and I'm always for that—but, as far as I can gather from Sarah, this is not a real possibility."

So there it was. Twenty-two years. More since Timmy had introduced them in the get-together at Eliot House, since they'd gone on the ski trip to Stowe. Years and years, and now it was on the operating table, and here was Sullivan leaning over with the scalpel.

"In my view, separation is a halfway measure. It only means that neither of you can date"—the incredible teenager's word—"and nothing is really fixed. There is no halfway possibility here. You can only go toward reconciliation or toward divorce. If there's to be reconciliation, it should come now. And I see—judging only from Sarah's appearance, her health, her feelings—that this is not likely."

"I suppose not," said Merriwether. And he had to bring out a handkerchief, blow his nose, shake his head. Why not? Let the man see the job he did on people.

"Sarah says you've always been an excellent father. She has no reason at all not to let you have every reasonable visitation privilege. Indeed, I am sure the court will leave that to your discretion. Here is the statement of charges." A packet of typed onionskin came over the desk, Merriwether glanced at it: *cruelty, neglect, adultery, all money in savings account, stocks, bonds, the house, the car.* "My God," he said. "What is this? You don't expect me to sign this? Adultery is not to come into it. No one else is to be brought into it."

"Don't worry about that, Doctor." The thin hands pushed air his way. "It doesn't mean a blessed thing. We state the worst as something we could—but won't, I hope —draw on. You and Sarah can draw up a list of stipulations which you both sign. And that will be that. The grounds will be mental cruelty. This is just for legal purposes. It means nothing. Sarah wants only child support. She is planning to work. But the court maintains permanent jurisdiction in divorce cases. If a situation changes, say you were to inherit a lot of money—"

"My parents are dead."

"Sarah could feel that she wants the children to have some of it—of course you would want them to anyway— and we could come back into court."

So it was no longer just Sarah and he, no longer even Sullivan and Sarah and he, it was a large machine made after thousands of years of mismatched coupling, contrived as the guillotine had been, for merciful conclusions. For a minute or two they were its case.

"I don't have a lawyer, Mr. Sullivan."

"If you are planning to contest this procedure, then you better get yourself one." The lawyer sat back, the revolver uncocked, the face wrinkled in general benignity. "Otherwise, though I can't act for both of you, I can advise you. You won't need a lawyer. I'll file for you. You have to pay my bill anyway. I better tell you the bill will be a great deal steeper if the divorce is contested. Even now, the court would award me—on the basis of what Mrs. Merriwether has told me of your assets—fifteen hundred, maybe two thousand dollars."

"My God," said Merriwether. "I understand you can get a divorce for under fifty dollars."

"A kind of divorce. No guarantees. No counsel. That might be all right when there are no assets, or when there is perfect agreement. But Mrs. Merriwether has already consulted me. So there's already a fee. But I am not going to charge you what the court would award me. I am going to charge you half-fee. If there is a stipulated settlement, the fee will be eight hundred dollars. You couldn't match that anywhere in Boston."

He'd come in here, breathless, running to be on time, sweating, taking off his rubbers—it had looked like rain—this odd-limbed box of a man had been waiting for him by his secretary's desk, perhaps ready to file charges if he'd been a minute late, and from that human moment, he was now buying—what?—the end of his domestic life, it was called "freedom." Sarah was buying it. It was a product of the machine. A bill of divorcement, *a vinculo matrimonii*. Had the American machine been made in Rome? Sumeria?

Each state had its own. His sausage was made by Massachusetts. Divorce—*di-vertere,* to turn from. *A litus et thoro.* From bed and board.

He put on his rubbers, Sullivan helped him on with his raincoat, and they walked through crowds to the Civic Plaza, and took an escalator up to an enormous room, where scores of people behind windows took and distributed papers. Sullivan joked with a black woman who stamped a paper Sullivan told Merriwether to sign. "It's nothing. Read it. It just acknowledges that you were served. You save ten dollars by not needing an officer of the court." Merriwether made out a check for fourteen dollars, accepted the papers, and saw that he and Mrs. Sarah Wainwright Merriwether, Plaintiff, had a long file number. While Sullivan read other papers, he noticed that the papers he'd signed were full of mistakes: the wrong date for their marriage was given, the wrong name of a Savings Bank, his own middle name misspelled ("Stil" instead of "Still"). Good. Grounds for appeal. But what kind of appeal? He and Sullivan went down the escalator, and at the bottom shook hands warmly. "I'll be in touch with Sarah as soon as I have a court date. The whole thing'll be over by March. God be with you, Doctor. Don't worry. Everything is going to work out."

The sun had come out, the sky was a profound, a thoughtful blue. He and Sullivan parted and the lawyer went off in the direction of his office; Merriwether followed his long, scissoring forks and apish arms till he was lost in the crowd.

Amidst the people fanning out of buildings toward restaurants, Merriwether walked vaguely toward the MTA. Ahead was Old South Church. For some reason he walked over and stood by it, taking in the sun, the chill, the gaseous air, the sense of the crowd. Shards of sensation stuck on odd thoughts. Had there been a Merriwether at the meeting Adams had called in the church? A Still? A Wainwright? Abigail Adams wrote her husband about a Merriwether who overcharged for coffee, and was besieged by infuriated women. John Hancock was in Sarah's mother's family. He'd wanted to be president. His insurance building strutted in the skyline the way his signature did on the Declaration. Mental dazzle: Sullivan's overcoated back, Esmé's, Back Bay, Marblehead, boats, sails, the longest journey. His marriage was over.

On the train back to Cambridge, he fixed on the almost-empty car, the iron rattle, the plank seats, the white poles, the underground hole; this train headed him toward displacement. Nothing was going to be familiar. What to do? He had to talk with someone. Not Cynthia. Sarah. (The old Sarah.) Almost funny. A friend. Maybe a lawyer, but he knew no lawyer well. Maybe Stuart Benson. They were close friends again after a bad time a few years ago. And Stuart had been through divorce. He was probably at home; he worked there mornings.

At the Square, he ran up the escalator and called Stuart from the phone outside the Cambridge Trust. "Of course, Bobbie. Come right on over. If I'm in the bath, I'll leave the door unlatched."

"I'm very grateful, Stuart."

"I'm grateful you think of me, Bobbie."

They'd had a serious, almost adolescent estrangement. Benson was not an easy man. A brilliant one, an immensely learned one, and not only in science. His library was one of the great private collections of Cambridge. Some professors of English Literature, even specialists in the nineteenth century, knew less about the Victorians than Benson.

Benson was smallish, red-faced, green-eyed. He worked enormously, published several papers every year. A neurophysiologist, he'd lately done pioneer work in prostaglandins. He also kept up with more work in the biological sciences than anyone on the faculty. Unlike Tom Fischer, though, he had little sympathy for other men's work. He was vituperative to both pupils and friends; he had very few of either.

His two best friends were Merriwether and Fischer. Fischer's genius, accomplishments, industry, even his fine appearance, filled Benson's talk. He considered himself unattractive and was enormously sensitive to good looks, especially the good looks of young men, but he'd neither had nor seriously thought of a homosexual experience. He had married once, a graduate student, but it hadn't lasted. He had dominated her, even with his tenderness, which was proprietary. A non-stop talker, his tongue darkened her thought and life. One day, she ran off with another graduate student.

Benson was terrified of criticism; his life was ingeniously, though unconsciously, fashioned to escape it. As a professor in a great university, he was subject to no one but his scientific peers; the few peers he had, he'd recruited to his side by offers to lecture at Harvard and the company of his wonderful friends, Fischer and Merriwether.

It was a dinner for a visitor from Berkeley and his wife that led to Merriwether's year-long estrangement from him. The visitor was a friend of Merriwether's named Roger Trimpi. He and Merriwether had been graduate students together, and they had seen each other at occasional scientific meetings. They got along very well. Trimpi was a mild, good-humored man. A few years ago, he and his wife had divorced and he was now married to a woman twelve to fifteen years his junior. Mrs. Trimpi was along.

They went out to dinner in Boston. (Sarah was not cooking that month for his friends.)

The evening turned into a Benson monologue on the decline of every institution and virtue, the rise of ignorance, bad manners and minority violence. When Merriwether interposed that the Victorian era had had its share of social malaise, Benson extended the decline to Merriwether's own recent work. "Bobbie here's been making an idiot of himself trying to work out dipsologic models for cytologic pathogenesis."

Merriwether said, "I don't think you've kept up with what I'm doing, Stu. I'll show you in detail some time."

"I'm not interested in your showing me, Bobbie. I know every man has to eat a peck of dirt in his time, but I've eaten mine."

Merriwether turned away to an embarrassed Mrs. Trimpi and asked how her children and her husband's got on together. The meal passed without his talking again to Benson.

When they met on campus a week or so later, Merriwether nodded coldly and passed by. The next day he received a letter in Faculty Mail.

> Dear Bobbie-
>
> Why were you so cold to me yesterday? Have I done something awful?
>
> As ever,
> Stu

Merriwether wrote back that despite his affection for Benson, he could no longer tolerate his rudeness.

> We began, I suppose, on the wrong footing. I the junior expecting correction, you the senior, expecting to give it. But twenty years have passed. We are, if not equals, at least equal as friends, and we must put ourselves on a new footing. I very much hope we can.

Benson didn't answer this letter, the summer intervened, and the habit of association was broken. In the fall, Tom Fischer had tried to act as peacemaker, but left town without bringing them together, and the adolescent pride which American life fosters kept them apart. They worked in different laboratories, there was seldom occasion to see each other. Now and then, they sat across from each other at the semester meetings of the biological sciences faculty; they nodded, even smiled at each other, and then, one day, about a year after they'd quarreled, Merriwether went up, shook Benson's hand and asked him to have dinner with him. A new version of the old cordiality began: Benson was careful of Merriwether's feelings, Merriwether tender of Benson's.

Now he sat in Benson's small living room, comforted, rather than subdued by what Tom Fischer had once called "Stuart's mortuary of authority." "If there were a literal book worm," Fischer said, "Stuart's walls would be its gut." In the corridors, in every room but the kitchen where he ate, Benson's books were the walls. Merriwether sat under a massif of diaries, letters and memoirs of lesser Victorians. His *pot-au-feu* took in the names even as he talked of the divorce (Henry Rawlinson, Moncton-Milnes, Tom Taylor, Hartley Coleridge, Thomas Arnold, A. J. Munby). He showed Benson the onionskin indictment.

Benson's green eyes covered the pages in seconds. "Who

wrote this? Jonas Chuzzlewit? It's a monstrosity. Call your lawyer."

"I don't have one."

"Get one today. Go to your bank, now. Take out half your money and put it under another name. They've got you by the balls. This is a terrible document. Sarah's gone and got herself one of these mick sharpies. He's going to eat you alive."

"The man's not like that, Stu. He seemed very decent."

"You're a baby. You don't know. They're all in cahoots, judges, lawyers. They work it all out. You're a minnow. They'll snuff you up without knowing they've had a snack. *Decent. Indecent.* They're in business. They *appear* to be whatever is going to get results. *Be?* They don't exist as beings. They're functions of their bellies. This mick saw you there, mouth open, he could have drawn out your appendix with a lump of sugar. But they want your heart. Sarah's going to eat you. Take my advice. I've been through this. Get yourself the toughest lawyer in Boston. Call Wally Archer at the law school. Ask him to get you an iron man. This isn't the lab, Bobbie. This isn't your rats bleeding. This is you. These lawyers are going to strip your corpse."

Merriwether felt himself pounding. Sure Benson had taken off on his own rhetoric, his dough-ball face was streaked with excitement. All that Dickens had technicolored life for him, his hands balled in the air, gaveling, hammering. But maybe it was true. Maybe the lawyers gorged on Dickens too. They went for broke. Sarah was no Goneril, but he had seen the tiger in her. She'd given Sullivan the stuff of the document; it was not the "nothing" Sullivan said it was.

"It's hard to believe, Stu."

"It's hard to believe a nanogram of PG can leash a cell, but you know it's so. *Hard to believe.*" Out of his rolled-up blue workshirt, freckled forearms hoisted in a mime of incredulity; the right one swept up a wall of books. "What's all this about? The documentation of what's far more astonishing than that an injured wife wants to pound her husband into glue. What runs the world, Bobbie? Are you an eighteenth century biologist? It's the 1970's. Neuro-enzymatic labyrinths. Labyrinths? Helical tsunami. You and I have spent half our lives omitting everything but what we want to pinpoint in a tube. Professional life tries for the same simplicity: Three square meals, a comfortable chair, chamber music, journals, wife on call, now and then an aspirin for trouble out there. We know it's not even that simple in a macro-molecule. The damn proteins don't behave; it's a bleeding miracle when we find something to spank them with. Bobbie, you and Sarah are in the snake pit. Don't pretend it's Disneyland."

Merriwether mumbled some sort of assent and walked home. Dizzied, heart bumping arhythmically, sweat in eye sockets, breath irregular; vasoconstriction, arterial distension, glycogenic riot. In his head, visions of a stripped life, no children, no house, no money. Stripped. He walked through the Commons. The sun lay a gold blade on the cannon.

Sarah was in the kitchen. "I saw Sullivan," he said.

"Well?" she said, quietly. She'd heated a can of soup, and got a second bowl, poured, and set it at his place.

"He gave me this terrible thing here," he handed the sheets to Sarah, "then said it didn't mean anything, that you and I could work everything out together, I wouldn't even need a lawyer."

"That's what he told me."

They sat at the table. "I went to Stu Benson. He said Sullivan was a crook, that you wanted to eat me alive, that I'd better get a lawyer."

"Do you believe that?"

"No. I liked Sullivan. He's probably capable of shystering with the best of them, but I guess this is an easy eight hundred bucks for him. He feels we can do it together."

"Eight hundred?"

"Eight-fifty."

"I've paid him three already."

"Anyway, I don't think I'll get a lawyer."

"I don't think you need one, Bobbie."

At this use of his name in a tone that was nothing but sympathetic, Merriwether put his head on the table and cried. It had been decades since he'd done that. "Just shock," he said, still crying. He went into the sun parlor and tried to get hold of himself. Sarah came in. "It'll be all right," she said. "It's the best thing."

After a bit, he said, "What a waste." He touched her cheek with the edge of his palm. Plump, white, scraped cheek. He went upstairs. When he came down, he came down with pencil and paper.

They sat in the breakfast nook. He loved this room, the shelf of blue Meissen, the silver-point engravings of Assisi and Pisa. It was a bay, polka-dot curtains were on the circle of windows. A room of cheer to smooth out night's wrinkles. The chairs were battered, scratched, not of a set, but they belonged together. He sat in his usual one, a low, unupholstered armchair; Sarah's was higher—as Sullivan's had been.

"We'll go over everything," he said. "We'll do it right."

"All right," said Sarah. She was calm, her eyes did not

glitter, her hands, slender, veined, those of a thinner woman than she was, a pianist's hands, were folded on the table. He wrote, "The House." The asking price, seventy thousand dollars, seemed high, but there'd be less problem disposing of it than a thousand dollar bill in Harvard Square. "We can split the money," said Sarah. "I'm sure each of us can find an adequate apartment with what we'd get."

To his surprise, Merriwether found himself once again in tears. "I'm sorry. Pay no attention. It's strain. The house," he had to stop. "You and the kids." It wasn't necessary to go on, but he let himself go on, even relished her surprise at seeing this husband who had such little feeling for her show what he was showing. Again he left the room, partly to control himself, partly to let her see he was ashamed of breaking down, partly to have a little more of the relief of tears.

When he came back, they went over each child's needs: tuition, maintenance, summers. Sarah, in a dignified and decent way, moved toward a constricted, economical life, one that made her secure but which Merriwether, even in admiration of her decency, also feared as a constriction of the children's life. Why should they have their skies cut in half? He upped her figures.

In this spirit, each giving the other more than either would have wanted in a contest of bitterness, they avoided the war Benson's strategy would have started.

12

The Merriwethers had their usual Thanksgiving Dinner with the Calenders, Dev, Tina and their daughter Tibbs (babble-version of Clementina). The Calenders knew the Merriwether situation, only George and Esmé knew nothing. (Sarah had agreed they should have as much "solid family time" as possible. "We'll tell them after the holidays." Merriwether hoped to wait till the end of the school year.) At Thanksgiving, it still seemed remote; they didn't even have a court date.

They'd had Thanksgiving together in this house for over twenty years, the last eight or ten with the Calenders. The dinner was one of their ceremonial measures. Each year the children announced what had been best and worst in the year, and Merriwether worked up some Massachusetts story from Bradford's history, or the Mathers'; though he told it with deprecating irony, that was but easement for the pleasure in continuity he felt he could not, in this day and time, exhibit directly. The meal itself was the American marvel, the stuffed, trussed bird, the squash and beans and marshmallowed yams, the fresh cranberries, tureens of giblet gravy, platters of celery and black olives, the mince, pumpkin and pecan pies, the white wine and hot cider, all spread under the brass chandelier a nineteenth-century slave trader had brought back from Brussels. The dining room walls were oak-paneled; between the frames hung portraits of Merriwethers, Stills and Tiptons, old insurance men and merchants, preachers and professors. Thanksgiving in this room seemed the great American payoff to the children of New Jerusalem.

This year, neither Albie nor Priscilla came home. Priscilla was cooking a turkey for foreign students at Oberlin. Albie wrote that he had a Thanksgiving-to-end-of-term job writing papers for delinquent students. Merriwether telephoned him in Williamstown and asked him not to take the job. "I'd rather have you lying about detergents on television." Albie bristled, said everyone had the right to do his own work. "I'm just helping some kid who's got to write six papers in two weeks. I'm pretty good at it, and I learn something; if he reads it, so will he."

"I don't feel much like an example these days, Albie, and I don't want to impose my standards on you, but I feel this is so direct a repudiation of my life, I have to say something."

Albie's voice rose on the phone, became boyish. "It has nothing to do with you, Dad. I just want to earn a little money."

"I'll send you more money. I didn't know you needed it."

"I didn't want to bother you. I still think you're being hypersensitive. These guys have helped lots of people over rough spots."

"I don't want to argue, Albie. The heart of education is

ripped by this kind of thing. I know you'll agree with me when you think it over."

Up in his study, writing out a check for Albie, it struck Merriwether that Albie's choice could have something to do with the invisible poison of the household. Underneath the civility, Albie had suffered the decay; and now he was attacking another part of the moral structure. That Merriwether was enforcing his own moral authority with fifty dollars did not strike him as a moral matter. It simply removed a burr from this celebration.

Tibbs Calender brought a boy friend from Cornell. Tibbs was an ugly duckling who'd found her style two or three years ago. The Merriwethers had watched her grow from big-thighed awkwardness into grace. Physically a queen, tall, big-featured, black-haired, her nature was gentle and curious. Her presence was a kind of holiday for all the Merriwethers. Her boy friend was a thirty-year-old graduate student in physics. She'd met him when they made love for a pornographer's camera. The film, *A Little Bit of a Lot,* hadn't been released, but the pornographer was going to film another with them. "You're a great sexual team." Theo, the physicist, was wiry, big-eyed, he had a dark, sharp-angled Greek face. He'd answered the pornographer's ad in the Cornell newspaper, and he'd stayed for the sex, not the money. Now he and Tibbs lived together in Ithaca. They were both good musicians. Tibbs sang, Theo played the flute.

After dinner they went into the sun parlor for music. Sarah played the piano, Esmé turned pages for her, Tina for Theo. George lay on the floor by his father's chair: Merriwether could feel the body warmth against his leg. The music—Rameau, Purcell, Bach—was beautiful. Merriwether let himself sink in it, and in the old beauty of the parlor with its wallpaper of gold spindles and the little what-not tables covered with silver holders and dishes. Beyond dark drapes, dusk fell in the street. He watched George, chin in his hands, floating, large-eyed, in some George world, and Esmé, serious and unobtrusive, eyes on the music, reaching to turn, her arm hair—which she hated and habitually depilated—trapping fuzzy pockets of light. It was lovely, the delicate arm in the velvety funnel of laced sleeve. On the tip of one sort of beauty, ready to fall through adolescence into another. Soon Esmé would be telling her friends, one by one, that she was moving and that her parents were divorced, she'd be trying to figure out what it was that hadn't worked, comparing it with models in magazines and TV shows. Merriwether sank into a swamp of foreboding, half-sybaritically, half in the superstition of people who believe life's so strange that by imagining its worst turns, you force it into better ones. The melancholy beauty of farewell came through the music. Tibbs sang *Bist du bei mir* in her quavering, heartrending contralto. Vibrato was a feedback system to keep on pitch. Was all trembling, all melancholy so useful? *Geh ich mit Freude*. Beautiful.

Later, helping Sarah scrape dishes and stack them in the dishwasher, he thanked her for the dinner. "It was a lovely day."

"It was. A lovely family day. I know how you must feel. It doesn't really alter things."

He went upstairs and called Cynthia. "How are you, dear?"

"Fine. I celebrated with a double portion of cole slaw. How was your dinner?"

"It was very nice for the children. What are you doing?"

"Reading Saikaku. A contemporary of Madame de Lafayette."

"General Lafayette's wife?"

"No, creep. The first French novelist. I'll read you the opening sentence from this one, ok?"

"Sure."

"I'm not sure of anything." This was her first book in Japanese.

" 'A beautiful woman, say the old men, is an axe that cuts down a man's very life.' "

"Well, well."

"Am I so dangerous?"

"You're a beauty. I'll tell you a line Priscilla used to recite. I forget who wrote it. 'A wandering beauty is a blade out of its scabbard. You know that, gentlemen of four score. (May you know it yet ten more.)' You like it?"

"Do you love me?"

"Yes, I love you."

"Then I'll go to sleep. I'm tired of Saikaku. And Thanksgiving. And cole slaw."

In these days, Merriwether, like some drunken Aeolus of feeling, could not control his emotional comings-and-goings. One minute, he felt he could give up Cynthia, could even go back to Sarah—that possibility had fallen out of her in one of their sessions, though he felt she made it only to assure herself she'd *tried everything*. Yet he could never be more than an uncomfortable brother to her, could never go to bed with her. When he hinted this, the black eyes turned in, the nostrils took in extra air. "I'm afraid I need more than that." What did he expect?

"Of course you do. We both do." But the neural hyperbole of these days churned out a meaner version: The hangman thinks he's a surgeon; he wants his victim's gratitude, his adoration. He could not live with her except in a "live-and-let-live" house, this house. And it was already too late for that. Leslie Devereaux, a new Radcliffe Dean, a topologist, had made an offer for the house, too low in Merriwether's opinion, but Sarah, impatient, even fearful, had accepted it. The only good thing about it was that Devereaux was black and a woman. That was a perfect redemption: the house had been partly built on slave-trade money. Historical irony was the classic consolation of defeat. All those Harvard war-makers of the sixties should be bathing in it. (He remembered the general relief when Mac Bundy was passed over for the Harvard Presidency, though he'd made a damn good Dean. *Sic transit gloria Bundy* went the joke, supposedly Finley's, the Thucydides translator. *There* was historic irony.) That brilliant, brittle, problem-making, problem-not-quite-solving Bundy-Harvard touched Merriwether here and there, but it wasn't his. That was English Harvard, the Peabody-Groton world ("to rule is to serve" transposed into "to serve is to rule"), the top grades, the top marriages into the old mill and banking families, the *rouge et noir* routes (law and social science these days) into Running Things. Into the ground. The intellectual motors rolled too fast, the world hardly had drugs enough to calm those fellows. He knew—slightly—and liked—slightly more—a few of them, Chip Boyd, Mac Frothingham. They made him feel dowdy, slow, even while catering to him, drawing him out. Great Drawers-Out. Perfect Foundation men. He was glad the house wasn't going to them.

Sometimes, at night, behind closed doors on the third floor, rehearsing future solitude, he'd wake, loneliness so thick in him, he found himself calling out, "No, no, no, no, no." It was going to be this way. What would happen if he had a heart attack and couldn't reach the phone? This must be why people went into nursing homes. And then, George and Esmé, they'd wake up and know he was not there, Dad, the Fire-Douser, Burglar-Chaser, Blood-Stancher, Hugger-and-Soother. His first memory of his own mother was waking with some dream terror, desperate for her, calling out, and she'd come in from guests, he remembered her dress under his cheek, scalloped flops of silk, her softness, oh Mama. He'd been spared loneliness. Sometimes Tom Fischer called, voice hoarse from disuse, embarrassed at his helplessness; it was that. Now he understood the eagerness of the bachelors and widowers at the Faculty Club for the company lunch.

He had Cynthia, yet, as much as he loved her, delightful as it was with her (playing gin rummy, reading aloud, watching the midnight television interviews with transvestite lawyers and lady blacksmiths, watching her draw off her shirt, the soft half-moons of her body, making love), they could not live in the same apartment; their systems were contrary. They liked different music, different breakfasts, were different about heat—she turned radiators on, he off—about mealtimes (he was leisurely, she ate where she cooked, standing up at the stove). And she was still so fragile, she suffered so from the slightest slight or suspicion of it, the classic girl of high intelligence rocked by, well, yes, males like himself—and worse. He noticed the studies of Radcliffe girls of high intelligence doing worse than girls at Bryn Mawr or even Vassar. The fear of success. Broken girls. Who—half the time—broke those who broke them. "I'll be rattled on that emotional roller coaster. I'll be cackling in her road show." Yet, without Cynthia, he would enter the lists of Cambridge hostesses, be hung on the local Availability Hooks. Impossible. He couldn't endure the deferrals, the expense, the stupidity of courtship. No matter how minimal the sexual signal system, it would be consumptive, humiliating. He came back to Sarah, the pre-furious Sarah, decent, straight, generous; to the idea of growing old beside her, every event dipped into memory. The deepest feelings grew down where the nerve foliage reddened, the dendrite thicket. No new relationship could ever have that. It would take twenty years with Cynthia, though she was a girl of exceptional emotional depth. Even now, twenty-two, her memories were the richest part of her life. Her dream life, her fantasy life, was the past; the scenes were Carolina beaches, her grandmother's room (helping braid her hair, smelling her sachet); her memories of school triumphs were more powerful than her ambitions. Was it because love for him deflected them? Or because she had that poetic temperament which early accumulates so much that most of life is just finding a way to spend it. Or was this the wish of a benevolent tyrant? Maybe she'd only become what she could if he'd leave her. If she left him. She said that would kill her. It wouldn't. Yet people hardened around their wounds; abandoned and abandoning women turned into the *belles dames sans merci*, their children into Lola-Lolas.

A silvery comma of moon hooked in the capillary thorns of the acacia. His tree. His view. His street, his house. He'd wanted to die here. The children's children to die here. This time next year, a young Devereaux would be looking at this tree-hooked moon.

Where would he be? Sarah had already looked at places. He'd been to one apartment she'd picked out. A condominium on Temple Street. He'd insisted on seeing where the children would be living. "That's fine with me. Come along." They drove over together one snowy afternoon to a long chocolate box of a building with the shameful-secret look of a nineteenth century shoe factory or prison. There was a scrub lot across the street, and some old, washed-out, Ashcan School frame houses. The apartment was on the top—fourth—floor. (There was no elevator.) The present tenant was either a masochist or a Spanish priest. The place was dark, velvety, the walls filled with yellowy Christs, hung in angular wooden misery on long crosses; the tables were covered with missals, rosaries, monographs with red crosses on them, teak figurines of deformity and mouth-twisted transcendence. Three small bedrooms, a half-kitchen, the velvety living room, a sunless sun parlor. Merriwether felt impaled. "You want the children to do penitence for us?"

It was the wrong tone. Sarah, a bulge in an ugly herringbone suit under her tackiest cloth coat, had had too many years of such repudiation. Her plump, scraped cheeks went red, the eyes were black nails. "This is what we can afford. You made it clear we're not going to be millionaires."

The place was dense with heat. The penitent didn't reserve his suffering for the walls; it was a rehearsal for hell-fire.

"You're going to be well off, Sarah. You can afford almost any place in Cambridge."

"I've heard that little aria for years. Then I buy a dishwasher, and you shake like a leaf."

"I didn't realize that. But it's your money now."

"You're darn right. I've earned it."

"Ok. And we owe it to the kids. They're used to something special. And Albie and Priscilla have to have places to stay when they come home."

"Lots of people put up with bunk beds. Or we can get rollaways. We're just not going to be as comfortable as we were. The sooner everybody knows this, the better they'll be."

"I won't let them live here, Sarah. If I had any say, I wouldn't want you to live here. Please don't even show them the place."

She turned and went down to the car. But he knew her; she'd changed her mind.

One minute helplessness, the next minute the Efficiency Queen herself. "When are you getting those papers signed? If you're going to sell the garden to the Bowens, you have to do it before January first. Get on the ball." Sullivan was at her—telephonic—side, the real estate agent was on the wire half the day. "You better quit dragging your feet."

Then he would hear her on the phone with Albie, asking absurdly naive questions—"How do you go about getting a mover, dear?"—to show she was a weak woman in need of help. She leaned on the children while pretending to support them.

In his way, he did the same thing. So he'd keep George on his lap, explaining things to him beyond his capacity or patience. "The anthropologists—they study human societies—have found out that people who treat babies gently, feed them on demand, hold them against their bodies, turn out completely different from people who make babies cry a long time before feeding, keep them on hard floors—" till George would wriggle off. "I've got to finish my model before supper, Daddy."

There was no pattern in their feelings. They'd be alone in the breakfast room, he reading the *Times* and eating the instant oatmeal with the lump of maple sugar (he made it himself now). He would look up from an account of IRA bombs in a Belfast theater and find her eyes on him. "You've dehumanized me." It was shivering, he had not heard the internal monologue out of which it spilled, he couldn't speak, managed only to grip the paper hard and get out of the room.

He discovered he could hate her. Forty-two years old, he'd never felt genuine hatred before. Except, perhaps, once, as a boy, when it was mixed up with fear of a squat hater-fighter he'd finally fought, the only real fight of his life. Derek Lobel, a mean, bespectacled rich boy, now he'd classify him as a psychopath, then he was just a terrible-tempered, resentful sac of fat and hatred. But that was brief, without meaning; now, inside, he felt a kind of metallic hollow which something struck. The throb was hatred. The feeling Hitler had for Jews, a black boy for the white boy who insulted him. He hated Sarah who hated him. He wanted her hurt. She was driving him from everything he loved, she'd sent him into the sexual desert—Sarah was Sahara, he'd never thought of it before. When he found water, she pounced, her chance to revenge herself. For what? His tyranny. The whole culture of tyranny. Merriwether felt the hatred leaking out in the rhetoric, but he felt weak with it, shriveled up, the room was airless, he opened the window, then the storm window, and took in cold air. Monsters. They were both monsters. Inside them both was every animal in the zoo. Out of each other they brought tigers, wolves, baboons. How could he have thought for a minute they could live together? The one relief of it all would be freedom from her. This was what divorce was about.

Up in the third floor room, fatigued beyond ability to sleep, Merriwether felt a kind of pride: he was feeling things people were supposed to feel. Forty-two and emotionally he was a fetus. "About time I felt something more than hunger for dinner." Not that he hadn't felt tenderness, sorrow, passion, love, even despair, but if he'd been asked if he'd felt the feelings of the people he read and heard about or watched on newsreels of the war, he'd have answered, "Of course not." He'd never married his mother or ripped out his eyes with a brooch, or, thank God, lost a child (though fear of that brought him as close to the depths as anything). He'd regarded the feelings of the Lears and Antonys as emotional frenzies, seizures, hallucinogenic discharges in the pre-frontal lobe, overflows unrelated to real life. There were physiological checks and balances to protect the system from such feelings (the delayed manufacture of angiotension without which there'd be permanent hypertension, a killer in every heart). Yes, but now he'd felt for a minute what Hitler was like, and there was strange, maybe compensatory pride in it. Surely the Lears came out of such moments. Who knows if they wouldn't light his way into some bio-chemic equivalent. This was too much. Ridiculous. "I'm prescribing divorce for the comfortable: turn in your misery and collect the Nobel Prize. The scientist's Las Vegas."

Sarah found an apartment above the Davisons'. She was registered with all the agents in Cambridge; it got around the science circuit, and Mary Davison told her about the apartment upstairs. "It's a nice place," Sarah told Merriwether. "You won't feel the children are degraded by it."

Merriwether knew the Davisons' place, it was pleasant and in the heart of Cambridge, that is the Harvardian heart. He refused the *casus belli* in "degraded." "That's a big load off us. I'm very happy."

"It's a bargain. You'll enjoy that."

"It's your money anyway, Sarah."

"Well, you can have some for your place."

The old decency. "Thank you, Sarah. I think I'll manage, but thank you."

The idea of an apartment, the word itself, had a claustrophobic aura to one who'd almost always lived in houses, but the children would adapt rapidly. And it was a comfort to know Davison was near by. If not an absolutely whole part of the continent, he was at least peninsular; he could dial a phone.

A few days later, Davison came up to him in the laboratory. There was an Olympian throat-clearing, the blue eyes went over Merriwether's head to some Davisonian horizon point (it probably looked like a ribosome belt and Merriwether himself like some amino block to be hoisted onto the difficult building process of Davison's daily life). After a relishing moment, a bit cruel, Merriwether wound up the pulley. "Sarah told me Mary told her about the apartment. I'm very grateful, John."

This pumped Davison free of his tension. "Yes, we heard about you and Sarah splitting the—the blanket."

Could a good heart have such foul discharges? Merriwether conceded to it, conceded to his own relief at talking with someone else about the business. "Yes, we're getting a divorce."

"That's tough."

"Yes it is, John. But there it is. We're not telling people yet because the younger kids don't know."

"I understand that. I'll keep it close to the chest." Whom could Davison tell? He was the least gossip-prone man in Cambridge.

"I'd appreciate it, John."

"Count on me." Davison was getting restless. They were

both in white smocks, it meant work, there was much to do. Davison arched a giraffian neck, his scopes called. Still, he didn't know how to get loose. "You found a place?"

"Not yet," said Merriwether. He was having a little trouble now himself. "Any ideas?"

What a question. Davison looked hammered. Still, questions were questions. The eyes turned back from nucleotidal graphs to the exotic subject of housing. For a moment, he remembered something about the apartment upstairs, then remembered more. There was quite a pause. Merriwether said, "If you or Mary hear of a nice, smallish place, let me know."

"Sure will, Bobbie. I'll tell Mary tonight." Then a marvelous tunnel opened up to him. The long face lit with intelligence. "Seen that report on microtubular protein in *Science?*"

"No, I haven't. Good stuff?"

"First rate," and Davison launched into colchicine-binding, axoplasm, vinblastine precipitates and phosphate buffers. Merriwether had to interpose, or rather, withdraw. "I'll look it up, Johnny. Thanks for mentioning it."

"Yes, tell me what you think." He was off, but a vestige of the social worm must have nipped him. The long white back spun around at the door. "I'm awfully sorry, Bobbie." He scooted off. It was a terrific thing; Merriwether—mentally—embraced him.

Not everyone came through so well. In his skinned, semi-paranoid alertness, Merriwether reassessed everyone by the reactions to his news. Maxim Schneider was the first disappointment. The Schneiders had a garage thirty feet in back of their house. Its second floor was a lovely apartment. A graduate assistant had lived there five years and Merriwether had learned at a faculty meeting he was going off to Chicago. That night he called Max.

"I've got some news, Max."

"You've won the Nobel Prize." Max was a telephone boomer. Though under the boom, Merriwether's radar sensed a Max-ish fear. Since he'd moved into the history of science, Max became exceptionally alert to and nervous about his friends' scientific accomplishments. That wasn't rare, of course; but nearly everyone succeeded in training himself out of resentment at friends' triumphs. Max, however, remained particularly alert to Merriwether's not-lengthy list of honors. (Perhaps he was one of Max's coordinates of accomplishment.)

"Not yet, Max," but said with enough gravity to penetrate the boom.

"Something wrong, Bobbie?" This was the warmth of friendship.

"I guess you'll feel that way. It's about Sarah and me. We've been having trouble for quite a while. We've decided to get a divorce."

"Whew." A good pause. They had spent so many happy times together, almost always as families. "I'm overcome, Bobbie. I mean we knew your style was, well, New England, you weren't demonstrative people. We just thought you a measure of our vulgarity. Still do. I'm just thrown."

"You never know about people inside their walls. We weren't phony with you. We always had good times with you and showed it. But we've not been the way you and Jeanne are. As I think you are."

"I guess not. I'm so sorry, Bobbie. I don't know what Jeannie will say. We'll do anything for you."

For years now, as his marriage unglued, Merriwether

was conscious of the marital "we." He thought of it as an American shield against suspicion (of loneliness, debauchery, homosexuality, eccentricity). "We went," "We saw," "Josie and I," "Jeanne and I." Was it a proud flag of dependence or did the connubial pair exist only as a pair, as colonial animals exist only as colonies? Maybe it stood for genuine need for the absent partner. He had certainly used it, perhaps years after there'd been small love behind it.

"We can take the children for a while, Bobbie. Maybe you and Sarah would like to go off by yourselves to think things over. Whatever."

"That's wonderful of you, Max. I think we're beyond repair. There is, though, something you might be able to help with. You know, we're both going to have to have places to stay. Sarah's found a condominium, right above the Davisons', but it occurred to me that with Mitchison leaving for Chicago, your garage apartment might be free. It's so lovely there, and set apart—we wouldn't need to be in each other's hair. And there'd be room for the kids to stay over."

"That's right, Mitch is leaving. Not till September though. He's going to finish up his phage stuff this summer. That would be quite a wait for you."

Merriwether felt, or thought he felt, a negotiating briskness imposed on the sympathy. "I could hole up in a motel for a while." He was pushing now, against his grain, for it was suddenly clear to him that it would be an embarrassment for the Schneiders to have the shorn Merriwether living right there as a kind of memento of domestic death for their children, or themselves. "Maybe it would be a mistake, Max." Another crudity.

"I don't know, Bobbie. I do think Jeanne has people asking for it. I think the graduate students consider it a sort of plum. But I'll ask her tonight and let you know. I do wish we could make this business easier for you. Both of you."

It was a decency, but Merriwether felt it as an embellishment, more as a wall between Acceptable Merriwether and Merriwether-Pariah. A paranoid (he'd grant that) Pariah. He felt angry, he felt low, he felt betrayed, and all these even as he felt his own unreasonableness. Would his children feel the breeze of subtle pariahdom? This wasn't Beverly Hills were almost every child had step- and double step-parents. All right, maybe it would save his children from unthinking ease. Though contemporary life was fuller of stories about The Children of Broken Homes, "It'll work out, Max. Thanks anyway."

"Bobbie, call if there's anything we can do."

"Goodby, Max."

Like an agitated prophet, Merriwether tried to read his dishonorable discharge on the faces of old friends. He felt a terrible weakness in Cambridge. A solidarity of timidity. Yet collective morality here was probably higher than that of most of its members. Aerated by the world's great texts, taught every year, alluded to with more than urbanity, refined by worldliness (sometimes beyond application). But ironic self-deprecation was in many a Cambridge face. Like worldly Catholics who keep both sinning and in the fold by constant confession of unworthiness, Cambridge citizens could profess the texts of heroism, sacrifice, nobility, charity, grandeur and humility, and yet systematically defect from them with only a ripple of self-criticism. The average Cantabrigian probably acted and voted right in causes which did not make too many demands on convenience, yet, in some ways, Cambridge was more depraved than many communities whose texts were fewer and more remote. Simpler, poorer communities, in the country, in the ghetto, showed a solidarity with the troubled that put Cambridge to shame. The *noblesse oblige* here was more public than personal. Or so thought Merriwether in these strange, turnover days of his life. His view was outward, inside he was a chaos, and seldom realized that was part of what he discerned outside.

He began writing letters to friends and relatives about his divorce. *Making his case.* The responses cheered him; his friends were friends; everyone who wrote back was sympathetic. Timmy Hellman and George Nyswunder responded with the warmth of inside knowledge. They were bricks. But even the letters that were hardest to write drew decent responses. The hardest of all was to his Aunt Emilia, his mother's maiden sister, the last close relation in what to Merriwether was the judgmental generation. Emilia had hardened into an eccentric spinsterhood. After retirement —she taught English in the Lawrence public schools— she'd begun reading Marx, and now, at eighty-odd, conducted Marxist seminars in her house. She wore red hats with stickpin and feathers and long dresses of her mother's day. Her face was sharp and whiskery, the jaw, long, flat, fishy, the nose cubist. Looks and habits made her a local celebrity. Fame made her even dizzier: she indulged what she'd suppressed, lifted her skirts to show legs she'd been told—sixty years ago—were beautiful. The pictures of Aunt Emilia showing her gnarled walking-stick legs beside a grinning Boston outfielder made Sarah suggest he have her committed. But within this coral of display, there was a person of older, more parochial habits, the family guardian, historian, genealogist, the family memory and conscience. Every once in a while Aunt Emilia spent a night or two with the Merriwethers. She told stories she'd rehearsed for months, cooked her family-famous Indian pudding and mutton stew, visited an ancient lecturer in English who had been cast as her girl-time lover (fifty years ago they had gone to concerts together) and lapped up the children's laughter as homage and love (which, in part, it was). Her favorite was her niece-in-law—who despised her. He wrote:

> Dear Aunt Emilia,
> I have some very difficult news to tell you, news which is still very difficult for me to think about, but which I must. There is nothing to be done about the situation, it has been in the making a long time, perhaps from the beginning, and though I could tolerate a continuance of it as it is going now for the children's sake, Sarah cannot.

He tore it up; too indirect. Even with the very old, a cushion was only more knife.

> Dear Aunt Emilia,
> I have sad news. After years and years of attempting to hold together, Sarah and I have decided to get a divorce. It is in many ways heartbreaking. The thought of not living with the children, the guilt of failing them are almost intolerable to me. But there is no alternative. Sarah and I have been impossible for years. As always, there is a great deal of fault everywhere. I, surely, am most to blame. In her view, I have dominated her and left her no room to be a person. She responded in her way to this some years ago. The result was a physical hell. This led to other things.

Her answer came in two days. It was an Emilia new to Merriwether.

> My dear Bobbie—
> So the best was not good enough for you both. I am

so sad. Without reproach. I have had no experience of marriage, I have always been told of its bliss—and its troubles. You and Sarah seemed to have so much more of bliss than trouble. I must have been blind. I believe in process that dominates individual life. My way was solitary, abstention; I didn't choose it, or want it. I've read Frederick Engels on the family, I understand through him some of the contradictions families in societies like ours have. Reason is but the shadow of feeling—did someone say that?—it's true. I feel so for you, for Sarah, and your wonderful children. Your parents have been spared this sadness, a small warmth in this wintry news. If I can be of help in any way, remember I am your loving, grieving but almost-understanding,

Aunt Emilia

Merriwether showed the letter to Sarah. "I'm so surprised," she said. "It's so surprising what people have in them."

Merriwether also wrote to Sarah's sister in California.

Dear Pris,
I want to write you myself, because whatever pain and difficulty exist between Sarah and me is complicated by the affection I have for some like you who were part of the life we had together. Nobody could be better in-laws than you and James. You are wonderful people, losing you is a special sadness. The fault in our marriage is mostly mine, but that is not the concern. Sarah is so close to you that I know your love and support will be an important part of her restoration. If in any way, I can ever help you or your—to me very dear—children, I am still, in heart, anyway, their loving uncle. I don't know if it's customary to write such a letter as this, but I wish to. It needs no response.

Robert

But a response came.

> Dear Bobbie,
> Thank you for your wonderful letter. James and I have suspected for some time it wasn't all roses for you and Sag. That doesn't make us any less sorry. You're fine people; you'll both be happier and lead better lives. The children will be happier when they see you are. If there's anything we can do—let us know. I imagine you feel unique in a kind of spotlit disaster area. If it's any comfort, know that in Peter's class, there are more children from "broken homes" than so-called "whole" ones.
> Bless you for writing.
>
> Love from us both to both of you,
> Pris

13

Almost everything now was ticked with the valence of last things: the last Christmas of his marriage, the last in the house.

Albie and Priscilla came home, the house which had been so bare of company—the house Tom Fischer had called "the social center of American biology"—filled with the children's friends. Merriwether could see George and Esmé (who brought their own friends home) flower under the ins-and-outs, the telephoning, the door bells, the walks, car rides, games. It was civilized life, not the gloom of television loneliness. Not that Merriwether couldn't bear isolation—he believed it essential—but the coldness of Sarah's house—he thought of it that way—was an airlessness for the children.

He bought a great tree, they all decorated it with ancient ornaments, the house flamed with colors, mistletoe, snowy balls, gold stars, scarlet berries, green needles, peppermint canes, blue and sapphire robes on the Magi in the old crêche. The windows of Acorn Street were full of wreaths and angels, and the Meltons' gingko trees were fitted with Christmas lights. They made eggnog and glühwein, packages piled in downstairs closets. Christmas Eve, Merriwether filled the old hand-made family stockings with oranges, nuts, puzzles and checks; Sunday, they came downstairs in pajamas at seven. Merriwether turned on the tree lights, the carpet sheet was covered with a hundred packages, everyone giving to everyone. (The year before Albie had given no one anything, and his shame hung on for days, prodded by George's frequent proclamation of the meanness. This year, Merriwether had put a—superfluous—bee in his ear.) There was a slow, pleasure-deferring, pleasure-doubling opening of the presents, everyone marveling at everyone else's games, clothes, books, gewgaws. Sarah gave Merriwether a bright green cardigan—the year before she had given him nothing—he gave her the Pléiade Mérimée, and pecked her on the cheek; she'd smiled "thank you." He went around with an Instamatic camera flashing pictures—said Albie with a sliver of the wit that made him a success with the Bowen Group, "Commemorating last rites?"—he gathered wrapping papers and boxes and fed the fire with them. George studied the assemblage plans of his rockets—no manufacturer assembled anything anymore, the entertainment was in the assemblage—Sarah cooked up a hill of eggs and bacon and warmed a coffee cake. The children piled their own loot, Albie regarded his checks with a little disdain, pointed out the virtues of the presents he gave, was kidded by Priscilla, then sweetly recognized his excess and gave himself over to George's blueprints. Esmé played her new recorder, Priscilla tried on her new clothes, and began talk of exchanging them. The phone started ringing, new records were played, and Merriwether did his annual reading from the notebook of the children's sayings he'd kept for twenty years, "Better than photographs." For this, the children sat around his leather chair. He and Sarah drank coffee, the others orange juice. The children knew the stories, but loved this annual reminder of their old innocence and wit.

"What did Priscilla say about the wheel, Daddy?"

He found the page. "I'd asked Priscilla—she was five—how she thought the wheel was invented, and she said, 'Somebody tried to make a square and goofed.' "

"What did I say about the apeman, Dad?"

"It was New Year's Day, 1968. There was a story in the paper about another primate find of Leakey's, and I asked George, 'If you found a creature and could not determine for sure whether he was an ape or a man, would you keep him in a cage or let him vote?' George said, 'Why not let him vote in a cage?' "

"That's what they're going to do with Albie," said George.

Albie lifted George on his head, "Penny for your thoughts, George."

"Here's Esmé in 1964. June 20. She was disappointed we weren't going to Marblehead. I said, 'Sorry, dear, that's life.' Esmé: 'Everything bad is life.' " Laughter.

"Read the one about the baseball cards."

"That's way back." He thumbed the old ink-doodled book, a Royal Composition notebook bought 25 years ago to take notes in Human Pathology (the first page was headed "General Phenomena of Disease"). "Albie and Pris were trading baseball cards. You got a square of bubble gum with every picture. Pris: 'I gave him McDougall for the baddest player.' Albie: 'She choosed it.' Mom: 'Chose it.' Pris: 'I don't even know the names.' Alb: 'Either do I.' Pris: 'You knew McDougall.' Here's one, July 16, 1958. We were on Duck Isle. Albie (calling downstairs): 'Doesn't *de nada* mean "You're welcome?" ' Dad: 'Yes.' Alb (to Pris): 'See.' Pris: 'Well, you don't have to hit me!' "

"What's so funny about that?" asked George.

"I don't know. They all mean something to me."

"They're great, Daddy," said Esmé. "George doesn't get them all."

"I get exactly what you get. I know what's funny."

"They're not always funny, George. Like snapshots. They just remind you of different times."

"See, I'm right. You just said they're not supposed to be funny."

In the afternoon, Fairleigh Bowen came over with Tim Frothingham. The Bowen Christmas was a rapid affair; Fairleigh spent most of his Christmases at the Merriwethers. A hearty, quick, bulky boy, full of strange knowledge, he was both skeptic and open. "Hyponastic" was the word that came to Merriwether for his physical type: Fairleigh's bulk was in his legs and rear, his torso curved almost delicately from it; his head was a small, dark, bright-eyed bloom, a Beardsley surprise on that lower trunk. He was, again surprisingly, a fine athlete, clumsily rapid with a great instinct for the play of the ball. He reported the family Christmas. "The table's covered with presents, there must be a hundred for the three of us. We come in from breakfast, we don't say anything. We open our own stuff. Without a word. Now and then there's a grunt from Dad. In five minutes, the room's a blizzard. Ribbon, boxes. We give one 'Thank you' to the air and take off with the loot. It's the way we eat too. We're a graceful lot."

"You just like farce," said Merriwether.

"No, sir, it's more maniacal than I say. We gobble, we burp, we split. And that's it for Mr. C's birthday."

Tim was another semi-permanent holiday guest. A long, fair, taciturn boy, he came to life only when he played the guitar.

It had been snowing since noon, densely; the streets were Siberian. George wanted a snowball fight. Muffled and booted, everyone but Sarah went out. Four o'clock, the light off the snow was the strange, sad, half-bright light of snow-days.

While the others cossacked up and down, packing, hurling, chasing, Merriwether looked from the steps. Receding into the rectangle, they looked like silhouettes, their voices bodied in the cartoon balloons of their breath. The street lights went on in the iron lamps. Bluish fluorescents under iron caps. "I love you, Acorn Street," said Merriwether.

He was called. In his plaid lumberman's jacket and high boots, he ran the street, packed snow, hurled, was pelted, pelted. Esmé came to his defense, then Priscilla. They made a Custer nucleus within the flickering, snowballing Indians. Priscilla tossed like Albie, Esmé with the pivoting elbow and limp wrist of the classic girl. Merriwether, dodging and getting hit, pondered the difference. (Bone structure? Estrogen supply? Early tutelage by Albie?) So much in his daughters was signaled by these throwing styles, Esmé the scorner of games, the dreamer, poet, lover of fairy tales, Priscilla the competitor, a runner, a puncher (judging from Albian boasts and George's complaints), matter-of-factly feminine, hardly using make-up.

Fairleigh, leaping—a trunk with wings—turned coat and fell on Albie, Tim summoned general attack. Albie and Fairleigh rolled into snow men, Priscilla fell on them both. A free-for-all. Merriwether retreated and watched from the steps. They were charging like miniature Panzers, breath came in spumes, they were wearing down. From the Hawthorne end of the street, they walked back, a snow line of Teutons. Faces lit like holly balls. They desnowed on the porch, stamping, slapping hats, mittens, and scarves against the pillars. "Acorn Street is going to be mighty quiet next year," said Albie.

They drank cider and glühwein. The fire was still going on a mix of logs and Christmas boxes. It lit eyes, cheeks, the silvery tubes of George's model cars, the brass pokers and shovels; never had it seemed so beautiful to Merriwether. Sarah, happy in the moment, as Merriwether could not quite be, wore an African djellabah Priscilla and Albie had given her. White with red trim, it lengthened her, relieved her plumpness, brought out her Christmas coloring, red cheeks, black eyes, fair skin. "She'll be able to find someone," thought Merriwether suddenly, happy in the thought, then uneasy. When she's good, he thought. He went for more glühwein so he could pass her, to pat her arm. She smiled, sweetly, sadly, but did not look at him.

Tim got Priscilla's guitar from her room—Merriwether was always surprised at the young people's unquestioned ease of access—and plunked out carols, French ones, which he sang alone, German ones he sang with Fairleigh, ones in English with everyone. Merriwether tended the fire, filled glasses, passed Christmas cookies, Pfeffernüsse, sugary almond crescents, flat yellow stars with jellied nuclei. Esmé went upstairs to play new albums, George to read *The Hobbit*. Two more boys—arcs in what Merriwether called "Fairleigh's Circle"—arrived, there was loud discussion of not, happily, pro bowl games, but the demerits of the mighty. Tim talked of the wasted decades of Einstein and Newton, Fairleigh of the low IQs of painters. Each boy seemed to have a specialty he riddled. "Sons of professors," thought Merriwether. Evangelical, paternal, he suggested they'd grown up too familiarly with men of accomplishment. "You take them on their parlor behavior, which, at best, is par. What counts in these people is the work they do in private, stuff they can do over and over until it is right. That's why they say tenacity's so important."

"So you're saying there's really no special talent."

"No. Only that an ingredient of it is the hunger for solution. And a nose for half-baked solution. An unwillingness to stop before the result looks, sounds, or works right." He was talking for Albie: the straight and narrow.

"Trial and error is what mice do going for cheese in lab traps."

"You're exalting mice, not degrading humans. But the mice live only in the present. Humans try until the painting looks right, till the economic policy reduces inflation, till the tumor disappears."

Sarah, making domestic application of this patient tenacity, said it was beginning to seem like a seminar. "I'm for carols."

"Mother," said Albie.

"I agree," said Merriwether. "Fewer words, more tunes."

But connubial "conciliation" was patronage at this date. There was a small chill in Sarah, and in a few minutes it spread. The boys went upstairs, Sarah and Merriwether sat alone, dead meat between the racket upstairs and the small fire noises in the parlor. Each was on the edge of speech. But what was there to say? Merriwether got up to spread the logs. The motion released Sarah. She went upstairs. He managed to call out, "It's been a nice day." She managed a "Yes."

14

As Sarah's February Court Day came on, Merriwether felt suspended in nostalgia and melancholy. "This is the last Monday of my married life." And the day itself: "So it's really here. It's all over." That morning he lectured his undergraduate class about the evidence for thinking the genetic nucleus had been formed out of the symbiosis of two organisms. "As, say, the word 'another' is independent of both 'an' and 'other' yet is clearly their product. So the older, rather inflexible transmission capacity of cytoplasm gave way to this superbly organized method." The analogy in his notes was marriage, but today he couldn't talk of the "family unit of transmission." There was a fly in the analogy. Divorce was not meiosis, not division for reproduction, it was not death. It would be the separation of symbiots into independent creatures.

It was the shank of winter. The tiny lawns of Ash, Acacia and Acorn were streaked with snow filth, the neighborhood dogs dropped their excrement in steaming cylinders

—why didn't Cambridge adopt London's system of doggy pick-ups with fines for delinquents?

Tomorrow, a new life. He was ready. He'd had the joys and difficulties of family life, he'd still have some of them, and always, always he would watch the children to see if he could fix whatever went wrong because of what he and Sarah had done. But now, fresh fields. Last night, he'd tried to drug himself watching television. He'd lasted through half the Late Late Show, could remember nothing after the MGM lion. He was just eerily conscious of this night, this last night as a husband, of George and Esmé sleeping yards away from the television set. They still didn't know. He and Sarah had agreed to tell them during the April Easter break.

He went to sleep, head a swirl of inarticulate trouble. He replayed the Super Bowl, himself a hero, blocking pass rushes, rifling passes, then on defense, laying linemen out, and throwing, literally, taking up the quarterback in one hand and throwing him twenty-five yards back. He got some sleep.

Sarah and he sat across the breakfast table. They did not say but felt, "The last breakfast in our married life." Twenty-two years. She called George and Esmé, they bundled up, he kissed them off and, at the door, touched Sarah's arm, "I hope it'll go all right, Sarah."

"It's been a long time."

Her court hour was two o'clock. He came home early.

"How did it go?"

"Quick and horrible. The worst was before. Sullivan read all the things I had to say about you. I didn't know if I could go through it. Tina too. Dev just had to confirm. The court hardly mattered, it was an assembly line. I suppose the judge was all right."

"What was he like?"

"I can hardly remember. I didn't look at him. The whole thing in court took ten minutes."

"So, we're not married anymore."

"The final decree doesn't come through for a while."

"I suppose I'd better get on the ball about finding a place."

"What about the Schneiders' garage?"

"I don't think they want me around. A domestic death's-head for their kids."

"I hope you can find a place soon."

"I'm trying hard, Sarah. The Faculty Housing Office says places show up around March first. The leases start coming in."

"I guess we can make it till then."

"I'd thought we could make it till the kids' school ends."

She shook her head and went into the kitchen.

Except for the astonishing fact that he was no longer married, after having been married since Albie's age, there was no further sense of change.

Though the next day, when he came home from work, he came home to the house that no longer felt his. It was now—at least till June—Sarah's. Yesterday it had been his. He was here now on her sufferance, she could tell him to get out, legally, as three or four times she had told him to get out emotionally. It was a strange feeling for him. "Maybe this is what women feel." He hadn't even felt this way when he was competing for tenure.

"I'm free without being free," thought Sarah. "Once again he's got the better of me." She went on cooking (or going out to supper with him and the children), she threw his dirty shirts and underpants in the washer and dryer and sorted them out; each throw, each sorting was a humiliation. He was home much of the time, and never had he been so sweet with the children. George and Esmé clung to him when he came in the door. "He's trying to cripple me with their love for him. He always has." She could not bear it, could not bear the sight of him reading in his leather chair, couldn't bear sitting next to him on the sofa when they ate in front of the television set. With the domestic tribulation of Dick Van Dyke barely ruffling the bliss of television domesticity, there he sat laughing and eating her food (a heated Stouffer's Salisbury Steak; she didn't have the strength for anything else). Every other day he suggested they eat downstairs. "I'm too tired," she'd say, or "I want to see the Olympic figure skating." She would take no more dinner seminars.

She could not bear to see him drinking wine and watching the news. "Some people don't have time to watch the news." (Looking at the children.) "Or even read the newspapers." When she took them to school in the morning, he would be finishing the *Times* in his torn blue bathrobe, which she knew he wore as an indictment of her lack of wifely—unwifely—care. (The symbols they threw at each other's heads.)

These days, it was as if there were ten thousand slivers of glass between them. Instead of air, glass. The glass was pain. That is, if they moved, if they said anything to each other, the glass moved, and it was painful. Impossible; but not impossible, for there he was; and every day put more glass in the space between them. It was not so long ago that there had been nothing, a neutral space, if not comforting, not discomforting. And before that, a warm space: how good to have you there across the lazy susan, the coffee cups, his, hers, the same as they used now, his blue with the gray vines, hers striped green, bought in the same store at the same time. By her. With "his" money. That old division of labor or of love had turned to glass and nails. Everything that had allied them separated them. Here in the breakfast nook off the bright kitchen off the wood-paneled dining room off the hall, the living room, the sun parlor, the bottom floor of the old house, here in this safe nook, cold and glass.

Pain found expression in money; money was the medium of hatred. Much that's said to begin in passion begins in money; and almost every human conclusion has a monied superstructure.

Sarah had never been greedy. If anything, she thought goods were tainted; growing up, she had battled the comfort of her own home, and since, especially since working in the poverty centers, tutoring poor children, her shame at comfort had an ascetic's force. Now, she faced the problem of permanently accounting for her own bed and board; she felt money as threat, means, as weapon, one that had been used against her, one she could use in defense.

When she and Merriwether had sat down to work out the settlement, the main thing for her had been quick, easy, reasonable division. Now she felt the weight of goods as things which could be replaced only with money. The money was her—proper—share of his income (plus whatever she could earn as a middle-aged woman teacher in a world that was not lavish with such people). One day, she'd have a little money from her parents, that other kind of money that meant you could afford to despise it, but now she had to carve her economic life, her ability to live, out of his. And he was no Rockefeller, either for quantity or charity.

It looked as if she could make it on the settlement; but you never knew, equipment could break down; the condominium's insurance covered only space, not goods, she would have to insure household goods, and then car insurance, and health insurance. What if the car broke down? If she broke down?

It was a time of fierce worry for her, and meanwhile she had to keep going, her degree was almost in hand, and beyond that was a job, some job or other. Her exams were the month before the household move; she did not know if she could make it.

Merriwether saw only the harsh outside, Sarah hardening, cursing. "That's full of shit," she said once after he told her she'd have no money troubles. She'd never used that word. She belched and passed wind, without apologizing. Once, when he frowned angrily at George for doing the same thing, she snapped, "How dare you. A person can't help that."

"I don't believe an eleven year old's sphincter muscle is beyond control," he said. "If there's a lapse, the tongue can atone for it."

"It's your calling attention to it that makes him uneasy."

Whacked up at every orifice, Sarah went on cursing, farting, belching. Merriwether connected it with what he thought of as her new greed. "Perhaps as she tightens in one way, she has to let loose in another." (He had not read the psychoanalytic literature on money and excrement.) The worst was at breakfast. Low blood pressure made it difficult for her to get moving. He supposed he was her morning coffee. She went after him about household money —he'd questioned her about a check, and said it was about time they had separate bank accounts—about his cheapness, about the pauper lives he'd made them lead all these years.

"Couldn't we live these last weeks in peace?"

"Easy for you to say. But you dog me for every nickel."

"Just for an occasional two hundred bucks."

"We've been needing a new dryer for a year."

"Wouldn't it have been simpler to wait till you moved?"

"I notice you're still putting your shirts in the hamper."

"That is unfair, I know. I'll do the laundry every other time."

"You better get used to it."

"Is it so hard?"

"Nothing's hard for you when I do it."

"Until now, no. I'm grateful."

"You're grateful. Go to hell."

When he got home that night, he found a note from her on his bed. (It bore neither salutation nor signature.) "You'll have to get out, whether you find a place or not. You can have till March 20. Here are the things you can take with you: your books, your grandmother's bed (this was the one he now slept on), your mother's oriental, any presents the children gave you, your desk and desk lamp, etc., the Brueghel baboons (a print of the two apes chained to a barred window which he'd bought at the Albertine Museum as a joking anniversary present at a time when it was a joke), the blue vase . . ." (a crusted blue mug from Sicily which held his pencils: she had given it to him for his thirty-fifth birthday and had dropped it on presentation; he'd glued it together; badly).

There were seven other things, including "some wedding china." (Did this mean she would be giving no dinner parties?) He would refuse this memento, although there'd been a hundred wonderful—in his view—dinners, after which he and she had done the dishes in the kitchen, congratulating each other on the dinner's success, recalling the choice moments, the best remarks.

"Some extra pots." He would take these. Another world. He would buy a cookbook. Did she give him the pots as a reminder of all that she'd relieved him of for twenty years? Too much? Nothing was too much. Maybe it was a burst of thoughtfulness. A way of getting him out of mind and conscience.

He went downstairs; she was playing the piano. He stood by, waiting for her to look up. "Well?"

"There are a few other things that mean a lot to me. If you want to live among my family ghosts, all right, but otherwise I would like Grandpa's desk and the glass cabinet in the upstairs hall."

"Take them. I don't want them."

"And I want you—or the kids anyway—to have at least half the books. I want them to have books around."

"They have plenty of books. We can work details out later. The main thing is for you to get out."

"Is it so unbearable for you?"

She looked up from the piano, took the cigarette from the ashtray on the mahogany shoulder (she'd begun smoking constantly) and took a deep drag; he could see her drawing strength and peace from the—to him—repulsive cylinder. Then she said, quietly, "It is unbearable."

The nights, with their insomniac bloat and cardiac pounding, were the worst for him. He fought them with Sominex, music on the transistor by his bed, books. In daylight, there was his routine, now charged with his awareness of its transience. The house felt luxurious, the coffee and newspapers in the breakfast nook were a small heaven.

Going down the steps, up Acorn and Ash Street, across Brattle to Agassiz, crossing the Common, skirting the Physics Labs, and entering the quadrangle of his own labs. Much of his life was in that walk.

He saw little of Cynthia these days. The energy of love, the sexual energy, the excess which made for tenderness and generosity dried up in anxiety; his feelings circled George and Esmé. Luckily Cynthia had an enormous amount of work. She studied Japanese seven or eight hours a day. Yet loneliness crept in. She felt Merriwether's need to stay close to what he was going to leave, but the very feeling evoked a counter-feeling of resentment that she was secondary. This opened her mind to blackness. She could not think, only felt the nausea of emptiness. In this pit, she called him, he rushed over, comforting, holding, lying beside her. Mostly, she suppressed desires to make him demonstrate more, but now and then, she could not endure the resentment she felt he felt for her weakness. In such a mood, she saw his smile as stretched muscles and bared teeth, his tenderness a matter of pressure and gesture. Unbearable. "It's only a transition, darling. It's just these awful weeks." But time made no sense to her. Time wasn't weeks or minutes. It was outside the terrible blank that was all she was. "Weeks don't mean anything to a dead person." He didn't understand, or pretended not to.

Usually, though, things were easier. He'd come, they would drink wine, play cards, go over the day's events, the boys coming on with her in class, the stuff of lectures, hers, his. They almost never went out. He brought wine and delicatessen meats, they drank and ate, watched the news, and sometimes wove fantasies around it. She said, "Kissinger's having an affair with Madame Mao." (Kissinger had been a distant Harvard colleague, a rolypoly who ran the Summer

Seminar for foreign students. Merriwether had eaten with him once at a committee meeting which did little more than decide to dissolve itself.) "I know that's what's behind all this China-visiting. He's setting her up for Nixon. When we see them rolling around together, we'll know good relations are restored. All this diplomatic stuff is a cover-up." Cynthia sat bare-bottomed in her blue denim shirt, her hair tied back with a black fillet. She held him, and they rolled around in her sofa-bed. " 'Nixon and Mao's Wife Tussle Lovingly Before World's Love-Starved Billions.' That's what east-west intercourse is about." She spun out networks of world-orgies, the late De Gaulle and Jackie Onassis, Martha Mitchell and Jomo Kenyatta, Spiro Agnew "tied naked, front to front, with Pat Nixon," pictures taken, mailed to *Life* and *Paris-Match,* "unless Nixon stops the bombing."

Two or three times a week now, Sarah wrote notes to him. He'd find them on his bed, written in pencil on his stationery. (She was too distraught for delicacy.) Mostly they were defenses of her conduct and indictments of his. She was unable to say these things to him, could not trust her voice in his presence; she felt he always got the better of her.

One note was a defense of her years of sexual refusal. She said she was a naturally warm woman, but it had been clear to her that he didn't want her as a person, only as the nearest woman available. He wrote on the bottom of the note, "I understand. Naturally you couldn't be intimate with someone you felt didn't respect you." He brought it down and handed it to her. After supper—he cooked himself a hamburger, but ate with her and the children in front of the television set—she handed him another note: "Perhaps I should have been able to tell you what was bothering me. But it wasn't my way to open up like that." He wrote in ink over the penciled sentence: "How I wish it had been." Her note went on: "If sex is the basis of your relationship with your girl friend, it doesn't seem enough to me." In ink, he crossed out "is the basis," and wrote "was the origin." He gave her the corrected note and said, "Every time you say 'girl friend,' you make it sound like a curse."

"I pity her," she said.

Another note asked him to pay the taxes on the house. He told her the house was hers now, and she had more money than he. She said she'd call the lawyer.

"What did Sullivan say?" he asked her after the call. "He said I was legally responsible for the taxes. But while you're here, you should pay rent. It better not be long."

"I've been paying the bills; but I'll pay half the taxes." She took this with grace for a few days, then tracking him to the TV set, she said, "You were clever to transfer the property to me. Making me responsible." He saw the chemical rhythm behind her muted fury, but muttered something about his legal obligation to make the transfer.

"Then why are you here?" She was in a floor-length flannel nightgown, an outfit which made her seem especially vulnerable and could almost evoke his pity for her unhappiness. The drained face above the little lace collar of the gown was streaked with red, the eyes glowed with the battle she sought, the pain felt, the hatred for him; he felt something close to fear. Who knows what she'd be capable of in this state? "Why are you here? Get out."

"I haven't even told the children."

"Tell them."

"I thought we agreed it should be in two weeks."

"You assume I agreed. When it's to your advantage. Tell

the children Sunday. Anything you want. I'll tell them I was on the edge of a breakdown and would have had it if you'd stayed. Everyone says it's unheard of for you to be here."

"It is unusual. I only thought we'd decided we would manage it to keep the children as fine as they've been so far."

"You can't keep using the children to kill ME."

"Whatever it is that has made you a monster, I hate. I pray to God that if there's a hell, you and I will burn for what our monstrosity does."

"Does? To whom?"

"George and Esmé. Less to the others."

"It's not them involved. It's—" and she managed "US," though shaking at the inclusion with him, even as she made this last claim on it under the roof where they lived the last days of their joined, if long unbedded, long uncongenial, and, for six weeks, unwedded life.

The Sunday morning Merriwether had looked forward to with dread for months, which he'd rehearsed at night for so long, was a mild, beautiful one. They'd decided they would speak to the children at the same time, but Esmé had gone out after breakfast, and Merriwether thought it might be best to tell them separately anyway.

"George, want to come in here?" *Here* was their old room. Sarah lay in bed. Merriwether sat on the edge, George came in and jumped between them. "Mommy and I want to speak with you about something important."

The little boy's head sprouted a tense smile. This was not the usual bill of goods. He started doing push-ups on the bed, but Merriwether put his hand on his shoulder as he talked and George listened. "What I'm going to say may sound hard for a little, but Mommy and I have talked it all over, and we are sure it is the best thing for all of us." George looked up, the smile still there, but fading. "You know Mommy and I have our arguments, our troubles. Well, we've decided that we can be better friends and better parents if we don't have to live together as husband and wife. That's a terrific strain on people, especially those like Mommy and me who are so different from each other." George's head was down. "So in a little while, we will live in separate places. But, and this is what counts, we both love you and Esmé and Albie and Priscilla completely. We will always be your parents, we will work together for you." George cried. Sarah's and Merriwether's hands were on his head and back.

The door downstairs opened. "Esmé," called Merriwether. "Could you please come up for a moment? Mommy and I want to speak with you."

George scrambled off the bed and ran, head down, into his room.

Sarah and Merriwether looked at each other, their war forgotten. She had tears in her eyes. "It's hard now," she said. "It'll be all right soon."

Esmé came upstairs. "What is it?" The delicate face looked puzzled, but there was control in it, a dignity of preparation.

"We've just been talking with George, darling," said Merriwether. "You see even more clearly than he that Mommy and I have been having a lot of trouble getting along lately—"

"You're getting a divorce? Is that it?"

"We're going to live apart, yes. Because it's even best for those we love most in the world, you and George and—"

"That's all right," she said. "I guessed you would. I understand." She paled, the lips pursed, the eyes glistened, the muscles tightened in the cheeks.

"We wanted to talk about—"

"You don't have to say anything. It's all right with me," and she turned, went downstairs, and out the door.

Merriwether went into George's room. He was on his bed, under the yellow submarine, head in his pillow, crying. Merriwether took him up in his arms, George's back against his chest. The boy looked around and saw his father crying—something he had never seen—and reached around and held him.

Sarah, in her djellabah, came to the door, saw them, watched for a second, came in, touched George's head, and went back to her room.

"I better see about Esmé, George. I'll come back."

Esmé was sitting in the sun on the porch step, arms around herself, face dense with thought.

Merriwether, feeling her dignity, did not sit next to her. "It'll be all right, darling."

She turned away. "It isn't as hard for me at my age, Daddy. It's harder for George. I'm taken up with things."

"I love you so, Esmé, dear. I'll always be here. I'm glad it's not that hard for you. But you may have hard moments. Mommy and I will do everything we can to help you."

"Thank you. I think I'd better be alone." The voice led to the edge of the tears she did not want him to see. Feeling a depth of love absolutely new in his life, Merriwether resisted lifting her into his arms. "I love you, darling," he said and went back into the house, up to George. They stayed together without talking for a few minutes. George cried off and on. Then, spent, he smiled. Merriwether said it was time for a bit of good time now, they'd had the bad. They got out baseball gloves and had a catch in the street.

A week later, the thought came to Merriwether that the moments holding each other on the bed were the best he and George would probably have together; it was as strong a love as two human beings could have for each other without sexuality (stronger for its absence). "You who are made of me, formed from—and against—me, you whom I've seen grow from bulge to this, you George Merriwether, whom I named and who will—please God—have me in mind years after my death, you my beloved child . . ." Nothing in Merriwether's life had come close to the love behind this unvoiced invocation.

PART FOUR

15

The doormat was off to the side, not in place before the front door. It was not the only sign of withdrawn hospitality. The rubber cleats stippled into WELCOME had worn down: a splotched ELC remained, "as if some antlered mutant lived here," thought Dr. Merriwether, who was, for the summer anyway, the actual tenant.

The fifth or sixth day there, the first and only visitor showed up. Dr. Merriwether was glooming in the easy chair behind the picture window, eyes more or less on two hummingbirds sucking at a bottle of amber nectar hung from the pine tree. "The smallest things in nature make the greatest show." (This out of his Latin School days.) Out of the pines, came a young, Moses-bearded man in knee-high boots. He and Merriwether eyed each other through the glass. Merriwether beat him to the door, and the young Moses grumbled a social phrase: "I'm Bill Bender."

"Better than Bill Collector." Amiable Merriwether put out his hand.

No smile lit the beard. "I got to get something inside."

Merriwether had rented the place from a former graduate student, Henry Bender, so he stood aside, perhaps half a second before young Bender entered, then moved fast to catch him before he got to the bedroom. As much to assert Tenant's Rights as to protect Cynthia, he said, "There's somebody in there." Bender looked but did not quite say, "What are we going to do about that?"

"Let me see if it's ok."

Cynthia was asleep. She hadn't adjusted to the air almost two miles up here in the Rockies. What she did most, and most happily, was sleep. Her hair lay like a bundle of gold fibers over the pillow, her cheeks were red from sleep warmth, her mouth was open. Was Moses balanced enough to keep from leaping on her? "Ok," said Merriwether.

Bender looked once at bed and girl, but he had important business in the closet. He reached behind a cedar chest and came out with a shotgun. (Merriwether hadn't known it was there.) He broke the barrel open, snapped it, and tried the trigger, at which CK-CK Cynthia opened her eyes. Merriwether moved into her line of sight for reassurance.

"Kids trashed my place last night. You can't live without a weapon." He put the gun under his arm and strode out, Moses Nimrod, the Punisher.

Was the fellow going off to shoot his trashers? Merriwether saw himself interviewed by police. Another item in *Newsweek*. "Yes, he came in for the gun. He knew where it was." These melodramas of the heights. Maybe heights generated aberration. Maybe when scenery dominated, unsteady human beings became extravagant; to make their mark. Cambridge scenery was so humanized, so worked-on and worked-out, it was as much actor as scene. In the mountains, human actors were subdued. Solitude was the human mode for mountains. Since Cynthia and Merriwether had no company up here, the conclusion was a comfort.

Most evenings, Merriwether and Cynthia walked the roads behind the cabin, by forests of aspen and silver spruce. The loudest noise was a stream melted out of the Arapahoe glacier crashing on its rock bed. Rainbow trout swam in it, though not enough for fishermen who lined Barker Lake a mile down the road. On the back road to Eldora, Merriwether and Cynthia almost never passed anyone. At first the walks were tiring; though beautiful. Terrific sunsets pulled color out of the sky and the woods and laid it down on the water, recoloring what evening uncolored. Clouds were golden, runic. There were flowers everywhere. Merriwether bought a Colorado Guide Book and learned to recognize fifteen or twenty kinds: blue harebells, heads bent like boudoir lampshades, golden avens, scarlet globemallow, clematis, silver-blue lupines, avalanche lilies with their golden pistils going "Blah." He and Cynthia talked little. Occasionally, they pointed to fine sights, a horse drinking in the stream, dusk-lit peaks, glitteringly intimate, with snow in their lofted groins. The mountains were part of the Continental Divide. (They were on the Atlantic slope.)

Now and then, cars, lights high, drove by them. They judged the character of the drivers: some gave them wide berths, others skirted them savagely. "Fuckers," yelled Cynthia to their murderous rear-ends. On the walk back, the last colors would be pressed from the hills, streams of rose and frail gold, violet, orange. "What a palette."

"Wish you'd compliment me," said Cynthia.

"Your palette's fine."

"I mean cooking." At a loss without school assignments,

Cynthia had taken up cooking. "You didn't say one word about the fish."

"That kind of palate? I did. Didn't you hear me groaning with joy?"

"You're not a Chinaman. That won't do."

Bender had a shelf of cookbooks. Cynthia studied them as she studied the shogunate, underlining, analyzing. Then she shopped down in Boulder at King Sooper. She translated recipes for her diet, skimmed for whole milk, margarine for butter, imitation margarine for margarine. Her body was beautiful, but she was on a permanent diet and said she envied Merriwether his almost unfattenable body. "You're like something above the timber line. What a metabolism."

"My mother thought I was dangerously thin."

"She lived when diseases wasted people. You're perfect. I'd give anything to be like you."

"I won't be like that long, if you turn this place into Lutèce. Look at this." He raised his shirt and grabbed a fold of stomach flesh. There was precious little to grab. Out in the sun, chopping wood, walking miles, chinning himself on the pine tree under the hummingbirds' bottle, Merriwether was in good shape. He looked infolded around his bones. Until the Conference began in mid-July, he let his beard go for three and four days at a time; it grizzled dark gold and silver against his tan. He looked all right; and felt all right; his year-long Cambridge cough had stopped.

He'd come out here because of the Conference. At least, partly so. The Conference was an Intensive Study Program in the Neuro-Sciences sponsored by Massachusetts Institute of Technology and the University of Colorado. Merriwether hardly qualified as a neuro-scientist, but the semi-popular book he was writing for Timmy Hellman was about changing concepts in motivation research, and he wanted the latest poop. In May, he'd written Bender about getting a place in the mountains. Bender taught physiology in Boulder. He was also a rancher, and it turned out he was going off for the summer to buy cattle in England. His cabin was free from mid-June, so when the spring semester ended in Cambridge, Merriwether took off, driving out with Cynthia in a secondhand Mustang he'd bought one day after George said the six-year-old Dodge looked "worse than my worst dream." "You wouldn't have bought it if I'd complained," complained Cynthia.

In the weeks before the Conference started, Merriwether worked on the book. There was a void in his conception of it; he didn't know what it was. He told Cynthia he was marking time until something in the Conference papers hit him right. Still, every morning, he wrote at the kitchen table; and, now and then, he had a good session; mostly, though, it was pure relief to finish his day's chore. As noon came on, he found himself looking up every few minutes at Bender's Swiss birdie clock. (The birdie came out but didn't chirp.) He stopped on the non-chirp of noon. After lunch, he walked, read, or listened to music and news on the public educational channel in Greeley; once or twice he went with Cynthia to ride a glue-footed nag on the mountain trails.

Mostly he read at Bender's library, poetry anthologies, books on real estate—Bender was apparently a land shark —a novel called *Poor Plutocrats* "by the Hungarian Balzac, Jøkai," a Dutch novel with the beautiful title *Old People and the Things That Pass*. The library was in two parts, the first in shelves built under the stairs, the second, towers of paperbacks piled in the attic like a miniature San Gimignano. The shelf library was full of medical texts, dictionaries, cookbooks, and books about the West, the geomorphology of the Rockies, mountain plants and minerals, histories of Denver and Leadville, treatises on silver and tungsten mining. You went upstairs to the attic with a flashlight and a chest full of breath, knocked into a tower and came down with a handful of—it could be anything, six mysteries of Margery Allingham, an anthology of western mystics (Julian of Norwich, Meister Eckhart, Thomas à Kempis) histories of the potato and Venezuela. By August, the towers were down, the little Tuscan city was sacked. The day before they left, Merriwether reconstructed it.

Until George and Esmé came out to Colorado for ten days apiece, their only human visitor—there were lots of dogs, rats, rabbits, bugs, birds—was young Bender. He showed up every few days to fetch or inquire. The second time he came for cartridges ("I'm going hunting."), the third for his VA check. (Merriwether picked up Bender's mail.)

"I didn't see anything for you."

Apparently young Bender had been wounded in Vietnam and lived on a disability check. Ed, the Fina Station owner who serviced Merriwether's Mustang, told him Bender had a plate in his head. "He is a strange guy. He's wrecked three cars in the Canyon. Comes buzzing up from Boulder and piles into a curve." When Merriwether told Ed about the trashing, he said it didn't surprise him at all. "He lets these STPers crash in his place. They've got a month's fog between the ears. They get cold, they can't chop wood, so they break up the chairs."

Since Bender's first visit, Merriwether had been locking the cabin, so he was relieved that trashing just didn't come out of the blue. "Though who knows," he said to Cynthia, touching the pile of pages for whose sake he locked the door, "this may have been destined for trashing."

Cynthia, in flowered underpants and blue denim shirt,

was gobbling yoghurt. (Home-brewed.) "You know you have more to say than anybody." He occasionally read to her from the manuscript. "That part about conation is like a poem. You're the best scientific writer in the world."

This extravagance undercut the praise. More and more, Merriwether relished accuracy. How much had his early surprise, then humorous puzzlement, dismay and then anger at Sarah's inaccuracy deformed his marriage? For his birthday Priscilla had given him *A Room of One's Own* and *Three Guineas*. Otherwise he might have sloughed it off with, "Women." Though perhaps the protein chains did register the millennial enslavement. No. "And Education more than Nature's fools." Radcliffe was full of careful, alert, fiery girls; and in her own work, Sarah was precise, accurate, full of interesting distinctions. Nature-nurture, whatever, that was over. But he did not relish this extravagance in Cynthia, no matter how charged it was with love.

This was the first summer in years he had no official employment of any sort. Most of his colleagues relished these untethered months, he'd always felt more comfortable in some sort of harness. Writing a book was a loose commitment. He was going to have to discipline himself in a new way.

Everything about the summer was remote. He hardly heard from the children. Priscilla was working for the Muskie campaign in Spanish-and-Italian-speaking districts of Boston. Albie, like some fusion of Hercules and Candide, worked in the stables and gardens of a Long Island estate. George was in an Ozarks "Survival Camp," Esmé with Sarah at Sarah's sister's in California. George was coming out to Colorado in July. He would stay ten days and be exchanged for Esmé at the Denver airport. The logistics were worked out in notes from Sarah, who, after twenty-two years of marriage and five months of divorce, still could not bring herself to head them with salutation or conclude them with her signature. As if to say, "You know my hand, I know yours. Minimal recognition is all that's left for us." Merriwether had been raised by courtly people, and though he understood the revolutionist's view that courtesy was the mask of refusal, why should it dissolve between him and Sarah? Hadn't they had enough harshness? And what was that? Was proximity like gravity or altitude? Every thousand feet of altitude meant three-and-a-half Fahrenheit degrees of cold. This could be translated into air pressure and wind convection. But what were the forces which made love grow and die?

Those hovering jewels with the cinnamon glass tails stabbing their bills into the amber bottle hanging from the pine branch were not capable of it. But was there a connection between their feeling for the bottle and his for, say, the Acorn Street house? The Merriwether house. Did anyone feel for it as he did? Weeks ago, Priscilla had stopped by to get the mail and written that it was already being glassed and mirrored. The barnacled old shell would have as much relationship to the interior as the Merriwethers did to the Devereaux. The Devereaux would put in new chairs, who knows, maybe bulge the floor into sitting, eating and lying areas, nail slashes of color over the old walls, or knock them out for windows to make the fight against Cambridge dark less of a losing battle. And that was fine, all fine, but the million connections of that house with Merriwethers and Tiptons were cut.

Merriwether hiked the trail up to the Arapahoe Glacier. Cynthia dropped off below the timberline, and waited for him in a rock cranny by a waterfall with a Penguin Mencius and a carton of low-fat cottage cheese. Merriwether carried a lunchbag with a nectarine and a Gorgonzola sandwich. For pauses—and these became more frequent—he had a pocket *Bhagavad-Gita* on the flyleaf of which he'd written notes on mountains from a geomorphology text inscribed by Bill Bender. Apparently Nimrod had studied—as well as wrecked himself in—the mountains. Merriwether sketched varieties of the regolith in the empty pages of the *Gita*. "Might as well know our neighbors," he told Cynthia, who saw this "greed for information" as masculine dysfunction. "All this naming of rocks and birds limits your feeling for them. You see little more than the name. Didn't you tell me biology didn't advance till it unburdened itself of nomenclature?"

"Not quite," he said, kissing her to take away even this small sting. (She could not take much contradiction from him.) "You're reacting to eighteen straight years of school. Adam didn't assign names to the animals just for attendance records. Anyway, these geological names are wonderful." He read out, " 'Vug, till, scree, kane, drumlin.' I guess they're Scandinavian or Celtic. They sound like primitive gods."

"More like Henry James characters to me."

Up on the mountain, fifteen hundred feet beyond the timberline, there is nothing but rock. It is a sight that has less of ease than most Merriwether's seen. He counters his uneasiness by identifying what he sees, trying to discriminate between glacial and alluvial debris, checking on the stone shapes by comparing them with the squiggle drawings on the flyleaf. A mantle of unconsolidated gray stuff, the mountain on which he feels himself but another stone, looks miles across gray air at its brother lumps. "The newest part of the earth."

Walking up here is no joke. He has to stop every fifty or

sixty yards for breath, though, aware of oxygen narcosis and sensitive to its giddiness, he tries not to gulp the air too greedily. Less is best. He pokes into the lunchbag: the Gorgonzola decomposes, and its fumes have contra-narcotic force. "Every nose its own eco-system."

The first hour's walk was all color: meadows, black hawthorn with purple thorns, white aspen, chokecherry, tiny waterfalls, then a thinning in the grass, the bone-show of the rocks, the plates of snow. Beyond were the hundred shades of gray stone, split, sheared, cracked, broken, ground, dusted, the world's trash coat, its vomited foundation.

When the sun speared out of a gray diarrhea of cloud, it turned into script—a celestial Linear B. The light struck fluorite crystals sunk in the vugs. Quartz, amazonite, corundum, beryl. Merriwether himself is most of what's colored up here: blue jeans, red LaCoste sportshirt with the green alligator, dirt-blotched white sneakers. Colorful, but not the official climber's outfit.

Now and then, booted climbers clumped past him in descent, some of them clearly annoyed at his fool's guise. It is July, but it can squall and snow up here, it would be a lesson to this gold-and-silver-stubbled fellow to end up frozen on the rocks.

Merriwether spotted a climber spiraling down, a girl, and up close, saw her great legs, bronze face. She is high-colored, buck-toothed, has the open face and squinting eyes of the mountaineer. "Hi," she called.

"How's it going?"

"I'm beat," she said. "Thought I'd better turn around. My friend went on."

"Make it to the glacier?"

"I saw it. You?"

"Not yet. I'm debating now."

The girl leaned on a rock opposite Merriwether's own ledge. She adapted J. P. Morgan's answer to the man who asked if he should buy a yacht: "If you're debating, better not."

"Is it that far?"

She nodded to the peak. "When you get there, there's a dip, you go down, then up, down and up again, and from *there* you see the lake and the glacier. It'll take you at least an hour. It's mosquitoey. But nice."

"How far is it?"

"A mile, maybe more."

"A mile up here's like ten below."

"You know it. Well, have a good climb, up or down."

"You too. Have a good day."

After he lost sight of the climber's back, he felt for a coin to flip for his decision; he had none. He'll find decision in the *Gita*. "And now, Krishna, I wish to learn about Prakriti and Brahman . . ." Nothing squeezable there. He tried again and found "Freedom from activity is never achieved by abstaining from activity." "That's the ticket." He pushed himself up, hands pushing on his thighs; five easy, ten hard steps, a stop, two more, one more. His chest felt pummeled, his lungs raw. He made for a ledge, let his head fall on his chest, sank into himself. Whew. He has had it. He stripped sweat pips from the eye sockets, massaged his neck, rubbed his chest. Ok, he is almost ok. He leaned back on the ledge, took in the sun and slowly recovered. He ate the nectarine. *Life*. Fruit, Merriwether and the *Gita* against molecular junk. He read, "I am not bound by any sort of duty, but I go on working nevertheless. The ignorant work for the fruit of their action, the wise must work without desire." Pure New England. No wonder Emerson and Thoreau loved it. From sense objects to senses, senses to mind, mind to intelligent will and that to Atman, "the Godhead in every being," said the Glossary. Like the crystal in the vug, no, like life in the rocks, a grain in the grain of the universe. Easy to believe up here in this high, gray, messageless debris.

Every morning, for a month, he has written on tropisms, instincts, taxes, stimuli, vacuum reactions. Just this morning, he wrote up the gonadal hormones which seasonal light released in swallows to drive them north. Neither duty nor desire. No choice.

He, however, had a choice. He did not have to finish this climb.

It is the coldest July day in Colorado history. By the time he and George drive up Boulder Canyon on the way back from Denver Airport, there is hail-ice on the windshield. Still, George is thrilled by the beauty of the mountains, the terrific cliffs—"They really are Rocky."—the waterfalls. His little face glows rosily in the long frame of hair.

Two hours before his plane arrived, Merriwether kissed Cynthia off at hers. She is visiting Weej in San Francisco. "It'll do you good to be with people under ninety." (Merriwether, though, has to ride herd on a run of uneasiness about what she might find there.) "You can sleep with anyone you like. Not more than twice with the same man."

"I don't want to even look at anyone but you. But if you get horny . . ."

"I'll buy a copy of *Playboy*."

"You can sleep with a hippie. Just don't infect me."

She's in tears at the gate. "I don't know if I can last three weeks away." She takes off her flowered straw hat—her hair is balled into a nugget of gold cloud; how beautiful she is. They kiss while passengers break around them to go into the tunnel.

That night, George sleeps in Cynthia's bed. (It is years since Merriwether has slept so near his son.) He sleeps with his mouth open, makes sleep noises, sometimes talks—once he counts to sixteen—a Wainwright family habit. Can it be genetic, or is it anxiety? When George babbles something about fires, Merriwether reaches over to touch his hair, but George groans and turns away. He has a pre-adolescent sensitivity to being touched, perhaps deepened by some internal decision to stand on his own.

The next day, when Bender calls for his mail, Merriwether asks him about fishing rods for George. Bender's language is action. He goes up to the attic and comes down with a rod and rig. "You can get bait at Sargee's." (This is the general store.)

"Thanks very much."

"He's under fifteen, he doesn't need a license," says Bender and clumps off through the pines. He'd returned the shotgun. "Too many dumb kids around in the woods. Liable to kill one."

Merriwether goes with George to the stream behind the cabin; there's no one in sight. George fishes just beyond a wooden dam which converts the drift of the glacial stream into a small torrent. Merriwether has never fished, but remembers his father's instructions about casting. George is good at it. When Merriwether goes back to the cabin, he is whipping the line halfway across the stream.

Merriwether puts on his working record—Chopin mazurkas and ballades—and does his morning chore (the behavioral input of the memory transplants done by the Planarian Research Group).

Around noon he looks out the window to see George in

his blue jacket and black cowboy hat—borrowed from a Bender shelf—walking down the rock path holding his rod and, wonder of wonders, a fish. His face shines with triumph.

"You're terrific. I don't believe it."

"Just hooked it. Right above the dam. It wasn't too hard. Maybe it didn't want to live."

"Maybe, but it's struggling now." The fish was hopping around the hook, panting, gills flapping. A rainbow trout, speckled black on the silvery flanks, banded with orange. "It looks like Aunt Emilia."

"It's slippery. I can't take it off."

Merriwether gets a paper towel, holds the fish and removes it from the little hook. The trout arches its head, wriggles around, gasps. Not pleasant.

"Would you kill it, Dad?"

"I'm not that kind of doctor, George. And it does look like Emilia. You'll have to finish it off. Knock it against the sink. I'll clean it."

George grabs the fish in the paper towel and clouts its head against the sink. That does it.

Merriwether finds a carving knife and serving fork, lays the fish out and slits it open. It's been quite a while since he's slit so much flesh. There are the gonads, the heart, the spinal cord. He goes over it as well as he can for George, opens the head, points out interesting features, picks off the gills, describes the circulatory system.

"Shouldn't we eat it, Dad?"

Merriwether fries it. There's enough for four or five bites apiece. "More tender than Aunt Emilia would be."

"And not as salty."

George is almost visibly getting older. His face is thinning, and rich with expression. Priscilla tells him George and his friends look through sex manuals, have signs for fornicating (an index finger poked through a thumb-index circle). Merriwether didn't know one end of a woman from another till he was a junior in high school. "How'd you like to live on what you catch or raise, George?"

George says he wouldn't mind if they had seeds for Mars Bars.

It is a fine ten days for Merriwether. Now and then, he misses Cynthia, but he is busy and George is a good companion. They go into the mountains or down to Boulder. Every few days they ride the trails.

"What's for today, George?"

"What do you want to do, Dad?"

George senses his father's new sensitivity to his wants. He knows it's a mark of love, but it's a bit much. To have constant choice is to be constantly obligated to enjoy what one's chosen. Merriwether knows George feels this, yet he continues to offer blank checks. It is another form of his desire for ease. Even in the simplicity of this life—no dressing up, little or no shaving, no obligations, following little more than the earth's schedule plus old habits of three meals a day and a certain amount of sleep—he's burdened by the complexity of want. He will never be able to satisfy anyone, no one will ever satisfy him. Human flesh is born to itch. He and Cynthia will always disagree about pleasing each other, he and Sarah lasted as they did because of the very silence which eventually separated them. Maybe human beings who love each other should only present their best face to each other, saving their miseries for silence, dark and the pillow. Only masochists can tolerate lifetimes of complaint. Watching George read science fiction while rock music plays from Greeley or playing casino with him till they take their night walk to the stream and back is as close to human interdependence as he wants. (At least until he feels other needs.) In any case, George is permanent; he will always be his son as triangles will always have three angles. When it's time to exchange George for Esmé at the Denver Airport, though he knows he will miss the boy terribly (and sees how George will miss him), he knows, and sees George knows as well, the deep sense of this permanent geometry.

The ten minutes with Sarah is tensely civil. She cannot bring out a smile for him, can barely nod. She is tan, plump, her eyes are brilliant, but strained. She is completely natural kissing George, speaking with him and Esmé. Not with him. (What does he want?) She lets him carry her bag to the gate, but barely manages to hear his news about George, his questions about the others. He hands her the envelope with the month's check and kisses George goodby. "Will you come to Duck Isle, Daddy?" (George hasn't grasped the geographical limits of divorce.) Merriwether says if he can finish his book, perhaps he will, anyway he'll see him soon in Cambridge and will speak to him on the phone before that. Esmé gives George a rare kiss of farewell, embraces Sarah, then takes his arm. "Goodby. Have a good time. See you soon."

Esmé sleeps upstairs. Merriwether has knocked out the sealed windows, put up screening, swept the place, pushed the books into a corner and made up the cot. "I thought you'd like a bit of privacy, darling. If it gets too hot or cold, come downstairs with me."

It works out well. Esmé is self-sufficient. She reads, writes five-page letters, plays Bender's records, goes for walks, sketches. In the afternoon, they swim, ride, climb. Now and then, they go to movies in Boulder, they see *The Marriage of Figaro* in the Central City opera house. The final forgiveness scene—the abject Count, the benevolent Countess—makes them both uneasy, but otherwise it is a delight to be with each other.

Esmé is lengthening, she has a sweet, loping awkwardness, is secretive, funny, oblique, sharp, self-contained. "Do you think it's going all right?" he asks her one afternoon. They are sunning on adjacent towels after a frigid dip in Rainbow Pond. They are alone with dipping loons, sunning, shivering.

"What, Daddy?"

"This business with Mom and me. Are you used to it?"

Esmé is lying on her belly, wrapped in a red beach towel. She arches her long head, hangs it. The hair is wet, a fair, jungly tangle. "I think so. I worry a little. Maybe about Mom more. She doesn't have anyone." Merriwether swallows. "And I think you have a girl."

"Yes," he says. "I do have a fine friend. Whom you'll meet, if you want to."

"We'll see. I'm glad for you. I think it's working out."

Merriwether towels himself dry. "You're terrific. I'm a mighty lucky *père*."

That evening, Esmé hears a funny little noise near the garage shed in back of the house. She goes inside and finds a two- or three-day-old kitten sticking out of a Total box on top of the garbage can. She runs to Merriwether with the almost inert pile of fur in her not-large palm. "Can you save it, Daddy?" She's close to tears.

The kitten has a tiny, scrounged-up, monkey face. "They don't usually make it if their mother doesn't keep them for seven or eight weeks. We'll try though. Can you get the medicine dropper from the bathroom?"

They heat skimmed milk, mix it with water, then manage to drop a bit around the unwilling little mouth. "He hasn't learned to suck anything, probably not even his mother."

"Who would have thrown him there?"

"Someone who couldn't kill it outright."

By afternoon, the kitten snuggled against Esmé's shirted breast and accepted a few squirts of milk from the dropper. By evening, it managed to take feeble steps in front of the living room window. Its cry was like a pin drawn against glass. The next day it had a tiny little motor.

"It's learned to purr, Dad."

Esmé names it Figaro.

"Is it a boy?"

"I think so," she said. "From the way it peed on me."

The kitten's monkey head poked in Esmé's shirt buttons. "It wants my breast."

But the kitten died. They went to see *Cabaret* in Boulder, and when they got back, the kitten was snuffling and threw up the milk Esmé gave it. Esmé's face lengthened with misery; she held it close.

"It probably has pneumonia, darling, I'm afraid it won't make it. Keep it warm. Their temperature is higher than ours."

Esmé wrapped the kitten in her sweater and kept him on the floor beside her bed. In the morning, Merriwether woke to the sound of tears, went upstairs in his pajamas and found Esmé holding the four inert inches of dead kitten in her arms. "It died when I was asleep."

Merriwether spaded a foot of earth under a pine tree, Esmé lay the kitten in it, and they covered him with the earth, then a stone which they surrounded with pine cones and larkspur.

The last thing Esmé said to him at the airport was, "If

you remember to put flowers on Figaro's grave every now and then, Dad, I'll feel better for it."

He bequeathed this chore to Cynthia whom he picked up an hour after he kissed Esmé goodby.

The haphazard survivor. This was the anti-Darwinian notion which Professor Eigen repudiated in the great address of the Boulder Conference. Electrons got the jump on positrons, and this universe is made of matter, not anti-matter. So the linkage of nucleotides and protein cycles accelerated into the nucleic strand which survived the decomposition of other "information units." A Paradise of Phage, but the very "mistakes" of the enzymes provided the new information which led from steady-state—and inevitable decomposition—to new information; to evolution.

Slim, beautifully articulate in English, moving rapidly from blackboard to podium, gesturing, pointing, smoothing his silver hair, Eigen's modest but accelerating power, like his own triumphant life chain, elevated the conference from a kind of factual soup to that vividness of being which marks individual triumph.

The talk had begun with a tribute to Eigen's friend Katchalsky, the Israeli neurobiologist who'd died a month before in the massacre at the Tel Aviv airport. Eigen began with Katchalsky's work on the analogy between electrical and chemical systems; he concluded with a comparison of the nucleic transcendence to the transcendence of the synaptic feedback system which gave promise of what his nineteenth century countryman would have called an *Übermensch.*

The marvelous two hours sent Merriwether up the

mountain in a kind of ecstasy. He felt, without detail, without conception, that Eigen's notions would fill the void in his own book. He left Cynthia in the cabin and walked down to the stream. Pine odor saturated the air. Survivors, DNA, Eigen, the structure of truth, and yes, Merriwether felt it—himself, his children. Behind them, the contributing dead, Katchalsky, the decomposed states, the house, the family. States decay, survivors survive. The misery, the waste, the trash of the last years somehow led here to the moonwashed water in which the trees stood out with a clarity obscured by the very color of daylight. You need darkness for clarity (moonlit darkness). A jet light moved above the mountain, followed, seconds later, by a bridal train of sound. Charged by everything, Merriwether feels something there. Yes, understanding trailing event. Light and sound issue together but register separately. The depth of love after loss. The way of human beings. Self-catalytic forms, fed by errors, and so perpetuated. Love, family, Cambridge, mentality. Linkage. Transmission. Evolving.

"Are you ok?"

Out of the dark. He looks up, Cynthia calling from the road. He can make out her hair holding light.

"A-1," he said. "I'm on my way up."

AFTERWORD

RICHARD Stern's *Other Men's Daughters* is the story of a man's loss of innocence on two levels: the loss of his family—his wife and children—and the loss of his naive assumption that he would always have his family. The sense of loss jumps out of the frame of fiction and moves us, too, on a third level, for when we read it now, nearly fifty years after its first publication in 1973, it makes us realize how we, as well, have lost a precious world of our own innocence, a world in which good and intelligent people could still have what we would grandfather in as a stunning naiveté about the possibility of having it all, if you are a married man who has an affair with a much younger woman. It has been well said that you have to read a classic every few years to see how you have changed; reading this richly evocative book now we suddenly see how our emotional world has shifted so much that the moral ground has been pulled right out from under our feet. On the one hand, we have become shockproof. Philip

Roth rightly remarked, when this book was first published, that it was as if Chekhov had written *Lolita*, and *Lolita*, first published in America in 1958, still held the power to shock in 1973. Of course, the sins of Stern's protagonist, Merriwether, are mild compared with those of Humbert Humbert: Merriwether is innocent of statutory rape (the woman, Cynthia, is much younger, an undergraduate, but not that young), incest (she is no relation at all, not even his stepdaughter), or even academic sexual harassment (though he is a doctor and she his patient, raising certain ethical eyebrows). But now, after the public exposure of the Clinton erection (as the Japanese might have called it) and the Augean flow of child porn, the offenses committed even by Professor Humbert Humbert, let alone Dr. Merriwether, seem literally child's play. And it is, after all, not Nabokov but the Chekhovian Stern, sharp eyed but gentle tongued, who guides us through the pages of *Other Men's Daughters*.

Yet, on the other hand, we have also become both more sensitive to and more litigious about the sexual vulnerability of the young, and our erotic imagination is often grounded, even before it takes off, by concepts of abuse and agency that would have been Greek to Merriwether, who knew Greek. Stern also constantly makes us feel the force of the difference in the age and power and status of Merriwether and Cynthia; Merriwether himself wonders, "Was part of his feeling for her the joy of learning about a new species?" Stern also depicts them so differently; he is almost always called Merriwether, or Dr. Merriwether, and only rarely addressed as Robert; she, by contrast, is Cynthia even before she is Miss Ryder, and remains Cynthia throughout. She is also alone in Cambridge, while he carries on his back, like the earth's orb on Atlas, the world of Harvard, and his great house just a short walk from Harvard Square, and his many colleagues, and his ancestors, and above all, his immediate family, his wife and children. Yet both Merriwether and Cynthia fall into bed with only brief, gossamer qualms, and at first it does seem that they will get away with it scot free. And, indeed, they do get away with it; they are together, and happily together, at the end. It is in many ways a great relief to read about a careless, thoughtless indiscretion and not worry that it will end with the murder of the children's pet rabbits; when Merriwether casually remarked, "I don't believe in fatal attractions," how could he know what his words would mean to readers who had seen that film in 1987? (There are other, charming, incidental time-warp moments, such as the evocative description of streaming cylinders of dog shit everywhere in the snow, with a plea for Cambridge to adopt London's system of doggy pick-ups with fines for delinquents. We have cleaned up that mess now, but not, alas, the human emotional mess so well depicted in this novel.) It is a great relief to be in the skillful hands of a nonjudgmental omniscient narrator.

At first, we are shocked, shocked at the immorality of the man; he doesn't seem to care about the damage he's doing to his family. He doesn't try to conceal his affair, and other people don't seem to mind it. When he meets his wife's friends, people who have known them both for years, they just say, "Well, be careful; you're going to get hurt," with not a word about potential hurt to those caught in the cross fire, Cynthia, or Merriwether's wife, Sarah. Cynthia's father is so impressed by Merriwether's aristocratic ways that he aids and abets the affair; this is surely the realization of Merriwether's fantasy, the two powerful father figures reaching out to shake hands high above the head of the young woman who loves them both. The novel therefore moves us all the more as it subtly and movingly leads the happy couple out of their private passion and deeper and deeper into the social labyrinth. For there is, as Richard Stern's University of Chicago colleague pointed out, no free lunch, not even with adultery; Merriwether pays a terrible price, one that we feel all the more sharply precisely because we are at first entirely caught up in his blithe expectation of not just a free lunch but a free *super intime*. Much later after his initial meeting of great minds with Cynthia's father, Merriwether confesses to him that he's afraid Cynthia will commit suicide if he leaves her.

The pain begins not with Merriwether or Cynthia but with Sarah, who is no feminist (though she knows all about it) but simply a woman who has given her life to her husband and now feels that she has been robbed of it. Her devastation is magnificently evoked, and it is through her bitter eyes that we read the final verdict on the affair near the end of the book: "She felt as if she were looking in the rearview mirror at an accident; their own life cracked up there." She gets it long before he does, but he gets it, too; eventually he begins to understand Sarah's dilemma, though not very sympathetically; we never do learn, as he no longer remembers, what made him love her once, or her him, though we learn a lot more about what went wrong. His initial total lack of consideration for the effect that his affair will have on his family is gradually replaced by an intense and beautiful evocation of his love of family when he loses it, culminating in a stark, vivid description of his tears. And he begins to indulge in self-indictment: "I practice the golden mean: gold for me, meanness for others."

Merriwether's failure to see where the affair is leading until it has blown up his life is made all the more shocking by his brilliant meditations on most other aspects of his life, his wit, his erudition, his skill with words, his philosophical awareness, all captured for us by Stern's skillful writing. The novel abounds in mots that are not only bons but make you keep thinking about things long after you've closed the book. Like the following:

"He said that when he talked with John Van Neuman, he felt that he was asleep and Neuman awake." "By the time you're my age, [love is] but a combination of lust and nostalgia." "He had the comparatist's lust for analogies, unexpected symmetries, historical metaphors." "I feel about her the way Galileo did about the telescope. My feelings for her enlarge my feelings for other things." "[I]t was a grand day, one of those designer's preview shows of autumn that New England stages around Labor Day." "[N]early everyone succeeded in training himself out of resentment of friends' triumphs." And finally, significantly, "For years now, as his marriage unglued, Merriwether was conscious of the marital 'we.' He thought of it as an American shield against suspicion (of loneliness, debauchery, homosexuality, eccentricity)." How can a man who is capable of capturing such thoughts, and putting them so carefully into perfect word cages, fail to understand where his life is taking him? The implicit answer to this implicit question is the power of love.

At first, it seems to be sexual love (there is a great description of Cynthia's perception of two kinds of orgasm, "some lightning-fast and radiant over the surface, some rumbling and revolving deep with her, almost unendurable"); though we are told that Merriwether and Sarah had been good together physically even after the marriage soured, they have stopped sleeping together, and then this beautiful young creature knocks on his door. But the dominant love in this novel turns out to be not adulterous love but the love of family, and not just the family consisting of Merriwether's wife and children; we learn most about what makes Sarah and Cynthia, too, interesting by seeing them with their families, Cynthia with her dominating father, Sarah with her background so different from his. The sense of loss is brought home to us by the skill with which Stern depicts the family, and Merriwether's love for his ancestors and his children, culminating in the heart-wrenching Thanksgiving scene in which Merriwether is simultaneously there and not there. The ambivalence is also wonderfully captured in his free association as he watches his son Albie playing football: "He'd watched with tears—he didn't know why. What was a father's stake in a son? His dissociating head flashed a bloody, literal version of this phrase. Odd." Not so odd, as the story goes on, and people get hurt.

The love is in the details: the hilarious poem, composed by Merriwether's grandfather, about marine insurance; the same man's memoirs written in red ink on the left-hand pages of a ledger book, in a script like a healthy cardiogram; the notebooks that Merriwether kept with the children's sayings in them, one of them being the idea that the wheel was invented when someone tried to make a square and goofed; the children's voices in cartoon balloons of their breaths. It is with his children that he has talked about whether the human goal is happiness or pleasure, which turns out to be what the whole story is about. The Merriwether House, which we meet in the very first words of the first sentence of the novel, and which we learn to love in great detail, a house still perfumed with Merriwether's strong sense of the ancestors who haunt it, is the receptacle of many displaced emotions, seen in the rearview mirror that teaches us that we never know the true value of things until we lose them. After the breakup, Sarah remembers the things that she bought with his money and other things bought with money from parents, money that meant you could afford to despise it. What begins with the great house ends with the cups and saucers. This is the best novel about divorce and the anguish of a lost family that I have ever read.

—Wendy Doniger

OTHER NEW YORK REVIEW CLASSICS

For a complete list of titles, visit www.nyrb.com or write to: Catalog Requests, NYRB, 435 Hudson Street, New York, NY 10014

J.R. ACKERLEY My Father and Myself*
HENRY ADAMS The Jeffersonian Transformation
RENATA ADLER Speedboat*
LEOPOLDO ALAS His Only Son *with* Doña Berta*
CÉLESTE ALBARET Monsieur Proust
KINGSLEY AMIS Dear Illusion: Collected Stories*
KINGSLEY AMIS Girl, 20*
KINGSLEY AMIS The Green Man*
ROBERTO ARLT The Seven Madmen*
U.R. ANANTHAMURTHY Samskara: A Rite for a Dead Man*
WILLIAM ATTAWAY Blood on the Forge
W.H. AUDEN (EDITOR) The Living Thoughts of Kierkegaard
W.H. AUDEN W.H. Auden's Book of Light Verse
EVE BABITZ Slow Days, Fast Company: The World, the Flesh, and L.A.*
DOROTHY BAKER Young Man with a Horn*
J.A. BAKER The Peregrine
HONORÉ DE BALZAC The Human Comedy: Selected Stories*
VICKI BAUM Grand Hotel*
SYBILLE BEDFORD A Favorite of the Gods *and* A Compass Error*
FRANS G. BENGTSSON The Long Ships*
GEORGES BERNANOS Mouchette
MIRON BIAŁOSZEWSKI A Memoir of the Warsaw Uprising*
ADOLFO BIOY CASARES The Invention of Morel
PAUL BLACKBURN (TRANSLATOR) Proensa*
RONALD BLYTHE Akenfield: Portrait of an English Village*
NICOLAS BOUVIER The Way of the World
EMMANUEL BOVE Henri Duchemin and His Shadows*
MALCOLM BRALY On the Yard*
MILLEN BRAND The Outward Room*
ROBERT BRESSON Notes on the Cinematograph*
SIR THOMAS BROWNE Religio Medici and Urne-Buriall*
ROBERT BURTON The Anatomy of Melancholy
DON CARPENTER Hard Rain Falling*
J.L. CARR A Month in the Country*
LEONORA CARRINGTON Down Below*
EILEEN CHANG Naked Earth*
JOAN CHASE During the Reign of the Queen of Persia*
ELLIOTT CHAZE Black Wings Has My Angel*
UPAMANYU CHATTERJEE English, August: An Indian Story
ANTON CHEKHOV The Prank: The Best of Young Chekhov*
GABRIEL CHEVALLIER Fear: A Novel of World War I*
JEAN-PAUL CLÉBERT Paris Vagabond*
BARBARA COMYNS Our Spoons Came from Woolworths*
ALBERT COSSERY Proud Beggars*
HAROLD CRUSE The Crisis of the Negro Intellectual
LORENZO DA PONTE Memoirs
L.J. DAVIS A Meaningful Life*

* *Also available as an electronic book.*

ANTONIO DI BENEDETTO Zama*
ALFRED DÖBLIN Bright Magic: Stories*
JEAN D'ORMESSON The Glory of the Empire: A Novel, A History*
ARTHUR CONAN DOYLE The Exploits and Adventures of Brigadier Gerard
DAPHNE DU MAURIER Don't Look Now: Stories
ELAINE DUNDY The Dud Avocado*
G.B. EDWARDS The Book of Ebenezer Le Page*
JOHN EHLE The Land Breakers*
J.G. FARRELL The Siege of Krishnapur*
KENNETH FEARING The Big Clock
M.I. FINLEY The World of Odysseus
THOMAS FLANAGAN The Year of the French*
MAVIS GALLANT Paris Stories*
GABRIEL GARCÍA MÁRQUEZ Clandestine in Chile: The Adventures of Miguel Littín
LEONARD GARDNER Fat City*
WILLIAM H. GASS In the Heart of the Heart of the Country: And Other Stories*
WILLIAM H. GASS On Being Blue: A Philosophical Inquiry*
GE FEI The Invisibility Cloak
JEAN GENET Prisoner of Love
NATALIA GINZBURG Family Lexicon*
JEAN GIONO Hill*
ALICE GOODMAN History Is Our Mother: Three Libretti*
PAUL GOODMAN Growing Up Absurd: Problems of Youth in the Organized Society*
HENRY GREEN Blindness*
HENRY GREEN Living*
HENRY GREEN Party Going*
WILLIAM LINDSAY GRESHAM Nightmare Alley*
EMMETT GROGAN Ringolevio: A Life Played for Keeps
VASILY GROSSMAN Life and Fate*
OAKLEY HALL Warlock
THORKILD HANSEN Arabia Felix: The Danish Expedition of 1761–1767*
ELIZABETH HARDWICK The New York Stories of Elizabeth Hardwick*
L.P. HARTLEY The Go-Between*
ALFRED HAYES In Love*
PAUL HAZARD The Crisis of the European Mind: 1680–1715*
ALICE HERDAN-ZUCKMAYER The Farm in the Green Mountains*
YOEL HOFFMANN The Sound of the One Hand: 281 Zen Koans with Answers*
RICHARD HOLMES Shelley: The Pursuit*
ALISTAIR HORNE A Savage War of Peace: Algeria 1954–1962*
GEOFFREY HOUSEHOLD Rogue Male*
BOHUMIL HRABAL The Little Town Where Time Stood Still*
DOROTHY B. HUGHES In a Lonely Place*
RICHARD HUGHES A High Wind in Jamaica*
INTIZAR HUSAIN Basti*
YASUSHI INOUE Tun-huang*
HENRY JAMES The New York Stories of Henry James*
TOVE JANSSON The Summer Book*
RANDALL JARRELL (EDITOR) Randall Jarrell's Book of Stories
JOSEPH JOUBERT The Notebooks of Joseph Joubert; translated by Paul Auster
YASHAR KEMAL Memed, My Hawk
MURRAY KEMPTON Part of Our Time: Some Ruins and Monuments of the Thirties*
GYULA KRÚDY The Adventures of Sindbad*
SIGIZMUND KRZHIZHANOVSKY The Return of Munchausen